The Pinewood Gardener

The Ninth Catrin Sayer Mystery

ALLAN JONES

Cover: White Spiderlilies in the Kuala Lumpur
Bird Park (author photograph)

THE CATRIN SAYER MYSTERIES

The Chinese Sailor
The Scottish Colourist
The Falmouth Model
The Carnforth Double
The Powys Deacon
The Stratford Hunter
The Thornham Copyist
The Chiswick Chauffeur
The Pinewood Gardener

OTHER NOVELS

Canons

*All novels are released as ebooks
and Kindle Direct Publishing paperbacks.*

CONTENTS

"I would prefer even to fail with honor
than to win by cheating."
Sophocles, *Philoctetes*

"It's morally wrong to allow a sucker
to keep his money."
W. C. Fields

PROLOGUE. HEATHROW

"Go to work."

Mair Gwendolyn Sayer Treneer repeated her father's words to her. Nearly two years old, she was be-coming an authoritarian conversationalist and a control freak.

"That's right, mummy's going to work, on a plane," Chris Treneer repeated.

"Plane!" squealed Mair, pointing at the mural. Somehow, the picture proved more interesting to her than the real aircraft visible in the distance.

At Heathrow Airport on a grey, damp morning in September, the family were saying their farewells, standing outside the entrance to a security suite belonging to the Airport Police. Several yards away, waiting patiently for Catrin Sayer, stood two other police officers also in plainclothes. They would accompany her.

Her first long trip away for work since Mair was born, the packed itinerary filled four of the five days.

A shorter trip when Mair was eleven months old had been far easier, in terms of separation. She had driven to

Wales for the funeral of an aunt. Away for a day and a half, it seemed strange to sleep in a bed without listening for her child's nighttime sounds.

Catrin gave her daughter another hug and kiss. "Be good for Daddy and Chloe. I love you."

"I love you," came back at her.

Chloe was the nanny they shared with their friends Jean and Melanie and their own daughter, Lili. Chloe planned to occupy Mair's attention later with a special 'Wheels on the Bus' game added to the children's activities. Chris, like Catrin, also worked for the Metropolitan Police, in his case, in a civilian role. He would take Mair home to Spitalfields before going to work for the afternoon.

As he picked up his daughter and kissed his wife, he said, "It's only five days, and you get to see Jian Li at the end. Think about that."

She nodded, lips tight, then she blurted suddenly, "I will. Love you." She turned to move forward and join her colleagues.

Detective Inspector Andrew Collard gave her a smile and DC Rita Tully a sympathetic look. "It's so hard, the first time," Collard whispered. He had two small children.

"Tell me about it," she said, turning for one last wave as she moved forward, raising her warrant badge for the security officer controlling the door access to read.

Overwhelmed by both the separation from her family and the work issues ahead, she had not slept well at all last night, recalling the recent weeks of errors, rushed decisions and the 'if only I–' demons of guilt that developed. The thoughts lingered, hard to dismiss.

She felt almost as bad as on her return to London from Scotland years ago, as a detective constable, recovering from emergency surgery. Her boss had accompanied her then, making her aware of the diplomatic war going on between the Scottish and English bureaucrats over an arrest Catrin had made days earlier. Recent events now weighed as heavily on her.

The three officers were on a difficult and depressing task. At the end of the visit lay the one bright spot Chris had reminded her to focus on. She would meet with her friend Jian Li Yeung for a day, to catch up and see in person her godson. Catrin and Li had first met in Wales years ago, while Catrin was a new detective constable and Li was a law student.

Detective Chief Inspector Catrin Sayer went through the door that swung open, followed immediately by her two team members. They had over thirteen hours in the air ahead of them. She could catch up on sleep while on board, hopefully more peacefully now that she was committed.

For some reason, her mind went back two months, to the events around the first time she encountered DS Emmie Shand with the South Wales Police, yet another casualty in the current mess they were unravelling.

Sayer was experienced enough to know that all serious incidents have complex causes. There are many events that wind together to create a tragedy. The meeting with Shand was a component, but it was nowhere near the beginning of the case. And she had no idea when this one would end.

Others, reviewing the file many months later with much the same thought process about causal factors, would point to a young man from Kos, Nigeria, or a land purchase made to assist the aims of the British Lichen Society, or the zeal of an ambitious detective sergeant in

Lewisham. All would agree that a house purchase in Iver, Buckinghamshire became a critical element, made around the time Sayer was a detective inspector immersed in art crime. Together, they led to a serious injury of one police officer and the violent deaths of two other people.

PART 1: EMERALD

1 IVER

The house on Pinewood Road in Iver, Buckingham-shire was constructed of old brick but devoid of any part-icularly attractive features. It had a nice address, though, attractive to prospective buyers. Buckinghamshire, being a ceremonial county derived from history, laid claim to a Lord Lieutenant rather than a member of parliament. Electoral, local council and civic parish names were different, but Iver, Buckinghamshire sounded more up-market than Iver, Iver Heath.

It was home to Pinewood Studios, the centre of the British film industry. Living there, you may run into the stars doing their weekly shopping at the local market. Or not.

Of late-nineteenth century construction, the Victorian gabled roof over the front entrance and its associated ornate woodwork showed the house's general condition. They both needed repair. Any prospective buyer could see firsthand the evidence of additional costs to come, even before entering the home. What loomed for the unwary in the major parts of the house?

The local neighbours feared that a developer may buy the property for the land, tear it down and rebuild. The sizeable rear garden stretched about one hundred yards to a small copse of trees at the boundary, with an old stone wall bordering the minor road behind. Five houses in that part of Pinewood Road benefited from the privacy the copse provided, with a bonus; the woodland was undevelopable. It had species of lichens growing there, now under a protection order amicably agreed between the owner, the council and the British Lichen Society.

The concern around property redevelopment arose partly from the construction work that such a major transformation entailed, with the surrounding mess and noise for the months of construction. Longer term, the spectre of one of those miserable, modern blocks of tiny apartments appearing drove their fears. It would be a more permanent blot on the neighbourhood.

Logistics would be a problem, too. More cars for too few parking spaces and apartment occupants who commuted into London during the week and morphed into noisy party freaks at weekends.

A collected sigh of relief filled the local gossip when the house sold to a couple with money, Amaechi and Hasanna Akanni. The pair came from Nigeria, but now had British citizenship; dual nationals, the rumour mill shared, who were relocating from the London suburbs.

He was a wealthy business executive and Hasanna enjoyed gardening. They could integrate nicely, as everyone around them was supportive of cultural diversity, of course, providing the standards of the neighbourhood were maintained.

The Google searchers discovered that Akanni was in his early-to-mid forties and his wife owned up to being some ten years younger. He appeared stocky, of medium height and looked suntanned, rather than black. She turned out to be slim, slightly taller than him, a beauty with ebony skin, a ready smile and warm, flashing eyes.

During the two-month period after the 'Sold' sticker covered the 'For Sale' sign, the neighbours saw only the builders and renovators there. The new owners made fleeting visits during the work, mainly the wife.

Before they even moved in, Hasanna searched out and joined the local horticultural society. That bode well with the locals.

Hasanna Akanni's idea to invite neighbours and a few members of the Iver & District Horticultural Society to an informal 'get to know you' reception raised some issues. The timing was out of season and the garden looked a mess. Overgrown and shabby now, it once had been a traditional English garden, with a large trapezoid-shaped lawn tapering nearer to the copse. Flowerbeds and shrubs filled the border areas and a new greenhouse had replaced the former vegetable patch.

A late frost on the morning of the event gave everyone a sense of the approaching winter. At the back, the shrubs and outer areas had grown quite wild. Token efforts to keep the main lawn area neat while the house was vacant only contrasted with the weeds and overgrowth else-where. The prior owners of the house had been unable to cope in their later years with either its size or the labour involved.

At the front of the house it was a disaster; the series of vans and trucks, building equipment and workmen had left their mark. It, too, would need a lot of attention. But Hasanna wanted a garden planning party, not a traditional garden party.

The second reason, unstated, was that Hasanna and her husband knew that Iver and its surrounding areas were not the London suburbs. A couple with mixed race and black ethnicities stood out in the area. But Hasanna and Amaechi really wanted to settle here and were bold enough to make that known.

The event was a great success, as it turned out. Some people came out of curiosity, to see the renovations and the state of the rear garden. For others, it was an opportunity for free food and drinks, or to get a feel for the new neigbours.

For Hasanna, it provided a chance to talk about the 'before' stage of a gardener's dreams and for others to offer their local knowledge of soils and pests. Hasanna was an unknown entity, but she had won a 'best microgarden' prize in Notting Hill several years earlier, they heard. And from talking to her, they learned she was no slouch horticulturally.

They also found that Amaechi was away a lot on business and, with some envy from other spouses, that Hasanna was more a homebird. She would travel with him if needed, or if the place particularly attracted her, but otherwise, she was happy to stay home.

"Being a tourist on your own while your husband is in meeting after meeting pales after a time. And we want a dog now we have the space. A dog needs looking after.'

One neighbour, whose husband travelled regularly, leaving her with the two kids and a dog and cat, felt she would jump at the opportunity to get bored with sightseeing and hotels.

The renovations and upgrades in the ground floor area had been tasteful and expensive. Amaechi talked about those as his wife conversed with people about prospects for the garden. He had an engaging smile and a warm, tenor voice.

"An interesting name, Amaechi, if I may say so. I have not come across it before," said Simon Coombs. 'And I have travelled a bit."

He pronounced the 'ae' like 'ee' and the 'ch' hard, like a 'k'. His bit of travel didn't include Africa, it seemed.

Akanni smiled. "Amaechi, like 'may-chee'. A Nigerian name, obviously, from the Igbo language, meaning, 'Who knows the future?'."

"Very true, indeed. We should not forget that. A good name," responded Simon, solicitously, hoping he had not been too nosy.

Amaechi wasn't going to mention that he was christened 'Charles Kingdom', not 'Amaechi'. He had chosen the Igbo name later in life. Charles was in memoty of his paternal grandfather, born in Kos. Kingdom was after his maternal grandfather whose family in Lancashire used it for religious rather than territorial reasons. Several men in the family tree had Kingdom as their middle name, a reminder of 'the kingdom of God'. Amaechi had chosen his new name as it was in line with his own philosophy on life and it could only be perceived as African. Being of mixed race, he had wanted to be clear in his chosen identity.

"Do you golf?' asked John Lucas, the third man, in a conversational lull.

"Badly, but I enjoy it."

Simon laughed. "It doesn't matter if it gets us out of gardening serfdom."

They had already identified their common bond. Unlike some others there, none shared their partners botanical passions; they just did the heavy lifting and mowing of grass.

"What do you do, can I ask?" John enquired. The Akannis obviously were monied, but the golf club to which John and Simon belonged was a little choosey about prospective members. He wanted to feel out if Akanni would 'fit in'.

"I am the co-founder and CEO of Serval Enterprises. We have small divisions in investment, import and management services. I have one hundred and eighty employees currently, based in three locations."

And, understanding full well the question, he added, "And I have just finished a term as a member of the board of the University of South London."

The two men listening nodded their approval. USL may be a polytech upgrade rather than an 'old school' institution, but still…

John continued, "Perhaps we could do a foursome some time with another golfer we know? Simon and I are both members of the Coverley. There are a few other golf clubs in the area, but ours is a little more traditional."

"And discrete," added Simon, "with Pinewood Studios in the village."

He left it unfinished. Discretion, wealth and celebrity went hand in hand, he inferred.

Akanni responded, "I'd like that."

The conversation moved to golf courses and prospective dates. Simon finished with, "As I hinted, we have some interesting members and visitors, with the film people close by. I can't give you any names, its just not done and against club policy; but you'll know of them, I'm sure. We'll see who is around at the time we play."

Amaechi Akanni smiled.

John added, "You know, some people even move here because of the studios; not just for the jobs there, but to be around the history and the actors."

Amaechi responded, "I moved here because it is ideal, being fifteen minutes from Heathrow. I do a lot of international travelling, to Africa and Asia."

John laughed, "You and Simon should talk. He took early retirement from British Airways two years ago. He has contacts."

For some reason, Akanni muttered a pleasantry, but did not take up the hint. He was suddenly lost in thought, staring through the window, past his wife, at the trees beyond the garden.

The reason he moved to Iver, and the view of the trees seemed to have occupied his whole attention. John followed his gaze and checked the treeline, not seeing anything.

~~

It was some weeks later when the Coombs and the Akannis spent an afternoon together. Well, the men golfed; the women did something else.

Frances Coombs, also a keen gardener, asked, "What do you think, now you have seen Pinewood Studios?"

Hasanna mused on the question. They were having afternoon tea at Frances' home following the tour. For Frances, it was a ritual, to show newcomers the studios.

"I wasn't sure what to expect, but it is very industrial; factorylike. All in a village setting. All the magic goes on in the sets inside; I see that. The buildings are pretty..."

"Utilitiarian? Quite." Frances responded. "It's very much a production environment, so it has to be efficient. The audiences are in the cinemas, not tourists coming through the gates."

They heard the noise of Simon and Amaechi returning. Frances mused, "I wonder how the golf went?"

When the men came in there was a slight tension evident, but nothing was said. They joined the wives and Frances made fresh tea. The talk was a bit about golf, a bit about the club, a bit about the visit to Pinewood. It was all very pleasant.

For some reason, a comment from Hasanna, that 'the tricks and special effects all went on inside these ordinary-looking buildings,' made Amaechi laugh. "The art of trickery," he responded, "is just that; to hide the cleverness in plain sight."

"I thought it would be more like Hollywood sets. You know what I mean."

Her husband smiled, clearly happier now.

After the Akannis left, with many thanks for the afternoon events, Frances said, "It was a bit frosty when you came in."

"It was the strangest thing. We agreed two pounds a hole, just for fun. It was pretty even as we played. At the end, I won the round by a stroke and Akanni came in third. I wasn't too sure he liked that. He didn't say anything, but... he takes his golf seriously, perhaps."

Frances replied, "Or he doesn't like to lose at all."

Simon mused on that point. "Perhaps. His mother was from Lancashire, and met his father in Kos, Nigeria. She went over as a schoolteacher and stayed. His parents know Hasanna's family, that was how they met."

Frances responded, "Hasanna is a lovely person, but I get the impression she is totally under his thumb and doesn't even realise it. At one point we talked about kids, and I went on about the school that ours attended. She said, 'Amaechi doesn't want children' in a matter-of-fact tone. I asked her what she wanted. She struggled with the answer."

"Funny. He seems very self-assured, a bit forceful. But she seems happy to me."

"I think she's found a way to enjoy life within the confines he creates. I suspect her garden is her life because he doesn't let her do much else other than go with him on business trips."

2 COMMISSIONER

Catrin Sayer's eyes wandered to the armed security aide, a uniformed sergeant who stood several feet behind the new Commissioner of the Metropolitan Police.

Josephine Ursula Worthington, OBE and a former Olympian athlete, (for rowing), was visiting Lavender Hill Police Station in south London. After a tour of the main areas, she visited Operation Undertow, part of the Serious and Organised Crime Command structure, located in their own suite upstairs.

Undertow's three senior officers, DCI Catrin Sayer, DCI Ken Osborne and Superintendent Gerry Lauder clustered together, standing to one side of the Commissioner.

The visit formed part of Worthington's itinerary today. She had been diligent in her promise to visit the working police stations in London during her first year in the job.

Taking in the smartly dressed aide, Catrin thought of the two years she spent in a similar role as the security officer to an assistant commissioner. The times on the daily itinerary among fellow police officers were easier than those in public areas. You could almost relax, but never completely.

In half an hour, she thought, this sergeant and his important charge would be elsewhere and, silent and in the background, he would be alert for any threat.

Laughter brought Catrin's attention back to the tall, older woman in her summer uniform.

"I hear that within these walls you refer to yourselves as the Lavender Hill Mob and aggressively object to any outsider using the term. None of us are old enough to have seen the film when it was released, obviously. Well, I'm not, though sometimes I feel it."

She paused, a questioning expression on her face as she focused on Superintendent Gerald Lauder, who shook his head.

"Nor me, ma'am. Though in my case, I look old enough to have been a bit player in the film."

The Commissioner continued, taking a more serious tone.

"I appreciate the brief tour and the update on current investigations.

"Operation Undertow, as you know and guard, is one of the more confidential operations within Serious and Organized Crime Command; indeed, within the Met. The work you do is a crucial part of our response to the increasingly sophisticated world of organized crime. You understand that.

"Operations at the front line are on the edge. They can generate success, but also incur failure. Well, it's easy to support success. The 'brass' always turn up to give every-one a pat on the back, don't they?"

That comment, too, brought smiles.

"If something goes wrong, we need to correct the core problem, whatever that may be, but never doubt my support for your team and each of you as police officers during those times, too. At such moments, you need to know that I stand with you."

Her head moved, surveying the room for a moment.

"I have one request of you before I leave. It was mentioned how well the undercover operations programme is working for Undertow, including the secondment of officers from other services in the UK and the National Crime Agency. And I'm pleased that several officers from your teams have undertaken similar work for other police jurisdictions. I encourage that and will support it in the future. We must break down this sense of protectionism between geographical segments of UK policing.

"To look after our own mandate, our own citizens, is a given, but not by making things more difficult for other people doing the same job and facing similar challenges. Be open to cooperation. Don't fall into past stereotypes. Together, the police services of the United Kingdom will be more effective against those who would hurt, exploit or abuse our country and our people.

"My best wishes to you and my every expectation, I should add, for your continued success."

In the applause afterwards, the commissioner shook hands with Sayer and Osborne. With Lauder in tow to accompany the Commissioner to her car, they left the suite, heading out to their next appointment.

As he left, the security aide gave Catrin a knowing smile and a nod of recognition. She may be a detective chief inspector now, but the small group of people with the job of protecting the Executive Team, past and present, knew each other through personal contact or reputation.

Now, Sayer thought, let's get their heads back into the

work.

Opertion Undertow, as the Commissioner said, focused on organized crime. Unlike most Metropolitan Police operations at the borough level, it did not deal with incident response or laboriously work its way up from the street level to the people who ran criminal gangs. By various means, including digital intelligence work, undercover officers and careful planning, it targeted directly the people at the top. At the right moment, arrests were made and charges were laid. Like the tidal analogy it had been named after, it took the top people's feet from under them without warning. As inferred in the Commissioner's speech, little was known about its teams or its activities by other units or the general public.

Catrin Sayer led Team A, her colleague, Ken Osborne, led Team B. Specialist sub-teams provided support for both.

Still in the process of wrapping up the evidence for a six-week operation into a major housing development fraud, Team A was receiving a new assignment.

Lauder said, "This is smaller, easier, for a change, the London end of a trafficking operation, bringing in women from Eastern Europe for the sex trade. The primary operation is led by the Hamburg Police. We will coordinate our work with them, to wrap up the UK end as they make their move on the organizers."

Catrin was listening as she read the briefing document passed to her boss from Commander Moore.

She looked up. "This involves a company called Warminster International Transport. I have met their CEO at a gala dinner. He received an award."

"Is this linked to your pottery work?"

"Yes. With Jean and Melanie."

Lauder gave the impression he had little time for events like charity galas.

"Do you know him?"

She shook her head. "We just sat at the same dinner table. That's all."

"It isn't an issue, then. The Germans say they hope to close this lot down within the next three weeks, so you'll need to get moving. There are at least three Warminster employees involved and probably more."

She was still scanning the document. "Warminster has main depots in London and Swansea. Any linkage with others in Wales, for the Swansea end?"

"No. Not yet at least. And given the timeline, I suspect anything there will be part of the follow-up after the main arrests."

He smiled. "No, you don't have time to go liaising with the Welsh Police, despite the Commissioner's plea. It's just the London focus for us at present."

She returned the smile. "Pity. I could have taken Mair with me, she could spend time bossing my mum and dad for a change, instead of me and Chris."

Sayer grew up in Pontypridd, South Wales. Her parents still lived there.

If she had known what was to come, she would have been more focused on Port Talbot than either Swansea or Pontypridd.

3 MAESTEG

When his phone rang, Howard Kirkland had just completed a sixty-one finish in two darts; an outer bulls-eye followed by his favourite, double eighteen. The tavern where he played darts was called The Pig Iron, in Port Talbot. Others watching him made noises of congratulation or annoyance, but on seeing the number that flashed up on his mobile, Howard waggled the phone and moved away.

Rosilyn, his sister, was calling. They hardly spoke these days, so it must be something special.

Ros said, without preamble, "Gareth's gone, Howie; he died today, a heart attack at home. I feel so alone."

She burst into tears, sobbing. "I can't even believe I said that."

Howie stood stock still. His friends just watched the colour drain from his face. Something was wrong, they saw, and several stopped talking, waiting to hear what Howard would say.

"We'll be right over. I'm sorry, sis, I really am. It's shocking news."

In the following silence, the background noise from the pub made Ros realise that Howard was playing darts. If nothing else on this crazy day told her, she knew it must be Wednesday. It had been a ritual of her brother's life for years. Wednesday, darts; Saturday afternoon, football. Rituals never changed, his or hers.

"How come he didn't go to the hospital?" he asked.

"The paramedic told me he suffered a massive heart attack. He'd never had one before. We had no idea…"

As she started crying again, he asked, "Who is with you; anyone? Are you at home or what?"

"Joseph is on his way back from Exeter. People from the Tabernacle are here, being good, but…"

She didn't finish. Her son was returning home from university. The people there now were church friends but were not family. She left it in the air, unsaid.

Gareth Harris and Howard Kirkland had spoken less than a dozen times in the last ten years. Their worlds were different. When Ros and Gareth moved to Maesteg, it meant the families were separated by only a twenty-minute drive. That provided a breathing space; an excuse to miss normal family gatherings.

For Howard and his wife Donna, Gareth's religious zeal and snobbery alienated them. He may have done well financially but he had dragged Ros into a life of church and home. Both felt as uncomfortable in Gareth's church as, on the occasion they came to Howard's fortieth birthday party, when Gareth and Ros appeared in the pub.

But sudden death brings people together and makes a mockery of past resentments. As they finished the call and Howard stood there, the cheerful banter around him seemed alien. Within a minute, after calling Donna, he left, walking back home. Donna would drive, she said. Howard drank half of his first pint before the call, but he admitted the news shocked him, so Donna should drive.

The Harris family being long-time members of the Maesteg Baptist Tabernacle, the support from their church community organized and carried Ros through the rituals of death. Having her brother and Donna as well as her son at the funeral helped considerably, she found. She had no other family to call on, really, since their mother had died. Her dad had died when she was ten and Howard was thirteen.

In practical matters, Donna turned out to be far more helpful than Ros had always thought her to be. That was a blessing, too.

The funeral and burial were well-attended. But in the period afterwards, as she began to adjust to being a widow and to act as the executor of Gareth's will, she needed support. It was several days later when the weight of the world added to her grief.

Joseph and Howard accompanied her to the bank, armed with various papers and the death certificate.

In the discussion the day before, Howard learned for the first time just how little his sister knew about her financial affairs. She had left all that to her husband. All Howard knew was that they were well off, always had a good car less than three years old and went on holiday somewhere every year.

It was Joe who said, suddenly, "Dad looked after everything. He was very controlling."

He looked guilty and went quiet. It sounded as if he was speaking ill of the dead.

At the bank, they met with a Mrs. Pearson and were taken into an office, seated beside each other across a desk from the bank employee. Mrs. Pearson had express-ed her condolences and pulled up something on the computer screen. Then she looked carefully through the documents provided by Ros.

As she suspected, things were missing.

"Mrs. Harris, do you have a solicitor to help you with the estate?"

Ros replied, "Mr. Quigley at church gave me his card and said he would be willing to help. I have not followed up yet. I thought my husband had one already, but it turned out he hadn't."

More's the pity, thought Pearson.

Howard, reading the bank official's face, asked, "What's wrong?"

Gareth had worked with the borough surveyor's office after qualifying. He had a career, he once said; he was a salaried man, not a wage earner. Howard had remembered that.

Mrs. Pearson explained as gently as she could the situation. Sizeable sums had been withdrawn from their savings accounts in the last two years. Six months ago, Gareth had taken out a short-term loan, the additional interest payents now being serviced from their accounts, as the repayment was overdue. Two investment accounts solely in his name had been closed out also.

Her recommendation was that Ros should get the help of a solicitor and, from what she saw, talk with that person about reaching out to the police, as the pattern had the hallmark of an on-line fraud. In doing the review for the meeting, she had seen that the bulk of the payments had been transferred to accounts overseas.

Ros was dumbfounded; Joseph was angry.

Howard asked, near the end of the meeting, was there any insurance or claim process with the bank they could go through, if this was a fraud thing, as she was suggesting?

He wanted to know, does the bank help? He got nothing but apologetic smiles and excuses. It was a private matter. The bank had no role.

"Unfortunately, internet fraud, scams like these, are common. Mr. Harris never talked to us about it and until recently, he seemed to be a very financially capable man. I talked with Mr. Griffiths, who set up the loan arrangements. He was under the impression that it was for major home renovations and a small loan to a needy church he wanted to support overseas."

"We had no renovations," replied Ros, "We had no need. He never mentioned any church other than our own."

Mrs. Pearson said gently, "Both you and your husband's signatures are on two key loan documents, Mrs. Harris. It is required by law. Can I just check it is your actual signature?"

She had printed off one sheet of a document. Ros looked at it. "Yes, that looks like mine. And Gareth had me sign some papers at different times, but I left all that to him, you see? He claimed it was routine stuff. We didn't talk about it much."

Or at all, thought Howard. He couldn't see Donna doing that. She had a better handle on their finances than he did.

The bank was sympathetic, and Ros wasn't going to lose the house. They helped where they could. She had her entitlement from Gareth's pension fund and some insurance policies; she wasn't in desperate financial trouble. But Mrs. Pearson recommended that she consider a more modest lifestyle. And to talk to the police.

~~

At home, energized, Joseph found the passwords for the home computer in his dad's desk. But it was Donna who dealt with the situation in a systematic manner, making sense of the mess.

She bought a portable hard drive and brought over her own printer and a stack of paper. She and Joseph downloaded various files and an email folder that Joseph found called, 'The Gareth Harris Home'.

It wasn't about Gareth and Ros's home at all.

The email printouts and other documents, sorted by date, were the size of a small book and read like a novel, albeit one which had a bitter reality to it. Gareth had invested in a firm in Nigeria, the business arm of a charity called the 'All For The Lord Foundation', abbreviated to AFTLF, its logo an ornate mix of the letters in its acronym.

AFTLF purportedly built small orphanages to take children from the streets and give them a home and education, bringing them up 'in the light of the Good Lord'. Each home was named after the major benefactor, who would be invited to its opening and, attend or not, be feted with thanks and blessings.

The bank statements and email correspondence showed a trail of initial small support payments to the charity involved. That had developed into a larger sponsorship recognition and, in the last year, to the supposedly short-term loan to the organisation, to enable the next stage of the grand plan; monies for a new orphanage construction, repayable in six months, it said. It would be called the Gareth Harris Home.

Repayment on Gareth's loan to AFTLF Industries was due two months ago, but nothing had appeared. Gareth had even met with a representative of AFTLF in Cardiff, it turned out, a Reverend Doctor Herbert Fisher.

Strangely enough, Fisher had given a description of himself for the meeting at the Cardiff Marriott, but in the world of today, hadn't even supplied a photograph.

"I'll be grey-haired and wearing my clerical collar, and I will have the biggest smile in the hotel foyer to greet you, my friend."

They found on-line a web site for AFTLF. It had no photographs of the people behind it, just names and titles, and reams of 'before-and-after' photographs of children and buildings in various stages of construction.

"It's useless. If I email that address, I bet they will try to scam me," was Donna's comment. "And these receipts and invoices Gareth received, they could have been written by Frodo Baggins."

Donna worked in Accounts Payable at the offices of a plumbing services company. She knew what an invoice was.

Whatever transpired at the face-to-face meeting in Cardiff, Gareth still had not recovered his money, but the emails showed his renewed zeal to support the work of the foundation and the possibility of raising more funds once his loan was repaid.

Ros was stunned. "Back when this started, thinking about it, Gareth seemed happier than at any point in the last few years. He had become a profoundly serious person, you know?"

Howard exchanged a look with Donna, her face telling him to stay quiet. Gareth had always been a miserable sod, as far as they were concerned.

Ros continued, "But now I see it. In the last weeks, he was worried sick about something, but he wouldn't say. I thought he had been to the doctor about his health without telling me, I was worried he was ill. He said I was imagining things. But I think these people not only cheated us, but they also brought on his heart attack."

It was while they were deciding what to do that the email from Reverend Fisher came in.

"Gareth, my dear friend in God, I am pleased to tell you that my trip back home to Kos was successful, albeit filled with pain as well as happiness. As I told you, the employee who stole the money from AFTLF Industries was filled with remorse and guilt once our President confronted him. It was as I travelled back to England two days ago that the man took his own life. He could not repent and face his sin and despair. His worship of the Devil who tempts all in this sinful world brought him to such a low point.

"President Adebyo insists that he will personally repay the Foundation's loss arising from his employee's act. He is placing his parent's home on the market to raise those funds. They went to heaven two years ago and he had kept the home in the village of his birth, praying for guidance as to its best use, which has now been answered. This process will, however, take more time than I told you in Cardiff before AFTLF can honour our debt to you.

"Please bear with us through these difficult times and soon we will travel forward together, I am sure, to fulfill the ever-increasing needs of children without hope.

Yours in the love of Christ,

They sat looking at the screen in silence for a moment, then Donna said, "Sleazy sod, whoever he or she may be."

It was only then that Ros realised that the letter could have been written by anyone.

It was that, more than anything else, which spurred her, with her brother and sister-in-law, to go directly to the police. Donna had said they should go there first before Ros meets up with Mr. Quigley.

"Let him bill you for doing the donkey work of the executor, not for giving you tea and sympathy over this," she said. "And let's give the police something to do, other than file it."

Donna's initiative at that point led to a reprimand at the police station later. Ros was surprised how much her sister-in-law's email response to the supposed 'Reverend Doctor' sounded like Gareth's other emails. Howard and Donna never went to church.

Dear Reverend Herbert, my friend,

Thank you for your message update and good news.

It is so sad that this sin brought the culprit for our common problem to the terrible deed of taking his own life. I grieve for his family and pray for his soul.

But is it not wonderful how the Lord provides for us in our times of need? As I shared with you, I was concerned at the impact of your problems at the Foundation on my own situation, but now I also have some good news for you in return.

My wife Ros has just had a wonderful gift from the estate of her Aunt Beatrice in Brecon, a god-fearing woman and a member of the Bethel Chapel. We will use it initially to pay the interest charges arising from the payment delays from AFTLF Industries, but I would like to meet with you again, to discuss how we may fund the start-up of a second orphanage. Could this new venture be called the Beatrice Rees House, do you think, in memory of that fine lady? It would be a wonderful memorial and mean a great deal to my wife, I am sure.

If it is convenient for you, I will be in Cardiff next Tuesday, for a work-related meeting starting at noon. Would a meeting at the Marriott again, early or mid-morning, be convenient for you, now you are back in the UK? The timing of Beatrice's inheritance requires decisive action that should be taken sooner rather than later.

If that is not possible for you in your busy schedule during your visit, please make a suitable time for us to meet. I need your wisdom and guidance on developments in AFTLF activities and the best path forward. I truly hope to see you again soon.

Yours in the work that matters,

Donna said, before sending, "Are we OK with this? I don't think giving the file to the police without an action to chase will guarantee any help at their end. If they have a chance to catch the sleazebag red-handed, it will be followed up."

They all agreed.

"Do we call them or go to the police station in Port Talbot, do you think?" Ros asked.

"Neither one," said Donna firmly. "We go to Cardiff. This isn't a local thing, this Reverend bloody Fisher from Africa."

Howard responded, "Bridgend is the headquarters of the South Wales Police. That's only halfway between here and Cardiff."

"Clue in, love. The police station at Cardiff Docks is only a minute or two's drive from the Marriott. We make it easy for them to say yes, not to pass the buck to someone else."

4 REL-COMM

Howard Kirkland would have been more shocked than his wife to learn that the attack on their family didn't come from a corrupt clergyman in Nigeria, or someone masquerading as one, but from a firm in Lewisham High Street, South London.

The office of Rel-Comm, a 'social marketing agency for the customer-focused client' was on the first floor of a building where most people were interested in the kitchen appliances in the ground floor shop. The ground floor occupancies of the entire block were retail shops, the first and second floors were offices and the higher levels residential apartments.

The separate entrance to the offices led to two facing staircases. Turn left and the older brass plaque took you to F. Healey & P. Styles, architects. Right, and the laser-etched, stainless-steel plaque announced you had reached 'Rel-Comm Enterprises'. Beneath the ornate name was the proud announcement, 'Affiliated to the University of South London School of Business'.

The day that Rosilyn Harris and her family received

the email from 'Reverend Herbert Fisher', Mrs. Armita Montaigne, Executive Leader at Rel-Comm, was disciplining the employee who drafted it.

"Miri, please take a seat," Mrs. Montaigne said, turning away from the view outside of the High Street and pointing at the small round table for four, moving across to join her. In the mix of people below, she had seen a parasol. It brought back memories.

As she entered the office, Miri Udoh, recently arrived from Lagos, had seen Mrs. Montaigne standing by the window, watching the people below.

"How are you settling into the team?"

"Very well, I think. The work is familiar, even if London feels different. I like the university, the office and the noise of London. It's so noisy! But I love it."

She smiled and pulled a face. "But not the weather. I still feel cold here, even in this summer."

Montaigne chuckled. "I remember that experience when I arrived from Kolkata. You will adjust, but it takes time."

Montaigne was Bengali but had lived in London for over ten years. Miri had arrived a week ago from Lagos on a student visa, to start an MBA course at the University of South London. Part of her program involved two hours each weekday afternoon as an intern in the offshoot business, Rel-Comm Enterprises, a short bus ride from the university.

Miri observed the expression on her new manager's face change from a welcoming smile to a more serious expression. Down to business, it seemed to say.

Miri understood that the work team members only met with Montaigne for briefings of the gathered teams, or at performance assessment review, others had told her.

She usually worked through her team leads. Jason Umar, her own team lead, warned her to be careful if Mrs. Montaigne called her in alone.

Miri was a tall, slim, twenty-one-year-old with her hair in ringlets and eyes that held the attention of male passersby, whether she wanted them to or not. The eyes were now revealing her anxiety. Montaigne was shorter and heavier, in her mid-forties, her skin considerably paler than Miri's, despite spending most of her life in India before moving to London.

Montaigne continued, "I want to be sure you understand the main direction of your tasks here. Your primary focus, of course, is your studies at the university. You know you must be in the top 25% ranking. There, you have a wide area of study latitude in your Masters' course. But two hours a day each weekday are to be spent on the specific work here."

She emphasised the word 'specific'.

"Do not confuse the two. Is that a problem?"

The two hours were fictional, they both knew, but complied with her visa work limits of ten hours a week. Miri had a daily work quota at Rel-Comm that took twice that time to fulfil. Whether a member of the morning or afternoon shifts, all students interning there had the same understanding of what two hours meant. Collectively, they formed about a third of its workforce.

"No, Mrs. Montaigne. I think I understand what you are driving at. The edits..."

Montaigne nodded slowly.

"The Kolkata auditor picked up on the changes. Coincident with your start here, he was doing a random audit of our region and saw the Danish translations."

She pulled two printouts out from a folder, each highlighted.

"Why did you change these?"

Miri looked at the first one. Her changes had been reversed and bracketed by someone.

I pray that you will receive my urgent message in a good condition. My names are Dr Hiram Piggott-Smith, i am the assistant chief accountant [auditor] in northen bank of Nigeria and also the official storage officer for [a] good ten years now. Through my last audit i discover[ed] a[n] abandoned box of gold bars worth $1.5million...

Miri's eyes widened. "They were just small changes. I wanted to see if the hit rate improved with a slightly better quality of English or Danish in the opening paragraph. South Wales and southern Denmark are suitable sized test sites and ..."

She stopped. Montaigne was shaking her head vigorously.

"And this one?"

Greetings to you my dear and [I am] sorry if this message came [comes] to you as surprise. I am writing you with the help of my nurse. I am Mrs Esmera Yula, a widow. I found your email address through my husbands internet [data] dater, the late Mr. Yula. I am presently in the hospital suffering from a lung [liver] cancer and broken hip from [a] fall. I have only a few months to live and I wish to Transfer the sum of $3,500,000.00 united states dollars to your account for good purposes...

"Well, the same reason."

Miri was looking anxious.

Montaigne pursed her lips. "You realise that Kolkata has responsibility for all global and regional stats analyses? The team there reports directly to Lagos. Lagos decides on the tweeks and changes in the primary emails, not us. We distribute those unchanged. You were told that. There are protocols."

Montaigne made it sound like a diplomatic incident, thought Miri, annoyed. She made sure her face didn't reveal that. Instead, she looked apologetic as she gave a nod of aquiesence.

"It's just with me now getting responsibility for the Copenhagen and South Wales coastline responses to the primaries, I was trying to see if I could improve the hit rate in my sectors."

Montaigne was adamant.

"You are mixing up the two tasks assigned. You have responsibilities for one of the primary spam distribution engines. It is routine work here, as it was for you back home. Those emails are carefully worded to filter in only the people who are either sufficiently unintelligent or emotionally susceptable enough to respond. Every word is considered carefully. If you change it, you pull in people who see the scam trap and react, and a lot of the effort at the next level is wasted.

"You are primarily in London for the bigger task; to develop the skills to handle the intitial catch, to learn how to draw them in further. I realise you have only just started that training, but don't mix up the two roles, please."

She pointed at the second email printout. "In this one you even changed the disease from the lungs to the liver. That will distort the disease spectrum sympathy rate. Lagos isn't happy with me about that, but thankfully we caught it early."

Seeing that Miri was now looking really distressed, she eased off, her tone warming.

"The primary work is like trawling for fish, for which

Lagos provides the primary emails. We work them automatically through the distribution lists built by our own email extractor software."

I know, thought Miri. I have done it for years. I was trying to improve it.

Montaigne continued relentlessly. "The net pulls in the catch. But the *mugus* are not flopping on deck yet, they can easily slip away. Here you are learning to be a spear-fisher; to target a respondent, draw them in, with their money."

Miri thought it was strange, to hear an Indian woman use the Nigerian word for 'total idiot', now a component term in the victimology of the world of scammers.

Montaigne took a deep breath and gave a sigh. "So, delete your revisions, resend the originals and set aside all feedback from your first change until now. You have a restart. And, because both Kolkata and Lagos are aware, I must give you a first warning. Understood?"

Miri was crestfallen. Before she left the Lagos office, she was told that London was the same structure; three warnings and you are out, back a step in the programme or out completely, depending on the seriousness of the problem you create. She needed to be careful. Ten days into her year in London and she already had a strike against her.

"I'm sorry, Mrs. Montaigne. It was the change, the stimulus on being here. I overreached. I will fix it today no matter how long it takes and, from now on, check everything with Jason in advance."

Montaigne appeard mollified by the response. "Do that. Jason is very experienced, so you must rely on his input. I have high hopes for you. Your draft response yesterday to the Welshman on the orphanage scam was excellent. I approved it and this morning, based on his reply, Jason has followed up to organize a face-to-face retention plan using one of our graduates now in the Midlands. You helped save a valuable account."

She smiled. "With your first degree being in English and German, focus your language skills on the higher end challenges, not finessing base-level correspondence."

As Miri left Montaigne's office and gave something between a smile and grimace to Jason, now looking at her from their work area, she knew she would have to toe the line carefully.

The thought of this evening, a volleyball practice for tryouts for new students at the university, made her brighten up. She and a new friend from her class, Clara, would be going. She would have to work hard this afternoon and grab a snack, miss dinner, to fit it all in.

Clara was local, from Lewisham; happy, she said, to make a new friend at university so quickly, someone all the way from Nigeria.

She had no idea that Miri had been a working fraudster, a scammer, for nearly five years and, now nearing twenty-two, was part of a small team within Rel-Comm stealing an average of thirty thousand pounds a month from people who made the error of trusting them. Collectively, the Rel-Comm teams made a significant contribution to their global organisation. The average had to be maintained or improved, otherwise the team would be collapsed and reassigned.

Clara thought, being a Londoner, she was helping a new friend lost in the different world. There was some truth in that, but Miri was a lot harder and more worldly than Clara would ever be.

As Miri returned to her computer, she consoled herself with the thought that Mrs. Montaigne had complimented her on her fix for the man from the village of Maesteg. Welsh names were as hard to deal with as the place names in Denmark.

5 SHAND

The outside of the entrance area to the police station in Cardiff Bay reminded Howard of a squat moon rocket, with brick wings extending at right angles, following the line of the streets.

"Waste of money on a fancy thing like this," muttered Howard, looking at it as they approached the steps.

Ros asked to see a detective. She was filing a complaint, as a victim in an ongoing fraud perpetrated by someone who would be in Cardiff on Tuesday. They could catch the criminal just around the corner.

The plainclothes detective constable, a DC Ticknell, was sympathetic rather than energized. Ros wondered if he had too much other work to do or whether the hot weather in Cardiff at present slowed them down. They needed a good bracing wind off the Irish Sea.

He took down the details for discussion with his superiors, to consider a course of action. His closing comment was not hopeful.

"Most of these frauds trace back overseas, Mrs. Harris. It's unfortunate, but generally we can do little about it.

People who promise to meet you never appear. But I will talk to Detective Sergeant Shand, and she will take it up the line if she feels it to be appropriate."

It was Donna who butted in. "Either you get off your backside and have the South Wales Police deal with it, or my husband and I will make the meeting with this so-called Reverend Fisher. The way these bastards have treated our brother-in-law and his widow is unconscionable. We'll make a citizen's arrest and Howie will beat the shit out of the man if need be; he has hands like meat plates. Then we'll go to the media."

Howard had stayed in the waiting area while Donna had gone into the interview room with Ros. His wife had a better grip on this affair than he did. He was blissfully unaware that the conversation inside the room had transformed him into a local superhero for the downtrodden of Maesteg.

Ros turned, looking at the sister-in-law she and Gareth had thought of as 'common as muck' with a mix of embarrassment and admiration.

Finding a live one across the desk, the officer called in his boss, a Sergeant Emmie Shand.

Within half an hour, DS Shand assured Ros Harris that there would be a follow-up action. They were not to communicate further with 'Reverend Fisher' or come to Cardiff for the meeting.

A police officer would visit Maesteg this afternoon and collect Gareth's laptop, temporarily at least, as potential evidence, and to continue the communication with the scammers, if necessary.

"Besides the emails, there will be hidden information on the source of the correspondence; IP addresses and so on."

Ros was mystified. Donna nodded, looking pleased.

As they left the building, Howard found the young officer looking him over, at his arms and hands, particularly focused on two scars on his right-hand knuckles, a legacy from a cycling spill.

"No funny stuff, sir, I warn you."

Ticknell pointed at the hands. Howard looked perplexed until Donna took his arm and replied, "We'll be good. You do your bit."

Then Howard realised that somewhere along the line he had been set up.

Outside, Ros stopped, as if uncertain which way to turn to get back to the car park. She had driven them to Cardiff. Her eyes were stinging, but she was smiling.

"You know, despite all this mess I feel as if I have my family back."

She burst into tears as her brother gave her a hug.

Detective Sergeant Emmie Shand was olive-skinned, dark-haired and short for a police officer. Currently she was working hard fighting her changing metabolism and commensurate weight gain with what she thought of as regional success; her waist was under control, but her rear end had a mind of its own. Thirty-five years old, born in Newport, she had joined the South Wales police directly after leaving school.

Emmie had progressed from others seeing her as a token non-Caucasian appointment, one often paraded in photo opportunities, to proving herself a capable police officer. For the last eight years, she had been a detective, promoted mid-way through that period to the rank of sergeant.

The turning point in her confidence had occurred years ago, during her second year in uniform. A middle-aged sergeant had said to another officer, PC Hywel

Jenkins, in terms of a response to a report of a brawl, "Take Philips and the Malteser with you."

Someone, weeks earlier, had suggested incorrectly that Shand's father came from Malta, given her complexion. The association with the confectionary had been used sporadically. She inwardly bit her lip and hoped the nickname would fade.

Jenkins had just passed his sergeant's exam. His response, loud, so that everyone in the room heard it, was, "If I hear you speak to Shand that way again, I'll report you. You could lose your stripes, so you had better shape up, Tom."

His gaze was fixed on his fellow officer, who muttered an apology to Shand, remarking it was 'light fun'. But after Jenkins spoke up for her, Emmie Shand took no crap on the issue of skin colour or gender from anyone.

She and her boss, DI Derek Farr, were looking at the photo of Gareth Harris that his wife had given them.

Farr said, "It's unusual, finding these scammers have a London link, but Harris' computer shows that it is someone there. So, we can put some effort into this, to catch the local talent if they show up at the Marriott. Anything else needs to be passed to the Met to sort out. But let's take this one into custody first.

"Robertson is your choice?"

The police officer who would substitute for Gareth Harris at the rendezvous.

Shand replied, "Yes. At a distance he would be suitable. Similar age and build, similar hairstyle and colouring. Close up, no. But across the foyer of the Marriott, if he was holding the email printout and looking down at it, it should work."

Her boss agreed. PC Robertson was asked to come

into work in plainclothes on Tuesday, wearing a sports jacket or suit, preferably. Ros Harris had said that Gareth would never go to a work meeting in Cardiff in less than that.

~~

Shand was seated in the lobby of the Marriott Hotel entrance, talking on her phone, it appeared. DC Lesley Ticknell, outside, was looking for a middle-aged grey-haired black male, hopefully wearing a clerical collar, the description given to Gareth Harris in an email in advance of the first meeting.

"A young black male, no one with him."

This was the third spot he had reported during the last five minutes. The Marriott Hotel was busy. Emmie thought that the scammer had chosen a meeting location at a busy time, it gave more cover.

She saw the young man come in, wearing a suit and tie and carrying a lightweight raincoat over his arm. The forecast was for rain, and it was needed.

She expected him to go to the desk or restaurant, move off their radar, but he looked around the lobby and suddenly spotted Robertson sitting there, apparently re-reading the email printout.

As he approached the chairs, the young man said, "Mr Harris; Gareth?"

As the police officer looked up and smiled, the young man continued, "It is my great pleasure to meet you. Unfortunately, the Reverend Doctor Fisher is unavailable due to an emergency and has asked me to come. I am Matthew Chukwu, with the Reverend Doctor's staff."

He returned the smile, pulling out a phone. "I am going to call a colleague now to see if Reverend Fisher can be freed up for a moment. He can lead us in a quiet prayer together, as we continue this blessed work and, if not, we can pray ourselves for guidance with the path forward for the wonderful news you have given us."

Robertson stood, assessing the man, who was slim, athletic and his own height. He gestured to the chair opposite him, while extending his hand to shake it. Whatever it was, once they were close, perhaps a distinguishing feature on the police officer or his expression, they never knew, but Chukwu's face changed.

Seeing it, the police officer moved forward to arrest the man, but Chukwu was faster, turning and running, seeing a woman stand and move towards him from a seat nearer to the door.

He's like a whippet, Emmie thought, but she had the angle to intercept him.

Chukwu veered further to the right, nearer to the registration desk, jumping over a pull-along suitcase placed just behind a couple checking in. Almost.

His trailing leg caught the top of the case, and he went down face first, arms outstretched, the case handle now tangled around his ankle. Unfortunately, his arms failed to help him. One caught in a railing, the other went wide of the adjoining panelled pillar separating the bar area from the foyer. His head made the first real impact, with the pillar itself, as his raincoat slid across the floor.

As he lay still, Emmie's first thought was that there were security cameras. No officer had touched him. He did this himself. Injury to a suspect caused police officers a lot of grief.

She brought out her warrant badge and headed over, showing it to the astonished couple checking in and to the desk clerk. As Robertson kneeled to check on the state of the man, she called for an ambulance and then reported into DI Farr.

The young man was breathing, but unconscious. DC Ticknell entered to assist, and they started to clear people away from the immediate area. Emmie went across to retrieve the man's raincoat.

She felt the lop-sided weight and intuitively placed the coat on a lounge chair nearby. She pulled forensic gloves from her pocket and donned them before reaching into one raincoat pocket, then the next. She knew what it was before she took it out and, in doing so, called Ticknell to bring an evidence bag, sharpish.

As she looked at the man on the floor, she thought the case was going to take on a new dimension. She waited until Ticknell reappeared and opened the evidence bag before withdrawing the small automatic pistol from the pocket, checking first the safety lever. There was a red strip showing; the safety was off; it could be cocked and fired.

"Les, note this. I am setting the safety lever into the safe position before placing it in the bag. For the record. Got it?"

He confirmed it. "Now, take this. Place it over there and stay with it. Call tactical and get a weapons officer to take it to forensics."

She returned to Robertson, still kneeling by the man. As an ambulance pulled into the front of the hotel, she said, "Go with him. As soon as he is conscious, caution him. We'll see how it goes at the hospital, but he will be charged with the possession of a weapon."

She checked Chackwe's suit jacket pockets, finding the phone still lit up. As she thumbed through his emails and texts, she saw another reason to call her boss. This wasn't an African 419 scam with a local contact in the UK, she realised. It had all the hallmarks of a fraud operating out of somewhere in London; and they had phone numbers and emails that seemed genuine, not cover.

Two hours later, the man was in an induced coma, with swelling inside the skull and a cranial bleed. Doctors were worried about pressure on the brain and operated to relieve that. Chuckwe was still unconscous after the effects of the anaesthetic wore off.

At the same time, Cardiff Police found the calls to be traceable to a London address, which surprised them. It was one of a set of eight Samsung Galaxy smartphones bought by a small company, Rel-Comm Enterprises, a satellite business arm of a private university in Nigeria, fitted into the startup business envelope of the University of South London.

DI Farrar saw an opportunity; as did his boss, DCI Ratten. After a call to their usual contact at the Met explaining the time-sensitive situation, they received a response from a senior rank Metropolitan Police officer, a Commander Karen Moore. That, in turn, took them to their own Chief Superintendent, Alec Williams, who knew Moore well, it turned out.

They were people of similar disposition, it appeared; both were action-orientated decision makers. DI Farr and DS Shand found themselves driving to London for a meeting later that afternoon at New Scotland Yard.

6 RAID

The same morning, DCI Catrin Sayer also focused on making arrests. With several colleagues, she waited in a car near the gatehouse entrance to a warehouse site on Knights Road, in North Woolwich. They needed one more development; a car to appear with a rather nasty character called Stefan Kiel and two illegal immigrants.

Inside the gatehouse, Filippe Ignez looked out of the window as a woman on a bike came to an abrupt stop near the curb and leaned over, staring at the brake mechanism. Something has jammed, he thought.

He was required to stay in the gatehouse, or he would have helped her. She was a tall woman from somewhere close to his own roots, he suspected, from Jamaica or the neighbouring islands. But he couldn't do that. To leave his post, there had to be another person to cover for him, as you never knew when a vehicle wanted entry or exit.

As he caught sight of a familiar 'Warminster Transport' lorry livery in the distance, knowing it planned to turn in their yard, Filippe moved across the room to the control box for the barrier, a sturdy cantilevered metal bar blocking the entrance. A passerby, a white male, had stopped and was in conversation with the woman as she fiddled with the brake.

Filippe raised the barrier for the articulated truck to enter, the driver waving as Filippe noted the cab unit number in his log book and the time. He was never sure why; all the Warminster trucks had satellite tracking and reporting, but he did as he was told.

The pedestrian sidedoor to the gatehouse opened, and the cyclist came inside. She is probably looking for tools, he guessed. But she reached into her pocket and pulled out an identity badge in a wallet.

"Police. Don't drop the barrier. Keep your hands in sight and step back from the controller. Now, please!"

Behind her the man spoke into a radio.

"Where the hell is the Volvo? It should be here by now!"

DI Andy Collard, coordinating the various units, sat next to the driver.

A voice came back. "It just veered off along Boxley Street, going north. Hang on, I see two traffic units, lights flashing, flying by the ambulance station. I think they spooked him. We are turning now to follow."

Collard asked, "Ma'am? Hills and Collings are in the gatehouse. Do we go ahead or cancel?"

Catrin hesitated only a second before she replied, "Proceed."

Collard called out the war cry for the operation to begin. With that, their car shot forward as three more unmarked cars and a Ford Transit van arrived at Warminster Transport, to drive straight through the entrance without stopping.

As the last vehicle to arrive inside the depot, Catrin

watched her team move to their assigned actions. There wasn't a rush, just a sense of purpose and deliberation. Seconds later, two men ran out of the second warehouse, to be pursued by three officers. She turned to Collard.

"Any update on the Volvo?"

He looked pained. "They lost it in those small streets. We had it on cameras by the Royal Docks, but it may have turned into Victoria Dock Road. We are looking for him."

There were two girls from Slovenia in the car with Kiel, both thinking they had good warehouse jobs arranged, unwittingly heading for a life of hotel rooms, drugs to keep them contained, and a parade of men paying for their bodies. That is, if Stefan had his way.

She didn't curse or berate anyone, but she wanted to know who sent Met cars down the North Woolwich Road and why.

"It's bad luck, really," she commented. "Let's get in and process them, then focus on anyone who knows where Kiel is likely to be heading, if he doesn't turn up here. Clear the vehicles from the front and have Loretta work with the gatehouse guard to make it look as normal as possible. Kiel may loop back. If not, he will head off to hole up somewhere."

Inside the office block, they found Gregory Clewes in his office, sitting in an easy chair away from the desk. A uniformed officer was standing nearby, keeping a check on him.

Collard and Sayer identified themselves. Behind her, Sayer could hear several people complaining or questioning what was happening. But Clewes just sat there, waiting.

Suddenly he said, "I knew it. I felt it in my gut. Sid

Oates' son wasn't right. We should never have taken him on. The day after he leaves to return to uni, you lot descend. He sold us out, the bastard, didn't he?"

He wasn't Oates' son, Sayer thought; he was an undercover officer playing that role. His name will never be known to you and the officer is on his way back to Humberside, not the University of East Anglia.

She eyed him neutrally. "I'm the one asking questions, Mr. Clewes. Where is Stefan Kiel heading now? He bolted. Where will he go?"

He sneered. "I don't know what you mean."

"He has two girls with him, picked up in Kent. We have people in the depot there now. Where will Kiel be heading if he can't get here?"

"How should I know, I'm not his keeper."

"You are his boss. You know."

The expression on his face showed his co-operation was as likely as a confession of his own sins.

The corridor door crashed open and a large man in a suit appeared, followed by an apprehensive female.

"What the devil is going on here? What's happening, Greg?"

Catrin spoke evenly. "Detective Chief Inspector Sayer, Mr. Walters. I must advise you that Mr. Clewes and some of your other employees have been using Warminster Transport for criminal purposes. They have been bringing people illegally into the UK, women mainly, for the purposes of prostitution."

Walters looked at Clewes, seeing the insolence on his face and the truth of the police officer's statement. The woman behind Walters stifled a comment she was about to make and whispered, "Oh my God! Greg?"

Catrin continued, "I was just coming up to see you, sir, to inform you and present the search warrants. Stefan

Kiel was due back with two women brought in from Hamburg, but he bolted. Clewes is the best person to help us track them down, so we came here first."

They underestimated the older CEO. He was putting on the flab, but he was tall and fast. He threw himself across the desk and landed a punch on Clewes' face that sent his head back.

"How dare you!" Walters bellowed at his Logistics Manager.

As Catrin and Andy pulled him back, the blood poured from Clewes' nose.

She looked at DC Stone, who had entered, hearing the noise. Catrin pointed at Clewes. "'Caution him and handcuffs. Take him in. Mr. Walters, I must ask you to control your-self."

Andy Collard looked at Catrin; she shook her head. She didn't want to arrest Walters. A charge of assault may be made later, but her priority was to find the girls before Kiel did something with them. Walters' co-operation was important.

"I'm sorry, I–."

"Don't speak about it, Mr. Walters. Can we go somewhere else? I'll bring you up to speed and ask for your assistance for my people, some of whom will be working out of here for a while."

Walters was breathing heavily, looking at the back of Clewes, being taken away by DC Stone. "Let's go to my office."

He looked at Catrin. "I've met you before, but I'm not sure where?"

Catrin was surprised that he remembered. "At the charity gala at Fulham, eighteen months ago. I was at the same table. I'm also a ceramic decorator in my spare time. My artistic partner and I were seated across from you."

"That's it. Now I recall it. You and she make expensive pottery."

That's one way to describe it, she thought.

His award at the gala related to his philanthropy, but also referred to his work in modernising and growing Warminster Transport. Unfortunately, Catrin had concluded, he had left too much in the hands of people he trusted who didn't deserve that trust. The company's reputation was going to be in tatters once the press found out.

She had more bad news to pass on before she returned to Lavender Hill to direct the interviews of the people arrested.

In his office, she told him that besides Clewes and Kiel, four other employees were involved. The smuggling operation was linked to an organized crime gang in Eastern Europe. "Our operation here is in support of a major investigation by the German police. These criminals are violent people. One informer has been killed over there."

Walters shook his head. "Greg has a good job. He's been here fourteen years. It's hard to take in. This will kill my dad, he's eighty-six. He started this company with one lorry."

We know, thought Catrin. We did a lot of work in the last two weeks before we came in today.

"We would like your cooperation with access to files and your system. We have authorisation with the warrant but any help –."

"You've got it. What do you need?"

"I was going to say, you should really contact your solicitors and get them involved. We don't think the company is financially implicated in this, it is the people misusing your systems paperwork and vehicles, but your own legal people will want to be informed, as will your insurance."

He looked overwhelmed.

She added. "It's probably a good idea, when you talk to your father, to make the distinction. This is not about Warminster Transport; it is about an international trafficking gang."

Fifteen minutes later, as the action divided between the search teams gathering evidence and the custody teams taking people to Lavender Hill, she asked Collard, "Anyone else missed, other than Kiel?"

"No, all five are in custody. Now comes the time inside small interview rooms and asking questions that never get answered."

"Well, you do Clewes, and get answers from him about Kiel. I'll check with Sarah. You head back and get started."

DI Sarah Mills was a forensic auditor by training. Finding illegal funds processed through legitimate businesses was her forte. Her team was one of the specialist units that comprised Operation Undertow.

Andy said, "Clewes was yelling for Walters to be charged for assault. I told him I saw the man trip and fall across the desk. It was an accident. He won't be happy seeing me."

He started to walk away as Catrin's phone rang. She checked it with the intent of not answering, but it came up as Commander Karen Moore, Lauder's boss. Moore was something else, and unpredict-able, so she answered.

"Catrin, how did it go?"

"To plan, ma'am, except a pair of borough officers in lit-up cars ploughed through as we started, so we lost one.

We are trying to find him now. The rest on the site are in custody."

"Well, get on. But that's not why I called. Have you ever had contact with a Chief Superintendent Williams, with the South Wales Police?"

"No, ma'am. Not that I recall."

"If you had, you would remember. How about a place called Maesteg?"

She pronounced it 'may-est-eg'.

"Maesteg, ma'am. A village inland from Port Talbot but no, only driven through it. It has a choir, though."

"I thought every place in Wales had one. Right. Go find your lost sheep. I'll be in touch."

She rang off, leaving Sayer staring at the phone. Collard had stopped, once he heard it was Moore calling.

"Go find our lost sheep, she said," shaking her head.

Collard retorted, "These sheep have a wolf with them. It sounded as if she was giving you a test on Wales."

Sayer looked at him, a pained expression on her face. "She will be in touch, she said. I don't like the sound of this. Go on, see what you can do. I'll be back in the station in less than an hour."

She stood, thinking. Karen Moore was acknowledged as brilliant and decisive, but unpredictable. When she gets an idea in her head, her people get turned around. The usual buffer between Osborne and Sayer was Superintendent Lauder. He was a counterbalance; experienced, measured, meticulous and demanding.

But Lauder had left on holiday the week following the visit of the Commissioner. He had assigned Ken Osborne to act for him. Catrin wasn't put out about that. Six months ago, she had done the same when Lauder went on holiday then.

The memory of a call years ago from Moore late at

night came back, to leave for Norfolk at 5.00 a.m. to assist an arrest at a farmhouse. "You being an artist and still being an authorised firearms officer, I said you could help." She had a gleam in her voice on that call, too.

Catrin had enough to do already with the Warminster Transport arrests. Perhaps whatever had caused Moore's sudden interest in South Wales would be replaced by something else. She hoped so, anyway.

7 INTERVIEW

"And I am tired of questions from the pair of minions. I demand to speak with the top man!"

The slur about their rank could also be a smart-ass reference to DS Stephen Wong's glasses, Catrin thought. Wong had made a similar comment as a joke when he appeared in the new glasses, with their round black rims and heavy temple arms. If so, DC Stillwell was incl-uded for good measure.

It was the early afternoon of the arrests at Warminster Transport. Of the five people held in custody, the first round of interviews identified their accountant, a Barry Chisolm, as the one most likely to break. Without any prior conviction, he was inexperienced in issues of cust-ody and police interviews. He also found it difficult to hold his temper. As the evidence was shown to him, piece by piece, he saw the writing on the wall.

In an adjoining interview room, Clewes, nursing a bruised face, was proving hard as nails in his interview with Collard. They were making no progress with him.

Catrin stood still in the monitoring room. The large

screen displayed the feeds from the different interviews. They could focus in and listen to any of them. Members of her staff were following individual interviews on their own screens, analysing the responses and giving feedback to the interviewers via their earpieces.

Chisolm had lost his temper again, which was great, they thought. He glowered, breathing heavily at Philip Wong and Pauline Stillwell, after giving his ultimatum.

Careful, thought Sayer, watching intently. But she said nothing to the others present. After a litany of 'no comment', question after question, this may give us a break.

His solicitor gave him another sharp warning look.

The accountant had just played into one outcome scenario for the second interview session. Arrested as a key player reporting to Clewes directly, he knew the money flows and the people.

In the interview room, Stillwell spoke up suddenly. DS Wong had led the questioning so far. Stillwell's voice provided a contrast; she kept it deliberately quiet, defensive and uncertain.

"Well, Mr. Chisolm, you haven't given us anything, so I'm not sure you have that much to tell, certainly not enough for us to call in a senior officer."

Chisolm exploded at her. "No? Really? How about the place Stefan pissed off to in the car with the girls, the arrest you screwed up when the horde from hell descended?"

Stillwell's face showed surprise and denial. She replied dismissively, "As if you'd know that! Come on, you're a numbers person, not…"

"Of course, I know that!"

Catrin spoke to the screen and to the others in the viewing room, "Well done, Stillwell. Tell Wong I am arriving in two minutes. First ask Mr. Chisolm what he wants; it appears he is ready for deal-making, the arrogant sod."

As Sayer walked in and closed the door, DS Wong said, "For the record, DCI Sayer is entering at 1.36 p.m."

Stillwell stood to make room at the table, but Catrin motioned her back into the seat.

"I'm not staying, so sit. Mr. Chisolm, I am the senior investigating officer. You want the head 'man'; I'm it. Thank you for your enlightened view of gender equality, it does you proud.

"Talk to your solicitor. Anyone above me in rank is now dealing with bureaucrats and politicians or working to reduce overtime costs. Closing down your trafficking business is my job and I'm enjoying it, thank you."

Her tone was combative.

She continued, "What do you want to talk about?"

"I want a break. I won't snitch on our people, but I know other things. Where the money is; and where Stefan took the girls. You are after the money mainly, right? Well, if I help with that, what do I get in return?"

He expected a cooperative response. What he got was a look of incredulity from Sayer.

"You should have talked with your solicitor, you know? I wasn't joking. I've got you on record, not just the words, but the image and the tone of voice. You know with some certainty where Stefan Kiel is likely to be right now. Don't bother trying to qualify or backtrack on what you said, it won't wash. So, you tell me that address, Barry, right now, or I walk out."

Chisolm looked at her, as if Sayer were stupid, missing a chance to access the money flows.

Catrin pressed on. "If I do leave, my next move is talk

to CPS and add to your charge sheet. I will press for the addition of kidnapping and false imprisoment. That's a twelve-year stretch with violent offender sentencing provisions. If either of those women are hurt, I'll be going for assault charges and, should your friend Stefan end up killing one of them, deliberately or accidentally, I'll push for a manslaughter term for you to be tossed into the mix. Because, right now, we have solid evidence that you are his accomplice and have the knowledge to prevent any of those things happening."

She leaned forward. "And as SIO, I have the ear of the Prosecution Service. You have been in custody for over three hours, with nearly two of those in active interviews with these officers. You've known where a wanted man with a record of violence has abducted two women and you have said nothing. This is your last chance. Cooperate on that point and I'll tell CPS that you did so, and if it leads to those women being freed, they will take it into account. But you decide right now."

She moved back a pace and leaned against the wall, folding her arms.

Barry Chisolm seemed stunned. "I had nothing to do with that end. I can prove it I was in the office the whole time. I want a deal. I need to talk more -."

Catrin butted in before he could finish the sentence. 'With my solicitor' would compel a break, or a digression to discuss that point.

"I'm going. I've had it. You know with some certainty where Stefan is. I've got that and I'll run with it. And a deal about the money? I've got accountants on staff that could teach you a thing or two. We already have enough factual evidence to bury you in the existing charges, so don't make me laugh!"

She was at the door when Chisolm spoke.

"Southfleet. He'll be there."

"Where precisely?"

He provided the street address. She turned, speaking a little louder for the record, being away from the microphone, looking at Chisolm and then at his lawyer. "If that's right, and if we get him there and the women are unharmed, I'll tell CPS you co-operated."

She looked at DS Wong. "Continue the interview. Get the details. We can see if he knows as much about his accounts as we do."

She walked out of the room and closed the door as Stillwell noted her exit, for the record.

Outside, she looked anxiously at DI Collard, brought out of the non-productive interview. Finding the women and Kiel was a priority.

Andy said, "I am organising a team to go to Southfleet to coordinate with the Kent locals."

The implicit question was, did Catrin want to lead that exercise, or not?

Appearing behind him, DCI Ken Osborne spoke up. He had entered the monitoring suite sometime after she left to join the interview.

"Catrin, a word, if I could."

It sounded a command, and urgent. He had settled quickly into his new role.

"A problem?" she asked. With the interview and her action, she meant.

He shook his head. "Not that, no; good call to play it heavy. Something new."

She looked at Collard. "You lead the follow up. Keep me in the loop."

She followed Osborne out of earshot of her team, perturbed. Something new, right now? That wasn't the way Undertow worked. It was a specialist unit, not an incident response team.

Then she recalled Moore's earlier phone call.

In his office, Osborne said quietly, "An internet fraud in Wales, apparently, originating in Lewisham. That's all I know."

He saw the flush of annoyance. "The timing is awful, and she knows it, but Commander Moore wants you and a DI in a meeting in an hour at the Yard. I told her you were up to your eyes and said I'd do it, but she wants you, specifically. I am to cover until you get back."

He looked up. DI Ed Franklin had appeared, looking quizzical, obviously called in by Osborne.

Catrin glanced at him and muttered. "She knows what we are up to."

She pulled out her mobile and punched a number. It was only as she spoke that both male officers realised that Sayer had called Commander Moore's direct line.

"Ma'am. This fraud case Ken has just mentioned. Isn't it a borough issue for Lewisham to handle?"

"It's my call, Sayer. Get over here. Now."

Moore cut the line. While neither Osborne nor Franklin heard Moore's response, it was written across Sayer's face.

She looked at Ed Franklin and shook her head. "Will this screw you up, too?"

With the Digital Intelligence Team now busy working on the set-up activity for Osborne's new investigation, she meant.

"A short delay isn't that much of a problem at this stage."

Osborne said, "I'll cover for you, if Andy or Sarah need anything while Karen unveils her next exciting idea."

Ed looked at them both and raised his eyebrows. "Just what we need today. You or me driving?"

He was around the same age as Sayer, a rugby player with scars to prove it, yet in charge of a team stereotyped as computer nerds.

Catrin said, "Me. Can you get back OK, if we split up afterwards? I have no idea how long this will take and if we get Kiel into custody and the women freed, I'm heading home. The rest can wait until tomorrow."

Over the year and a half at Undertow, she had grown to trust her staff and, despite the intensity of the current set of interviews, she was comfortable with leaving them to handle the follow-up. If Moore's meeting finished late, she wanted to go directly home from New Scotland Yard to Spitalfields, not head back south across the Thames. The last few days on this case had been long ones, preparing for the arrest phase. She needed to spend more time with her family.

She finished with, "And I have a gut feeling neither of us will get home early tonight, if Karen is wound up."

8 BRIEFING

Commander Moore surveyed the faces of the people around the table. Her entrance to the meeting room with her aide DI John Leigh had brought a momentary hiccup in the side-bar discussions of those assembled.

She took in the two strangers sent up from Cardiff. They had been present in Chief Superintendent Williams' office when she and Alec decided to run with this windfall. She went over and introduced herself. The female, the sergeant, seemed more ill at ease than her boss.

Returning to the top seat and looking around at everyone as she sat down brought the room to silence.

"Thank you for coming, rearranging your day and, in the case of DI Farr and DS Shand, driving here from Cardiff. They are with the South Wales Police, if you have not met them yet.

"This morning, a straightforward police investigation in Cardiff, to follow up on an internet fraud, took into custody one of the apparent perpetrators. He turned up in person to meet the victim. It now has two significant developments, one of which involves us.

"First, the man made a run for it before they could arrest him and he accidentally injured himself. He is unconscious, in hospital. Found in his possessions were two items; a phone with information that our colleagues from Cardiff will speak to next and a gun. The scam comes from our patch and appears to be an organised crime group, not a one-off computer *wunderkind* working from his back bedroom. More worrisome is the weapon, a small automatic often favoured by gang and contract killers for close-up work."

She paused.

"This is an operation where two police services can show strong coordination on a subject of public concern, the fraud of citizens via the internet. In this case, we may get to take the perpetrators into custody.

"Finally, to kick things off, I'll say that Chief Superintendent Williams in Cardiff and I are fully behind this. Not only that, small as the financial fraud involved apparently is, the case has caught the attention of the Commissioner. You know she is big on inter-service cooperation.

"So, let's see how we can work together."

She looked at the two Welsh officers.

"DI Farr, would you or DS Shand care to give the background in more detail, as you see it at present? We understand we are in the early hours of the investigation."

The Welshman nodded.

"Thank you. I'm DI Derek Farr. Several days ago, we received a report of an ongoing internet scam involving a couple in Maesteg. That is a village near Port Talbot. The direct victim died suddenly of a heart attack and, as the widow dealt with the financial affairs, the ongoing fraud was discovered. Her deceased husband, a religious man, had been drawn into funding an alleged overseas charity, going as far as taking out a large bank loan ostensibly for home renovation but used entirely to support the fake charity.

"Unusual for this type of crime, at some point there had been personal contact, in Cardiff, between a man calling himself 'Reverend Fisher' and the victim. Relatives of the widow persuaded her to set up a second meeting to trap the scammer, with information about a supposed financial windfall. They did that before bringing it to us, making it clear that, if we were not going to act directly in response, they would.

"The last thing we needed was a pair from Port Talbot playing detectives and making a citizen's arrest."

People were looking serious or surprised, except for Karen Moore, who had a glint in her eye. Catrin thought she liked the attitude shown, but Moore interjected.

"Given the gun, it was lucky they came to you, instead."

Farr gave a quick smile of acknowledgement but pressed on. "Yes, fortunately we made the meeting they arranged, not them. I'm going to ask my colleague to describe our next steps, as she led that phase."

Catrin saw the woman look somewhat nervous as she began.

"I'm DS Emmie Shand. We arranged to have an officer in plainclothes substitute for the victim at the venue, the foyer of the Cardiff Marriott Hotel, with two other officers in covert support. Instead of this Reverend Fisher, who is an older man according to emails exchanged in preparation for their first meeting, a young black male turned up. Almost immediately on making contact he tried to make a run for it. No-one touched him, although we were trying to intercept him. He fell over a suitcase and his head smashed into a post.

"I found the gun, with the safety off, in his raincoat. When we looked at his phone, it had emails and texts from some accomplice in London. We passed those on to the Met, after our boss, DCI Ratten, spoke with Chief Superintendent Williams."

Karen Moore broke in, "Thank you. Vic, you looked into it?"

Detective Inspector Victor Holsworth was a long-time detective with the Borough of Lewisham, something of celebrity due to an award for bravery early in his career. He was approaching retirement and made no secret of the fact he hated the thought of it. His opening introduction was typical of him; pugnacious and humorous.

"I'm DI Holsworth, Lewisham CID, shortly for the knacker's yard."

Moore interejected, "Retirement, Vic, retirement. Time to dust off that set of lawn bowls we bought you when you had fifteen years in."

Catrin recalled that earlier in her career, Moore had spent some time in the Lewisham borough; working with Vic Holsworth, it seemed.

He gave her a mock scowl and continued. "The phone is part of a set belonging to a business called Rel-Comm Enterprises, an office above a set of shops. We are looking into the details now. So far, we have found that a private university in Nigeria has ties to the University of South London and, in turn, this is a start-up enterprise associated with the USL business park. Convoluted, it will take some sorting out.

"Given the information we have, the next step should be a warrant, have a team move in on the place, go through the computers and interview the people. We will build the links and arrest this man's accomplices."

Moore jumped back in. She gave him a mischievous

look.

"We aren't going to do that, yet. When we do, though, Vic, it will be your team that makes the arrests, so be prepared. Don't think about swanning off to the bowling club just yet. It's why I asked DCI Sayer and DI Franklin to attend."

She looked at Sayer, who was reading a text on her mobile.

"Joining us, Catrin?"

Sayer looked up, nodding. "We got Kiel, and the women are safe. Just confirmed."

"Glad that turned out well. For our guests, DCI Sayer leads one of the teams in Serious and Organized Crime Command. From what you have heard so far, what's your first thoughts?"

Shand thought it strange that the introduction wasn't more specific. Just 'a team'. She saw the woman sitting next to DI Franklin, to whom she had chatted briefly before the meeting, speak up, directing a question to DI Farr and herself.

"This university business where the scammer's accomplices work, Rel-Comm. I take it they are still unaware of today's development. Do we know that?"

Emmie Shand was caught by surprise. Not by the question, though, but by the questioner. She was from South Wales by her accent, and she was Collard's boss, not his sergeant, as she had assumed earlier. The woman is about my age, it looks like, and she is a DCI already, she thought. It threw her for a second.

"There has been no unusual traffic on his phone since the incident, ma'am."

Sayer looked at Holsworth. "Vic?"

"Nothing at our end."

Sayer continued. "Is there any media coverage of the

hotel incident?"

"Not so far. It was described to onlookers as an accident, a man hurrying, tripping over."

Catrin looked at her watch. "Let's find out who cleans the offices of this group, if they use a janitorial service, and whether they are cleaned daily. Perhaps we can get someone in this evening as part of the cleaning staff. Meanwhile, we should obtain warrants to access their systems and phones. Have you done that yet, Vic?"

The older officer replied, "No, I was waiting on this meeting called by Karen."

Shand looked surprised by the scope of the idea and the speed of action implied, but most of all by the voice. She had it pinned down now as Valley Welsh. Shand saw that DI Holsworth had rolled his eyes fleetingly at Sayer's proposal and that Moore, also in her sights, hadn't missed that reaction either.

Moore continued. "What else? Ideas?"

Franklin spoke up. "This man is unconscious, you said; is he still out of it, and what's the prognosis?"

It was Farr who answered. "He is in an induced coma, with a brain bleed. We are waiting to find out more from the hospital."

DI Franklin looked at Moore. "I suggest there should be a leak to the local media but not from the police, that a man had an accident in the Marriott and was taken to hospital. Perhaps the people in Lewisham are expecting feedback and will check. That will give a temporary explanation for them, perhaps, as to why he hasn't con--tacted them. And another idea. If he comes to and the doctor permits, charge him on the scam but not the gun."

Catrin was nodding with the last point; some others were looking nonplussed or questioning why. The gun was the more serious charge.

Shand spoke up. "To hit him on the weapon's charge later, for leverage during the interview, after charging him for the scam first."

"Exactly," reponded Franklin.

She shot back, "We could tell him his coat was stolen, a diversion theft in the hotel while everyone was focused on him."

"That's more like it," said Moore.

She looked at the clock. "Stay in this room, work it from here, for now. It is less complicated that way. Sayer, you lead, but this is a shared, transparent operation with Cardiff – and Vic's people do the front-end stuff other than any undercover work."

She looked at Vic Holsworth, who was clearly skeptical about the direction the meeting was going. It was obvious to the others that he preferred a straightforward approach, to walk right now into the office in Lewisham with a team.

Moore addressed him. "Vic, now I've got you and DS Mortimer out of Lewisham, let's go and have a cup of tea. We can leave June to represent the borough team, do the work. You and me, we can catch up."

Holsworth looked at her curiously as DS June Mortimer waited for her boss's guidance.

"Think back," was Moore's follow-on.

He pulled a face. She added, "We'll talk about it."

Whatever it was, thought Catrin, Moore had her own agenda on this one. She couldn't decide whether there was something else, or the commander wanted him a out of the way while they went down this undercover penetration route.

From his expression, it did not fool DI Holsworth at all. He was out of it – until they needed the locals to act, he realised. At least he smiled and accepted it gracefully.

As they left, Sayer stood and moved nearer to the whiteboard, but first asked June Mortimer to 'do the honours', there, with the markers.

She began with, "Immediate actions for this evening first before we build the detail. Ed, pop out and call your team, get Bo or someone on system penetration. Tell them we will deal with the warrants from here, it will be faster. And who should go in?"

Franklin didn't hesitate. "Given our other activities at present, I'd say either Roe or Stillwell. Roe comes from Avery Hill and would obviously be a local."

Sayer responded, "Call him. This is a one-shot deal, tell him, one night. Then come back and bring us up to speed."

She turned to the table, looking at Farr and smiled, "From the top then. Names of victim and the perpetrator; let's begin there."

She nodded to June to scribe away as Farr started speaking.

Three-quarters of an hour after she left the meeting, Commander Moore popped back in to check on progress. The investigation was laid out on the board and DS Shand was now sticking photographs there. She was pleased to see a set of actions covering both London and Cardiff, but one operational envelope.

She addressed Sayer. "Take me through it."

Fleetingly, Sayer wondered where DI Holsworth was, but didn't ask.

Later, as the meeting broke up, Moore called over to Mortimer, "June, your boss went back. Call him. He's hoping that your actions from this won't be too early tomorrow. He's still a late-night man who hates mornings, I gather."

June smiled and nodded. "Yes ma'am."

DI Farr gave an anxious look at his watch, which seemed to make Moore remember something.

"You need to get back, Chief Superintendent Williams said."

"Yes ma'am. My wife is..."

Moore interrupted him. "Alec told me, so there is no need to explain. Look, are you driving, or Shand?"

"She drove here."

"We'll get you over to Paddington fast, you can go back by train. It'll probably be easier on you. I appreciate you coming for the meeting."

Catrin saw the man relax at the thought he was going home. She wondered what DI Farr's domestic issue was, thinking of the time two months ago when Chloe, the nanny who looked after Mair, called. Mair's temperature had rocketed. She had left everything to her team leads.

Moore turned. "Catrin, can you or a member of your lot look after DS Shand for the evening, and make sure she gets to Lavender Hill tomorrow for the briefing session; to decide on next steps?"

She looked at the whiteboard. "You can reproduce all that there, lead it from your place. I'm good with that."

Catrin nodded. "Happy to do so."

Moore made it clear she was leaving, but said, "Stick with this. There's something in it, I'm not sure what but..."

She stopped.

"But what, ma'am?" Catrin asked.

Moore spoke carefully. "Check out the structure of Rel-Comm. Who manages it? It is tied to the university, but to what faculty or department? It is also a registered company. Who are its board members, its financial backers? Dig into that, not just the Rel-Comm employees and students."

She picked up her file and left the room.

Catrin had worked with Moore on and off for years now. The tone of voice rather than the words spoken caught Sayer's attention. The activities she suggested were routinely part of these investigations, but Moore appeared to emphasise them for a reason, as if she knew something she wasn't prepared to share. Catrin wondered what that was and thought it might relate to her earlier comment to Vic Holsworth.

She turned to speak to the Welsh visitors. It seemed that she was getting home at a reasonable time, after all.

9 SPITALFIELDS

Shand said something to Farr. He nodded, then wished her a good evening and a safe trip back.

"Keep me up to date," were his last words to her as he left the room with DI John Leigh, Moore's assistant.

Franklin came up to join Sayer as she asked Shand whether she wanted to stay in central London and do some shopping or sightseeing. Franklin looked at his boss, wondering if he should offer to take care of the visitor or not.

"I need to follow the case, ma'am."

"There'll be nothing to follow until we get feedback from our officers this evening, unless you are informed about any development with the man in custody at your end."

If Shand wanted to sightsee, or go out for a meal, she would ask Collard to deal with it.

"No, I'm beat, I must admit, with the morning's events and the sudden decision to drive up here. A bite to eat, talk to my kids on Facetime, and an early night will do me."

She sounded tired.

"Where are you from?" Catrin asked.

"Newport. And you, ma'am?"

"Pontypridd. How about supper with my family and a small hotel nearby? I'll pick you up and drive you to our offices in South London tomorrow morning. You can leave your car here and collect it afterwards when we wrap up phase one."

"I don't want to put you out—."

Sayer said to Franklin, "I'll take Emmie with me. We can catch up on things in South Wales."

In Sayer's car, heading from the Embankment out to Spitalfields, they talked about the case and a little about Cardiff. In the middle of it, Sayer took an update call on speaker about the Warminster Transport case, which lasted a while. When it finished, Shand said nothing, conscious of the rank difference and that Sayer was in the middle of a large operation as well as this development.

"When did you join Heddlu De Cymru?" asked Catrin. They had been unconsciously switching between English and Welsh.

"In 2005, straight after school. It's in the family. My dad was in the Glamorgan Constabulary during the amalgamation to the South Wales Police."

"I joined the Met several years later, after finishing university at Aberystwyth. I did Fine Arts there. We must have finished school about the same time."

Shand looked at her. "You did art, then became a copper?"

She seemed surprised.

Sayer smiled.

Shand asked, "Why didn't you join us?"

"I applied there, and Bristol and the Met. I liked the

idea of London anyway, but the Met was the first to respond. Bridgend wasn't hiring many that year, or at least, that's the impression I got."

Emmie thought back. South Wales Police were into diversity hire at the time and Emmie knew her skin colour had been a factor. But all she said was, "And you are a DCI now. It's their loss."

Saye mused, "It is what it is. I worked on art crime a lot of the time; it is specialist activity."

Emmie didn't ask about the scar on DCI Sayer's cheek, or how a specialist job in art crime could get her promoted so fast into Serious and Organized Crimes. She wondered if the scar was job-related or not. If so, not everything had gone smoothly for Sayer.

She said, instead, "You wouldn't have got much of that sort of work in Wales, ma'am."

"True. That is one of the advantages of the Met, really. What's Emmie short for?"

"Emerald. My dad is Jewish, from Cardiff, and my mum is from Lebanon. Emerald is the gem of the House of Levi, my dad's branch, my mum said. She called me Emerald."

It sounded rote; the number of times in her life she had explained it.

"I like Emmie better than some other names I've been called. With my complexion, the word got around the station I started in that I was Maltese, a diversity hire. I've never been there. I was called 'the Malteser' for a while, but I put a stop to that. I don't take that sort of crap anymore. The irony is that Maltese people have a whole range of skin complexions. It was just pig ignorance."

"Nor should you. Me, it was the Lambeth and Brixton stations that picked up on the accent and the art. A couple of male officers dropped hints they would pose for me in the nude if I wanted to do a painting. I had to put a stop to that, too."

Emmie replied, "Sound like we both got through it, one way or another."

As Emmie entered Sayer's flat, she heard people talking. Catrin called, "It's me and we have a visitor."

In the lounge they found two women, a little girl and a toddler. Catrin said, "This is Emmie Shand, from Newport originally. That's my friend Jean, and our friend Chloe, who looks after these two during the weekdays. And here is my daughter Mair and Jean's daughter, Lili. And I hear Chris is home already, in the kitchen."

"Newport," said Jean. "My uncle Phil lives there, on Clyffard Cresent."

Catrin was focused on Mair walking over to her and Lili telling her how they had been playing together. Within seconds, Jean and Emmie were talking in Welsh as Chris came through talking about dinner.

Emmie had the feeling that this was the first normal thing in her day. She had been telling Jean she had a five-year-old boy, Siarls, and an eight-year-old girl, Eve.

"Not Efa, Eve?" Jean asked.

"No, Eve is a family name, we didn't change that."

Her mum lived close by and took care of the children after school, she added. Her husband was a carpenter.

Jean said, "I'm a potter. My wife and I own a little pottery store here. Catrin and I also make some art together; 'one-offs' that sell through a gallery."

Emmie looked surpised. "She's makes pottery?"

Catrin had been half-listening. "A ceramic decorator. Jean does the hard work."

Jean responded, "Yes, we work together. When she

finds the time, that is."

She smiled as she hurled the jibe. "I'd better go. I was just collecting Lili to head home."

Chloe returned from getting her coat and bag and gave the girls a hug. "They are good at it, too, the things they make. I'm off. See you tomorrow, you two. And nice to meet you."

Her accent was Liverpudlian, and Emmie could tell that she was transsexual. Her face was feminine, but her Adam's apple was prominent.

Lili said, "I'll see you tomorrow," as Mair echoed "tomorrow!". The girls were swarming her with hugs, clearly a regular ritual.

Within seconds, Jean and Lili left also, and Chris was asking Emmie what she wanted to drink, as Catrin took Mair into the kitchen to give her supper before bath and bedtime.

It was later, over dinner, that Catrin picked her husband's brains about scammers.

He had explained that he was an e-crime specialist, a civilian employee of the Met, but it wasn't his area of activity.

"I don't do much on that. My section has responsibilities for tracking large financial fraud transactions and I used to do child and vulnerable individual protection, sexual exploitation using the internet. But they all have a common root problem. The internet is loosely regulated and controlled and people like that. Yet they also scream about the pirates on the virtual high seas.

"You can track scammers. The problem is that it is a 'crime of the instant' and is international. If you could act on the instant, but scammers change IP addresses rapidly, law enforcement is national in scope, and no one want to put a lot of effort into a scam taking a few thousand pounds or less."

Emmie said, "This one is nearer to forty thousand pounds, and the scammer was from London, that's why I'm here."

"You stand a better chance then. If it is truly from here, not simply a mirror site for some scam activity from elswhere in Europe, Africa or Asia."

Emmie looked at Catrin. "You should get him to work on it with you, him being an expert."

Chris laughed. "She has experts in her team."

Catrin nodded then said, "Bo's working on it right now, I expect. With others."

DC Bo Digsby worked in DI Franklin's Digital Intelligence team.

Emmie asked, "I don't understand why people fall for the scams? We see a lot of stupid things as police officers, but those letters are so off the wall."

Chris smiled. "Deliberately so. They are carefully written – poor quality language but each one contains elements some people hold dear – religion, child poverty, exploitation of women. Some victims are simply motivated by greed or financial desperation, the perennial million dollars in gold bars needing transfer. Something for nothing. They know it sounds off, but what if it's real, and they can climb out of the debt problems that are swamping them?

"The scammers filter out the people who see through it immediately, to bring in only those who take the chance of making the contact. Then the real con work begins. The scammer tries to build a relationship, give promises, build trust. Then they drag the victim down.

"They ask for help with a small fee to clear the transfer. What is £150 if you are going to get five million?

Or £300 for the additional taxes on an airline ticket if you are helping a woman escape slavery and seek asylum? You are the hero who saved her. Then, when the victim is in for a small sum, they get pulled down further."

Emmie mused on it. "I don't see what we can do, easily."

Catrin said, "Now don't start him off. He and his mates are always coming up with ideas."

Chris said, "No, I won't get into that. Basically, I see scamming as social terrorism, not petty fraud. I'd change sentencing provisions, stop a convicted scammer from using any internet device for a long period."

"That's a bit hard."

He shrugged. "When I worked on child exploitation stuff, there were people we found I would ban from the internet for life. They were locked away for a time, but me, I'd never let them touch a computer or phone again."

He sounded adamant as he stood and reached over to collect the plate from Emmie's place at the table.

After dinner, Chris offered to walk Shand to the nearby Hotel Ibis, but she declined.

"I can find it. Thank you both for dinner and looking after me. I thought I had a busy life, but yours tops mine, I think. And I have an easier commute to work."

Catrin laughed. "I'll see you in the morning, then."

10 ROE

DC Richard Coe dressed in crumpled jeans retrieved quickly from his laundry hamper and an old sweatshirt he used for the gym. An hour earlier, he had left the Undertow Headquarters at Lavender Hill in a pair of pressed pants and a short-sleeved dress shirt. He'd started his day in in the car with DS Underhill, trying to find Stefan Kriel's path through Woolwich.

Some days, work was monotonous, but not today.

Lewisham is also on the south side of London, a half-hour's drive around the A205 from the Undertow headquarters. It took other members of Undertow less than an hour to ferret out the details of the janitorial contract for Rel-Comm Enterprises. The cleaning company was a large one, and had the contract for all the offices and shops in the block where Rel-Comm was located.

Within the same period, they had checked out the manager and district supervisor of the company. Neither had criminal records. DS Ian Underhill and Roe went along to the offices, explaining that they were conducting a check on a business there and needed access to the office.

"I understand, but I am not at all comfortable with the idea, despite your warrant. They are our client. How will it seem if we are involved?"

Ian Underhill responded, "How will your owners feel to have a personal call from the borough superintendent, appreciative of any help your company provides in the fight against crime? We will be in and out, one time only. They'll never know."

More interested, the supervisor asked, "Are you going to bug the place with concealed cameras?"

"No," said Roe. "I'll leave nothing behind that can be found or that would reveal your involvement."

"You'd better dress differently. You look like one of the workers in the office there rather than the cleaner."

He looked at his boss. "We rotate people through, so a change wouldn't be a problem. Sheila has been working there a while. If we say later that Richard is a new hire, a trainee that didn't pan out, I could put another new hire in tomorrow night with her, for training. Everything will be back to normal."

He looked at Roe. "You realise that sometimes the staff there work late? We often find that at Rel-Comm. At the architect's office next door, it's always empty by six-thirty. Rel-Comm and the lawyer's suite further along have the late workers."

Richard responded, "If people are working there at the time, that is even better. I'm not ransacking drawers. Just cleaning."

The supervisor smiled. "Sheila will make you clean the men's washroom. Make sure you do a good job, or she will give you hell."

~ ~

Sheila was in her thirties, with dark hair and a sense of humour. After ten minutes with her, Roe thought she had never heard of political correctness.

"You ain't even got the uniform, just the trainee vest. Keep it on. I don't want any of the other women cleaning the south part of the block thinking I've got a piece on the side. I won't hear the end of it. Where did you work last?"

Richard found himself under interrogation, inventing answers and thinking how different this was. Undertow usually prepared carefully. This seemed to be a fast 'wing and a prayer' job.

It became easier once Sheila left him to set up for the neighbouring office. She and Richard had two businesses in the block to deal with. 'The Stuck-Up Irish Cow', otherwise to be called Patricia, had only one big office to clean at present, as the other smaller office in her set had temporarily closed for redecorating. "But does she come around and help me, does she balls!"

In the minivan driving over, the cleaners were dropped off at the various locations. It was obvious that Sheila and Patrica were not bosom friends. Richard, trying to fit into the role had asked, at the first stop, "Where's the equipment?"

Patricia had laughed. "In each location, dearie. We don't traipse around with industrial vacuum cleaners in our little cars. We aren't bloody Molly Maid."

She gave him a salacious leer. "I'm sure Sheila will be looking after you."

Sheila had given her a stare of hatred. Richard was thankful this was a one-night job. Anything more, and he would be asking for danger pay.

At the Rel-Comm office, Sheila efficiently started Richard with the task of emptying the waste bins. "Do not touch the desks. Even if you see rubbish there, leave it. It's not considered ours until it is in the bin."

Roe worked his way along the desks, emptying the bins before turning back. He went to open the door to the internal room on the other side of the corridor when a voice said, "It's locked. You can't go in."

"Sorry, I though it was a meeting room. I was going to empty any bins in there. I'm new."

"No, it's just got equipment," the man said, already focusing again on his computer screen.

Richard pressed a key on his phone in his pocket. Seconds later, it rang, and he answered it. The man turned again, giving a brief look of annoyance.

"Sorry again. The wife."

He turned away from the desk area, facing the wall close by the door. "Look, I can't talk now. No. It's going fine. They are good. I'm picking things up, yes. I'm at a place in Lewisham, training."

He paused, pretending to listen. On the other end of the phone, Bo Digsby and a colleague were not. They were concentrating on the wifi signals coming from the routers in the locked area.

"No, I think I will be here tomorrow, but I don't know. I could be anywhere they service."

That moment, Sheila returned. "Richard, we don't take calls at work, not in the offices. You'll have to go outside. It's against the rules, as it disturbs people still working."

The man at the desk looked around and smiled at her, in agreement.

Richard said, "I have to go, bye." He touched the screen several times and put the phone in his pocket. "I've put it on mute now."

She looked at him. "Remember, don't touch anything on the desks. Dust the divider glass screens next, as they get dusty in no time. Then we'll vacuum the carpets."

It was as he started vacuuming that his phone beeped, as if he had a priority text. Sheila heard it and gave him a glance. Richard deliberately ignored both the phone and her. The incoming message wasn't a text. It was the Digital Intelligence Team saying they were finished.

It was outside, later, that DC Pauline Stillwell drove up with a van. 'How many?" she asked Richard.

"Three."

Three wheelie bins used by the cleaning company filled with rubbish from Rel-Comm were exchanged for identical ones removed from the van that had been filled elsewhere. Sheila had already gone home. Richard's last job was to move the garbage out for collection. She thought he could handle that by himself, at least.

It was a strange thing, he thought. A private university in Nigeria has arrangements with a public university in the UK. They introduce a start-up business operation, not located in the university business park, but in an office above shops in Lewisham.

Something wasn't right. Perhaps they would find out more from the waste. He would be interested in what Bo Digsby was finding out from the servers inside.

11 ROUTINE INQUIRY

On the drive into Lavender Hill the following morning, the forecast was for another hot day with higher humidity.

The discussion was all business. Catrin began with an explanation of her group.

"Operation Undertow has two levels, Focus and Core. Officers assigned full-time are core. We occasionally draw in expertise or people with a specific fit for a short time, for task-specific work. I did two Focus jobs before I joined full time. You aren't either of them, but we will consider you to have Focus status. This requires you to discuss only the case details back home. You will say nothing about Undertow. Nothing about my role, nor any of my people or my operation. Not even its name."

"But DI Farr has met you and DI Collard?"

"As police officers within Organized Crime Command, that's all. No-one mentioned Undertow by name yesterday. You will become more familiar with our operation. But the basis under which we operate requires that. Do you accept?"

Emmie asked, "And my boss, Derek?"

"Same thing. No mention of Undertow to him. If he were here, I'd take him though this, too. Clear?

"I've got it, ma'am. Clear and understood. I agree."

"So that you know, Commander Moore will make that a specific point with Chief Superintendent Williams. We want to work seamlessly, but we need you to abide by our own rules in the Met on that point. If it becomes a problem when you get back, pass it up to the Chief Superintendent. Say it comes from him."

At Lavender Hill, Shand took in that Operation Undertow was a large activity, big by Cardiff standards, at least, and probably by the Met's. It brought home that Sayer had done well to be put in charge of a team here.

They showed her into a smaller meeting room where a whiteboard stood, set up with the information on it they had built yesterday afternoon; familiar ground for her. Taking it in, she identified elements that she could update. A younger officer, DC Stillwell, took on the job of looking after her. She showed her the refreshment room and the door to the loos.

"We have a big operation building under DCI Sayer's counterpart, DCI Osborne. As well, we are wrapping up another case recently completed under DCI Sayer."

The implied message was clear; the meeting room, food and drink and the bathrooms were within bounds.

Pauline asked, "Anything else, anything bothering you, sergeant?"

"I still have my pool car parked at New Scotland Yard, from yesterday."

Stillwell hesitated a moment. "We can arrange for you to collect it, but let's wait until after the briefing, then see what's required."

I only grabbed things for an overnight stop, thought Emmie. I want to get back to my family.

In the meeting room, once assembled, Sayer led the discussion. She introduced DS Shand and gave a brief background to the reason for the meeting.

"Some of you are tied up in other operations, we know. This is not meant to be a long one for us, I understand. Emmie, why don't you give an update on developments from Cardiff's perspective. You talked to people there earlier this morning, I know."

Emmie stood and moved to the whiteboard.

"The real name of the man in hospital first known as Michael Chackwe is Peter Olowe, a native Nigerian. He has applied for UK residence status and is currently on a short-term business visa while the residence status is under consideration.

"Olowe is a graduate of the University of Lagos, a business student who arrived in the UK a little over eighteen months ago to do a Master's degree course at the University of South London, where he also worked at Rel-Comm in Lewisham. He relocated from there to Coventry, where he now lives, working for a division of a company called Serval Enterprises.

"Other than our discovery yesterday, he would appear a capable, developing businessman with no criminal record. We haven't checked with the Nigerians yet. DCI Sayer said yesterday she wanted to keep information about him confined. He has no known relatives in the UK."

Her finger moved to the photo of Rosilyn Harris. "This woman is the widow of the man who was conned by someone going under the name of Reverend Fisher, still to be identified. Clearly it is not Olowe. He's too young. As in most scams, these identities are fictional, anyway.

"Harris has been told we are still investigating the case and she is to alert us to any further contact, although we still have their computer. I gather a copy of the relevant files were sent to someone here."

Bo Digsby raised his hand, indicating himself, and she smiled at him.

Her hand returned to the photo of Olowe.

"As of 6.00 a.m. this morning, Peter Olowe was still in an induced coma. The doctors think the swelling is at peak and hope he won't need surgery. If everything goes as expected, and thinking positively, he could be awake this evening or tomorrow.

"We have a police officer there and he will alert us. One of my colleagues will caution and charge him him regarding the scam when he is awake, stable, and we have clearance from the doctor."

"Finally, from me, the gun. It is a Ruger SLR automatic, a smaller weapon, .22 calibre. Our forensic people have given it priority and they completed a ballistics test yesterday evening.

"The results are being checked against databases of gun crimes involving the same calibre rounds. We have also sent a notification of the weapon, without detail, to Interpol, given the international dimension. In due course we will provide them with the ballistic fingerprint.

"That's it, other than thank you for letting me participate in your operation."

Sayer pointed at Roe. "You're up."

"I'm Richard, er, DC Roe. Last night, well early this morning, we finished going through the garbage retrieved from Rel-Comm Enterprises, Pauline and myself. It's not a typical office, by a long chalk."

Stillwell added, "There were a lot of fast-food containers and snack food waste." She pulled a face.

Roe continued, "But office papers, printouts, notes with addresses or bits jotted down during calls, none of that – almost."

He held a printout of an image of a specimen bag, containing a chocolate bar wrapper as Stillwell showed an enlargement on the screen.

"On the inside is a scrawled telephone number, as if the paper hadn't been fixed in place, the slippery side making it move as the writer noted it down. And it wasn't in a waste bin, it was behind the bin, as I pulled it out. It could have been there for several days. But the person's hand and wrist have been in contact with the wrapper, so they are trying to pull DNA from it. But we were lucky; we have a provisional ID with two partial prints, a Miri Udoh, pulled from recent Immigration data sets. She arrived from Lagos only two weeks ago and is a student at USL. She is working part-time at Rel-Comm."

He moved his finger. "The telephone number is the general contact number for the Cardiff Marriott Hotel."

He held up another printout of an image.

"Second item. Found in the manager's office, belonging to a Mrs. Armita Montaigne. A pair of coasters on the desk. The other two are in a leather case for four, on the meeting table in her office. Pauline?"

She amplified the image on the screen and said, "When I saw this, I wondered about the connection. They looked like business gifts. So, I checked. Gresham Hall Services is a management group, a division of a company call Serval Enterprises, the same company DS Shand just mentioned. The CEO is another Nigerian, Charles Kingdom Akanni. He is now known as Amaechi Akanni. His first name was changed about fifteen years ago, and he is a former director of the boards of both the University of South London Business School and the private university in Kos, Nigeria."

She let it sink in.

"At some point, Montaigne appears to have worked at or attended a course run by Gresham Hall, but there is no other link at present."

Roe spoke again. "The final piece from last night from us is the late worker. There was one person, as I began my duties, sitting at one of the desks and he was still there when I left. I noticed he was working on both his phone, on emails, and had a database of some sort running on his computer. Bo has more on that. We were able to link into one of their servers. Bo?"

Shand saw the officer with Eurasian features sit forward.

"Their firewall is not too sophisticated, but the objective last night was to tickle the system a little, find out what was there, not dig too deep and let them know we were visiting. My read of it, knowing the staff list now, is that some people there do a lot of work off Samsung Galaxy smartphones, the same model as the one found on your man in Cardiff. Looking at the pattern, these are connected to the servers during work hours, as are the computers operating twenty-four/seven.

"I have been watching them come on-line there this morning. My guess is that most of the correspondence between the scammer and the victim is via these phones. Most of the victim location work, the phishing email distribution, is on the computers, several of which are working on various databases, throwing out thousands of emails an hour. I think that anytime we hit them, providing we stop them triggering any emergency data wipes, there should be a lot of evidence of what they are doing."

"That's it, ma'am."

They were now all looking at Sayer. She would be the one to decide on next steps. Shand was impressed by what she had heard. The team had not wasted any time since the meeting with Commander Moore.

Sayer said, "We have two options, I think; close them down or try to get more out of them, either through electronic surveillance or by placing someone undercover. We could let Richard clean their offices for another week, perhaps."

She pursed her lips, thinking. Shand noticed how the scar moved as she did so.

"I think we will test the water a bit on their sensitivity and reaction. DS Shand, how about a call to their office, a routine enquiry from Cardiff, you'll claim. You have a report of a man in hospital. It seems he has been involved in a fraud in some way and he has numbers on his phone that were calls to this office. Do they know him? Does he still work there? Can they help?"

"I could do that, yes."

Sayer looked over at DS Mortimer, who, like Shand, was clearly a visitor, one with 'Focus' status, Shand assumed. "June, are you ready to go, if this gets active?"

"DI Holsworth was in early, getting it ready. I can give him a call to check."

"Do that. Emmie, get your thoughts sorted."

It took a minute or so, then Mortimer told Sayer, "It's a go. They can be there in ten minutes from the off, earlier with more forewarning."

"Let's do it then. Act the innocent local copper assuming they are above board. And Bo, you and whoever you want, get prepped for seeing the aftermath of the call."

They were quiet as Emmie dialled the number.

"Hello, I'd like to speak to someone in charge, I am with the South Wales Police."

The male voice responded by rote, it seemed, half-listening. "We don't take marketing or fundraising calls, sorry."

"I said, I am a police officer in Wales. Either get someone to talk to me or I will ask the local station of the Metropolitan Police to send someone there who will make sure I get to the person in charge."

"Oh. I see. I will check if Mrs. Montaigne is free."

"How do you spell that? In case I am cut off."

He spelled it out, then said, "Hang on, she has come over. Someone told her."

There was a pause, then a more cultured female voice came on the line.

"Hello. This is Armita Montaigne, the executive director. To whom am I speaking?"

"Detective Sergeant Shand. I am with South Wales Police. Do you know a Peter Olowe?"

"Olowe, yes. Peter graduated last year and worked part time here. He is in the Birmigham area now, interning in a business position there. He has done well. Has something happened to him?"

"Well, Mrs Montaigne, yes, there has. He is in hospital after a fall in a local hotel. We contacted the police station closest to his address to call there, see if he has any family or relatives, but looking through his phone, he rang someone at Rel-Comm yesterday."

"Is Peter alright?"

"He is unconscious, he banged his head during the fall Does he have relatives here?"

"No, not that I am aware of. At least, when he worked with Rel-Comm while studying, he had no-one here I know of. I could check his file with us, or perhaps give you the name of the person at the university who could check?"

Shand paused, looking at Sayer, who signalled to roll on, here finger moving in a circle. Stage two.

"It's actually a little more complicated, Mrs. Montaigne, I am afraid. We don't understand the background yet, but Mr. Olowe may have been involved in some way in a fraud attempt. The person he was meeting with was expecting someone else, an older man, and Peter introduced himself by a different surname, Chakwe. I can't say more at this time. Can you tell me who has the phone ending in 537. That's the number he called?"

Montaigne sounded surprised. "Peter Olowe? No. That doesn't sound like the young man I knew. He was a good worker here, and a good student. I was glad to hear he had secured another position after graduation."

Shand said, "And the number he called, shall I repeat it, do you want the full number?"

"No, no need. I was just checking the assignment list. We provide local mobile phones for all interns, you see. That one is assigned to Miri Udoh, but she is not here at present. She has classes in the morning and works here in the afternoons."

Emmie replied, "Well, thank you. If you could give me her home or residence address and the name of the contact person in the university who may have more knowledge of Mr. Olowe, I will follow up with them."

Within two minutes, she thanked Montaigne for her assistance and closed the call.

Catrin said. "Well done. It came over as nice and routine. Now we wait. Bo, it's down to you. I need to get back to the Warminster file. Let me know."

She stood. "Emmie, you settle in for the duration."

"Yes, ma'am. I have other stuff to do, make calls, check with my boss."

It was less than an hour before Bo called the group together again. Things were moving. Including the phone assigned to Miri Udoh. It had been in Lewisham but began heading into London before being switched off completely.

12 PHONES

Montaigne returned to Rel-Comm with Jason, who was carrying a box of new phones. She first checked who was present, calling all the staff involved in scams into her office. They had turned up on time, both those working this morning and the scammers on the afternoon shift, dragged out of lectures, in some cases. Some were visibly holding the Samsung phones issued to them, brought along, as instructed. Several were looking anxious.

"I hope you have all been abiding by the rules," she began. "You get new phones, right now. Anyone not current on their cloud backups?"

No-one responded, but one or two looked more concerned.

She went on, "Anyone have unauthorised material on them?"

One student, Amanda, spoke up. "I have pics of my boyfriend."

Montaigne responded, "Which you had better have backed up elsewhere. You can start. Give your phone to Jason. You all get the iPhone 8 and will download your current client set from the Cloud."

Amanda suddenly asked, "Where's Miri, the new girl? Shouldn't she be here?"

Montaigne gave her a stony look. "By now, she's on her way to Heathrow for a flight to Frankfurt. She's going abroad for the time being, as will your old phones, permanently."

She motioned to another person to change his phone next. Jason checked that each phone still opened with the master password before releasing the replacement, then he made a note on a list.

Within ten minutes they had a stack of used phones in varying degrees of wear and tear, and a set of discarded phone covers. The software would be factory reset, the memories deep cleaned, and the SD cards replaced. They were heading for re-use in another country. Waste not, want not.

In Lavender Hill, Bo Digsby saw the ISP changes on the networks; new ones were appearing, downloading content, and existing ones were switched off. He recognised the signs.

In the meeting room, he said, "They are swapping out their phones. The new ones are iPhones, not Samsung. I think they will wipe the old ones and then reset the computers and storage drives for the affected file areas. That takes a little time, so they will probably do it in conjunction with the overnight backup schedule."

Catrin said to June Mortimer, "Give your boss the go-ahead, on my authority. As soon as they can, make the arrests. Bo will coordinate and shut down their servers. You'll head back, I take it?"

"Wouldn't want to miss it, ma'am." She was on the phone to DI Holsworth.

Stillwell asked her boss, "Apart from documenting all this...?"

Catrin responded, "We are done. Emmie, the point of contact from now for you and DI Farr will be with DI Holsworth at Lewisham. By the time this gets prepped for trial, it will show good cooperation between South Wales Police and the Met borough involved. Remember what I said?"

"No discussion of Undertow, ma'am."

She said, in Welsh, "And thank you for dinner last night. It didn't feel far from home, not like I was stuck on my own in London."

Catrin responded, "Safe journey home, then. And best wishes to DI Farr."

She looked across at Stillwell. "I think Emmie's car is still at the Yard. Can you get a uniform downstairs to driver her over?"

Emmie held out her hand and Sayer shook it.

As the other officers left the room and Sayer headed for her own office, she thought Shand was quite likeable and had a different experience in the Met for a couple of days. She doubted they would meet again.

She phoned Moore and brought her up to speed. Karen would be in the thick of it now – but at a distance, no doubt – bothering Vic Holsworth, purring about the strong co-operation with the South Wales Police. Then she went to update Ken Osborne, to close off with him on the sudden intrusion into their planned work.

Warminster Transport was still her primary focus.

~~

Montaigne had just closed her office door and sat down with a cup of coffee, re-running in her mind if everything had been addressed. They all had new phones, except for Miri, who should be in the boarding area waiting for her flight, if she had followed orders.

Jason had put the old phones in a box in her car boot, ready for her to take to the person who would move them on. The computer resets were scheduled. She had talked with the university contact about 'the disturbing news about Peter Olowe' and that she might receive a call from the police.

Now she had the difficult job of callingMcEwen to give him the bad news. Roland would not be happy at all, despite it being his decision to do a second perso nal follow up with a *mugu*. With her experience, she knew that direct contact happened rarely and only once, never twice, so her own reluctance to respond to the Maesteg request for a meeting had been overridden.

As she sipped the coffee, she concluded that they had no choice now but to wait it out.

She took a deep breath and dialled McEwen's number. As she brought him up to date, her computer screen shut down and she heard noises in the main office. Still listening, she stood and opened the door, seeing the consternation on people's faces, made worse now by the noise from the staircase entrance

She cut across his comment with, "The police are here." Montaigne closed the call and went towards the main entrance to the room. She wanted to be the first person the police officers spoke to. It would remind the others of their own roles, fiction they would need to hold to in person this time, not over the internet or phone.

Within seconds, five uniformed police officers were in the main area, telling them to place their hands on top of the computer monitors where they could be seen.

Montaigne noticed that the officers also wore cameras on their protective vests. Everything was being recorded, she concluded. They would have the position of each person on record, a face to link to each desk, each computer.

Behind them, three plainclothes officers came in, the person in charge at the rear, an older man.

In her best effort at outrage, she hurled the question at him. "What is the meaning of this? How dare you frighten and threaten us in this way?"

Vic Holsworth ignored the outburst. "I am Detective Inspector Holsworth, Metropolitan Police. Your computer servers, where are they?"

His glance took in the older woman, but he fixed his stare on a young man who, in reaction, just pointed at the door to the equipment room.

Montaigne asked, "Did you shut down our system? All our computers went down!"

Again, Holsworth ignored the question. He spoke to the room.

"We have reason to believe that an internet fraud operation is operating from this address. I realise that many of you are students from overseas. You will be cautioned and questioned at the local police station and, in all probability, released after questioning or, if the findings merit, released under a police bail.

"You will not, I repeat, not, be held in custody for long or transferred to a detention centre, providing you have valid visas. The more you cooperate, the sooner we can resolve the problem. You have nothing to be afraid of."

His superior had insisted on him calming any fears. "Some of these students will be terrified by the process of arrest and the potential for detention. You need to tread carefully, Vic. Understood?"

He thought he had done that.

~~

In Iver, Frances Coombs was visiting Hasanna Akanni when her husband came home later that afternoon. The front door slammed and Amaechi came in looking angry. Frighteningly so, to Frances.

"Problems?" Hasanna asked, looking agitated. "Can I get you anything?"

Whatever he wanted was given in a language other than English. He glowered at Frances, turned and headed upstairs.

"I'm sorry, Frances. Amaechi has had a bad day at the office, I gather. I had better go talk to him, get him something to drink and eat. He is incredibly stressed."

Frances was just as happy to get out of there now, and assured Hasanna they could pick up their discussion later by phone.

Talking to Simon that evening, she said, "His tone of voice was very disturbing."

Simon replied, "Perhaps it is whatever language he used. Some languages sound harsher than others."

"That may be so. He never brings Hasanna to the golf club, did you notice?"

Simon thought about it. "He only turns up with business acquaintances, that's right. Perhaps she doesn't like golf. Have you asked?"

"No." Perhaps she never has the opportunity, she thought. "I'll say this; if you ever spoke to me like that, I would pack my bags and leave."

She would talk with Joan. She trusted Joan and her

more thoughtful, less hasty approach. Perhaps if they met with Hasanna together, they could offer support.

Once he had calmed down, Hasanna knew that the next stage would be withdrawal and silence. Amaechi brooded a lot. At those times, she stayed quiet, surprising him with cups of fresh coffee or tea, or his favorite beer, predicting his needs and meeting them unacknowledged.

He had been in Newcastle when he heard, seeing a development at the new office location for a management services team. He broke away for a minute, listening to the news from McEwen. Swallowing his anger, he returned to the staff there, his face full of pride and positivity. His people locally deserved the recognition and encouragement.

It was in the car on the drive back that he could turn his mind to the problem. He knew that Montaigne would hold to the plan; she was trusted. The problem, he thought, were the students, being young and more likely to be intimidated. An example had to be made, probably with the person who screwed up whatever scam went wrong.

Also, he needed to know who was leading this attack on him, and he had a suspicion who that was. A raid by the Metropolitan Police didn't come out of thin air; this one took resources and was heavy-handed. Someone was behind that.

And he wouldn't do anything with the Lewisham police, they were too close to old ghosts for his comfort level. He lived there when he first arrived in England. However, he now had a name of a police officer in Wales, a DS Shand, who must be involved in some way. He would keep that one in mind.

Only then, thinking about it, did he warm up and smile

at his wife.

Hasanna silently gave a sigh of relief. Her husband was through this fugue, thank goodness.

13 ELEPHANT

By the following morning, Vic Holsworth began to wonder what had happened. Most of the employees were not involved with the computers or phones of concern; they seemed to be regular social marketing staff.

Each student linked to the computers tied to scam traffic had said nothing at the police station, other than to make a request for a legal aid solicitor. Once one was provided, they still said nothing incriminating. On release, each person accessed their consular services to express concerns about their treatment by the police.

Finally, rather than try to conceal the police investigation, they went out to the media to publicize it. Rel-Comm were not acting defensive, they were on the attack. Their complaints were various but so similarly focused, they reminded Vic of the chorus line at the London Palladium.

'The way they spoke to us is still giving me nightmares. They burst in as we were quietly working.'

'I was overwhelmed by the intimidation. It was all I could do not to agree to everything they said, simply out of fear.'

'Police beat my uncle back home and he still bears the scars. Every minute in the police station, I was reminding myself that this was England, and I would not get the same treatment. But I struggled with that, the way they spoke at times, these initmidating white men.'

It made no claims of specific mistreatment but the language, with video clips of young people looking serious or miserable, was prime media material.

Montaigne, who had no need of legal aid as she had her own solicitor, provided the core response, emulated in one form or another by her employees.

"They are students. We provide useful, course-orient-ated part-time employment for these people, as a coop-erative venture with the University of South London Business School. We do nothing wrong, yet we have been raided by police simply because we are who we are."

She repeated that to the media on her release.

Vic Holsworth's borough superintendent found him-self, with Karen Moore, in tense, difficult meetings with the Media Relations staff at New Scotland Yard.

Catrin said, "A study module in an MBA? This woman Montaigne claimed they teach students about fraud?"

Vic Holsworth sighed. "She had the story down pat, smooth as silk. Rel-Comm mainly does social marketing work. Students work at improving advertising campaigns or clients employ Rel-Comm to deal with on-line customer feedback. Their database, at first sight, seems to support that; they list some legitimate clients.

"They are tied to the USL Faculty of Business. Besides their commercial work, they also handle 'real world environment' exercises for MBA students. One of these concerns the analysis of ethical business practice versus customer retention goals. Different degrees of persuasive influence through to illegal scamming practices are explored and debated, as elements of the exercise.

"They suggested that their study module may contain duplicate names that linked inadvertently to a broader, real customer distribution base. If that happened, they were unaware of it and see it as a computer problem, not an attempt at fraud. The tech people will have a devil's job sorting that out."

He sighed. "It's a complicated mess at present. I've asked for help from the Fraud Squad. They are not too happy about that, not wanting to jump into the hole I'm in."

Catrin said nothing for a moment, the line remaining silent. Then she said, "Of all the cheek! They rip off people over the internet and now they try to scam us about their practices. What does Karen say?"

"I talked to her just before I called you. She was unusually quiet about it, I must say. You know her. Karen just said, follow the evidence, ignore the media noise and she will sort out the resources necessary. She said she wants to meet you and me together; so, expect a call.

"You'll be glad that Undertow is in the background all the time, for this one, at least. People at the university are starting to react to a police raid on a student business. Now some in academia are coming out in Rel-Comm's support.

"Apparently, some professor at USL called Darius Ward teaches the course linked to Rel-Comm. He and Montaigne developed it together, several years ago, he told June Mortimer. And we have a barrel load of solicitors taking an interest, in case we charge individual students. I even had a call from the Nigerian High Commission, wanting a briefing, closely followed by the

FCO, telling me everything had to go through them."

The Foreign and Commonwealth Office.

Catrin shook her head then said into the phone, "What about the information from the Harris couple from Maesteg? That's solid. The email came from a Rel-Comm employee; the Harris money sent overseas is a fact; the man in custody in Cardiff is a fact, he worked previously at Rel-Comm."

"They say Olowe is no longer there. He graduated. They are shocked and disappointed, blah, blah, blah, but claim he has nothing to do with them. And the woman he called, Miri Udoh, is now in Germany, visiting a sick relative; she flew out yesterday. Coincidence, they claim. We will keep at it."

"Anything from Farr and Shand?"

"Not much. Their guy is out of the woods and conscious, but still not fit enough to be interviewed, according to the hospital. And if the students at Ma Montaigne's Little House of Tricks are anything to go by, Olowe will be a master of non-cooperation in any interview, when it happens. Fortunately, they still have the gun charge in their back pocket. That's one thing they can get him for. His print is on an internal part, presumably from cleaning it, or something. They are just waiting on DNA confirmation."

He rang off.

Catrin couldn't see why Moore would want her at a follow-up meeting. It was now up to the Borough and the Fraud Squad. She could see it getting messy in the media, but she had her own priorities to deal with. Within half an hour, her mind was elsewhere.

It was two days later that she found herself on a videoconference call with people fom Media Relations,

Vic Holsworth, June Mortimer, their borough super-intendent, an Andrew Johnson, and Karen Moore.

The groundswell of ire in the media followed two tracks: heavy-handed policing of international students and stigmatising visible minorities.

The expected additional cases to the Gareth Harris file hadn't even turned into a trickle.

Catrin's part of the bloodletting was to update them on the Digital Intelligence Teams additional analysis of the computer tracking.

"We have provided names and contact information of some probable victims. Part of the problem is that the money flows are separate and generally involve a phone call. They only appear incidentally in the correspondence, as promissory payments or expectations. Digsby says the banking files must be on another system."

Vic was next to fall on his sword. "Several people we located who have been defrauded don't want to know. One is embarassed, others said, 'I was only in for a hundred pounds. Thank God that you stopped it, but–'. They don't want to be involved or support any charges."

In the end, a silence developed. No-one wanted to discuss the elephant in the virtual room. In this case, the member of the family *Elephantidae* was in her early fifties and going slightly grey.

Not one known for passing the buck, Karen Moore said, "It appears that I was a little too eager in the actions on this one."

The expressions on the Media Relations people seemed to convey that might be an understatement. They hoped it would simply die away, with no further actions by the Met.

Moore gave them only a half a present. "We will drop everything, except for this man Jason Umar. We have a solid link from Miri Udoh to him and on to the Harris's in Wales. But we will hold on that, for the time being, until South Wales Police interview Olowe, to see if they can solidify the link. I don't see this one dying away.

A Drew Urquhart, a new and opinioned member of Media Relations, said, "I hope it does. With what we've been dealing with, arrests like this should go the way of the billy club, damaging the Met's image."

His boss gave him a scowl. He would be the one to end up in a one-on-one discussion with Commander Moore at some point. Catrin thought it might set Moore off, tearing a strip off the man. But the commander said, "Truncheon. Not 'billy club'. Truncheon. I think we are done here."

~~

Amaechi Akanni had been in the executive lounge at Schipol Airport when he received the innocuous text from Roland McEwen about a possible new account. The firm was genuine, as was the name of their primary contact. If ever it was checked, they would be surprised; they had no interest in services from Serval Enterprises. McEwen could argue it turned out to be more fanciful than a true lead.

All it meant was that Akanni should contact him urgently, untraceably.

After that call, where Akanni received an update that the steps in their contingency plan had been implemented, he sat thinking about the issue. Putting Rel-Comm in Lewisham was logical, given the links to USL. But he had his own history there and the name Holsworth was tied to that.

McEwen's assessment was that the problem was now

contained, that the borough was getting enough feedback to give Holsworth an even earlier retirement. He was due to go soon, anyway. It was 'old policing', embarrassing the Met now. It was likely to die away.

They had that first-hand through a somewhat self-opinionated employee in media relations who liked to comment to his trendy buddies about how he was dragging the Met out of the last century single-handed.

For Akanni, he wasn't sure this was a last fling by Holsworth. He talked in private with Montaigne, a call which surprised her. It was only the sixth or seventh time in a decade they had spoken directly, and only days apart.

By the end of his visit to Amsterdam, Akanni had thought it through. In a follow-up call with McEwen, he told him what he wanted. Roland was convinced his boss was overreacting, but he knew him well enough, and his tone of voice when he was unswervable.

Roland McEwen was made of the same metal as his boss. He didn't lose a moment's sleep or a have pang of conscience when he followed the instruction.

Catrin had instructed the digital intelligence team to put aside the Rel-Comm analysis; not close it, just keep it on the back burner as they dealt with higher priority items. Kept there long enough, it would be filed in due course.

Two days later, it was nearly off her own radar. Until she got the call about Emmie Shand.

14 KNUCKLES

Emmie took the bus to and from work on the occasions she didn't have access to a pool car overnight. It was a half-hour trip, door to door, and a reasonably frequent bus service around her start time. Her husband took the family car to work from their home in Plasnewydd, a suburb of Cardiff. If she worked late, he would often collect her, as the buses were less frequent after the evening rush hour.

In the early hours of the fifth day after she returned from her sudden trip to London, he heartily regretted not doing that. By that time, he was at the University Hospital, anxiously awaiting news of her condition.

At 7.15 p.m. the previous evening, she said she would get the bus. Their daughter Eve had an earache and was clingy to her dad.

"Don't bring her out, keep the ear warm. I'll pop into the Asda and get the shopping, after I get off the bus. I should be home before eight. There's a bus coming right now."

It was nearly nine when, not getting a response from

her phone, he called his mother-in-law to come and stay with the kids. Something was wrong. Before the grand-parents arrived, though, he had the call from the police.

When Shand left the Asda for the short walk home, she had a small daypack on her back and a reusable shopping bag, both now loaded with items. She was embarrassed to say later that she should have seen it, and been more careful. A car drove past her and stopped as a man in a track suit coming towards her suddenly said, "DS Shand is, it. Emmie?"

Her mind was on her daughter, so she simply looked at him as someone pulled on the backpack, dragging her into the back seat of the car as the man who spoke to her pushed hard. Off-balance, she cracked her head on the sill above the car door and ended up awkwardly sprawled along the back seat. Something hard hit her shin as he pushed her legs inside and the door closed.

It took less than three seconds. The man pulling her bag was the driver. He got back into the driving seat. The other man calmly walked around to the front passenger side, seated himself and the car sped off. As Emmie levered herself up, saying, "What the hell is -."

She tried the door handles. Locked.

"Be quiet, there's a good girl, and everything will be alright."

"I'm a police officer. Do you realise the trouble you are in?"

They did not even bother to respond. Her groceries were all over the place and the male passenger was holding her backpack purse, his gloved hand stripping the battery from her phone

It took them less than three minutes to drive where they clearly intended to go, a set of storage units on a short track off a road near Roath Brook. Her heart pounded as she looked around vainly for someone to call out to.

As the car came to a halt, the passenger got out and opened the rear door on his side. Ready for him, she turned, pushing hard with her feet to make the door slam into him so she could make a run for it. But he was prepared, letting the door swing wide on its hinges, after which he reached inside and pulled her out by her hair. By then the other man, the driver, was by his side holding something. A hammer.

"We want one thing. No messing about, either. Who at the Met did you talk to that caused the raid on Rel-Comm in London? Who?"

Looking at their faces, she knew they weren't going to be fobbed off with, "I can't tell you that," or something similar. They had kidnapped her; they weren't messing around.

"The Borough of Lewisham, a detective called Holsworth."

The driver grabbed her hand, forced it on to the top edge of the bonnet and brought the hammer down full force, twice, on her knuckles. The second time, through the pain exploding in her head, she heard bones crack.

"Wrong answer. A DI wouldn't do that, not without orders. Who? You have two more left on that hand, then I'll start on the other."

In her pain and terror, she gave them a name, shaking at the thought of the hammer swinging again. For some reason, it satisfied them, as the passenger pulled her towards him and punched her hard in the face, enough to send her to the floor. Next minute her carrier bag was swept off the back seat, all over her, the loose grocery items and her purse following suit, except for the phone.

One of them, she wasn't sure who, dropped the phone bits on the floor and slammed the hammer into the screen. She shuddered and lay still.

In a moment she heard the car move. Thinking that they might drive over her, she rolled and scrambled closer to a storage unit door, but by the time she worked herself to a standing position, they were gone.

She realised that in her panic and fear, she hadn't even got the number plate. She felt foolish.

As she stood there leaning on the door, her damaged hand throbbing with pain now cradled in the other arm, a small Fiat turned into the area and a woman driver stopped, powering down the window closest to Emmie.

"Are you alright? Have you taken a tumble?"

By two in the morning, Shand was awaiting surgery to pin together the pieces of the fractured knuckles and reposition the bones of the hand moved by the hammer. The surrounding tissues were a mess of blood, bruising and swelling.

By 6.00 a.m., seven black Mercedes flagged in the zone of the attack on CCTV as 'possibles' had been followed up, most of their owners brought out of bed by phone calls and persistent door knocking. Not one of them fitted the description that Shand had been able to give.

15 WILLIAMS

At 6.30 a.m., Catrin received a call from Moore.

"Shand is injured. Two men abducted and used a hammer on her. She's in hospital and one hand is a mess. Be at my office by eight, please. And cancel your commitments for the day."

Catrin had been preparing, getting things sorted before Mair woke. As she asked after Shand, Moore simply said, "I'll update you at the office."

She rang off.

Catrin called Chris, who had just emerged from the shower. Plans had changed; she needed to leave earlier, and she was calling Chloe. Then she called Osborne with the news that he would have a full day leading both Teams A and B.

In Moore's office, she found DI John Leigh, Moore's admin assistant Barbara, and DI Vic Holsworth, looking bleary-eyed. On the meeting table was a large laptop computer, set up ready for a conference call. But no Commander Moore.

"She's with the Assistant Commissioner," Leigh said softly.

At 7.58 a.m. Moore entered and nodded to Leigh to make the connection. As the screen came alive, a uniformed officer, a Chief Superintendent, appeared.

Moore began with, "Here we have DI Vic Holsworth, DCI Catrin Sayer and DI Leigh. John Leigh, you know. Vic, Catrin; meet Chief Superintendent Alec Williams. Alec, how is DS Shand now?"

"Good morning. She is out of surgery, sleeping, after reconstructive work on her hand. The bones are back in the right places, at least. Farr says she is in a cast or support of some sort with pins in it. She has had a hell of a shock. Further surgery will be needed later and a lot of physiotherapy. But the surgeon says Shand stands a good chance of regaining most of the use of the hand, over time."

Moore was staring intently at the screen.

"Can you repeat what you told me about the attack?"

Williams looked impassive, except for the eyes. "Two men, clearly no amateurs, pulled her off the street into a Mercedes, drove a short distance to a secluded area they had obviously picked in advance. The motive for the attack seems to be straightforward; to discover or confirm the name of the person who ordered the raid on Rel-Comm. Someone with money and resources became exceedingly angry about that raid."

As Catrin realised what happened, he voiced her fear triggered by the call earlier from Moore. "The only link that we can see is that Shand made the call to Rel-Comm, at DCI Sayer's instruction."

He kept his voice very steady, but Catrin could feel his anger.

"She tried to reason with them in the car. Seeing the

hammer, their intent, she gave them DI Holsworth's name, as the borough team made the raid. That brought the first two blows. She then gave them your name, Karen. That seemed to satisfy them."

He took a deep breath. "I talked to her just before she went into surgery. She apologised, for Christ's sake. I told her she did the right thing. She said she kept her promise, whatever that was, to DCI Sayer."

Moore responded, "Operation Undertow. Sayer leads one of the teams and put someone into Rel-Comm to prep for the raid. We give no visibility to Undertow, for obvious reasons."

She looked at Catrin, who now had her elbow on the meeting table, her hand on her chin.

Catrin felt a mix of guilt, anger and puzzlement. Guilt that she had given the order that put Shand's name to people at Rel-Comm and now had Commander Moore in their sights. Puzzlement about the level of anger causing the retaliatory attack on Shand. Her mind went back to the dinner, to Shand mentioning her kids.

Karen Moore said, "Alec, it's my fault, in a sense. Vic, you tell it."

Holsworth spoke up.

"Commander Moore believes it is all down to a man called Akanni, Amaechi Akanni. The raid on Rel-Comm was to flush him out, get him visibly active against the arrests, talking to politicians or the media. He is currently on the board of Rel-Comm and has deep pockets. He has influence within the University of South London and formerly was on the Board of Trustees."

Catrin glanced at Moore, who was motionless. So that was the reason for her reference at the briefing meeting. "Check out the board of directors."

He continued, "Years ago, he lived in Lewisham. We

took him in as part of an investigation into a fraud operation. The commander was my DS back then. We had a lead to Akanni, who had been in the UK less than two years at the time, but no hard evidence. The informer disappeared, we never got any evidence and he walked out of that one."

"That's it."

"No, it bloody well isn't, Vic; and the rest." Moore had suddenly become animated.

"The commander thinks that she somehow was responsible for the witness, a woman called Anne Krell, disappearing; that she slipped up. I'd recently given her a dressing down for being too mouthy, too vocal, too pushy. She was, but I don't think she revealed Krell to be our source, despite her belief. And we don't know what happened to Anne Krell, anyway."

He looked at Moore, his face clearly showing his disagreement.

Karen Moore said, "She's dead, I'm sure. And the attack on DS Shand makes me more certain. It is violent, immediate and totally focused on finding the person who came after him. And he's got my name, and I'm waiting for his response."

Williams spoke up. "I understand the background, and don't want to get into a dispute on this, Karen, but you have a gut feeling and no evidence. I have an injured officer and need to approach the investigation systematically. We are still trying to track down the car, find some CCTV which could give us leads and identify the occupants. We'll get Shand to do a photofit when she is able."

Karen responded, "I think I do have evidence, Alec. Indirect but powerful. When Shand gave them Vic's name they used the hammer, when she gave them mine, they stopped. They had been briefed. Akanni suspected me and got an answer that fitted. In protecting Sayer and Undertow, she fortunately gave the one name he wanted. If she hadn't done so, the damage would be far worse, I suspect.

"Vic, you and your team are going back to Rel-Comm. Media Relations be damned. I want this woman Montaigne and Professor Darius Ward at the university interviewed again. Bring in Jason Umar also; re-interview him hard."

Catrin had seen Moore focus on a criminal before, sure of their involvement. But it was always based on hard evidence. This, she thought, was more obsessive.

Williams was looking a little uncomfortable. He was probably thinking the same thing, she thought.

Moore spoke again. "We are coming over, this morning hopefully, to see Shand once she's awake, even if she is groggy. I owe her an apology, face to face. And DCI Sayer will be with me. I suggest you place an armed guard on Shand, as she saw the two men involved, and also put one on your suspect, Olowe. He might be as dispensable as I think my informer was. And Akanni has far more resources, these days."

"We have an officer there, of course, but not armed." He paused. "But I'm not going to ignore a recommendation from a senior officer at the Met, am I? This morning, you said. By road or what?"

"Helicopter. John will send you the details. And, Alec, I am truly sorry this happened. It was my misjudgment."

Williams looked at the screen for a moment. "Karen, I think I am with Vic Holsworth on this, looking at his face. You are jumping the gun, at least, and taking on yourself something you shouldn't. All Shand did was make a routine enquiry, I understand. DCI Sayer, that's right, isn't it?"

"Yes, sir. The call was meant to be just that, and she did it well."

He pressed on. "Farr could have had her do the same, in the course of events. This response was totally unpredictable."

Catrin could see that Moore was unmoved.

"We'll see you later, Alec. I've more to talk about. Best done in person."

They closed the call. As they talked, John Leigh had gone to the door and opened it, to check with Barbara.

He returned to the table. "The helicopter is booked for 9.45 at the terminal, ma'am."

Unexpectedly, Catrin was going back to Wales for at least part of the day.

16 HOSPITAL

Emmie's husband was a carpenter, Catrin found out, talking to him in Welsh outside the hospital room. He came from Porth, close to Pontypridd.

"We are all in shock. But she's so upset about giving away information of some sort, I know. It's good of you and your boss to come down so quickly."

Cartin was keeping one eye on Moore, as she talked with Chief Superintendent Williams. They were waiting outside the hospital room while the doctor checked Emmie Shand.

When he emerged, he said, "Don't overdo it. She'll still be a bit nauseous from the anaesthetic. There are too many of you, but… she wants to see you together."

Catrin wondered how Moore would handle it. She wasn't a 'people person'.

Karen Moore moved forward and stood by the bed, taking in the patient. The hand and wrist, wrapped in dressings, were on a support frame. They could see the bruises to the face and other arm, hair torn out on one side and a badly cut lip.

Shand spoke first.

"I'm sorry I gave your name, ma'am. I told them I had no idea what they were talking about. The raid was led by DI Holsworth, I said. But, after the second blow, I –."

Moore reached forward and touched her shoulder.

"You did well. Very well. Thinking on your feet in such circumstances and keeping Operation Undertow confidential, as DCI Sayer told you to do. Me, I'm a known entity, it's no big deal. Don't dwell on that at all, hear me?"

Shand nodded.

Moore took in Shand's damaged wrist and hand as if she were examining an architectural structure. "And the hand? What do they say?"

"It is going to take a long time, the surgeon said. I don't know whether I'll be able..." She choked back the fear of losing her career.

Chief Superintendent Williams spoke up in Welsh. Moore got the sense of support from the tone, not the words. Sayer added something in the same language from behind her.

Shand smiled. "Thank you both."

Moore raised an eyebrow. "Could someone explain?"

Shand said, "Chief Superintendent Williams told me it will take as long as it takes, he's not letting me go. I'm a police officer and I'm staying one. And DCI Sayer said, if he did, she'd send a car for me. It would be her gain, Cardiff's loss."

Moore smiled. "Don't worry about that, either. Just get well. You'll have to do your bit. I expect it will take quite a lot of physio work, to rebuild the strength. Are you and I OK, then? On the same wavelength now?"

Shand nodded. "You've taken a weight off my shoulders. I didn't expect this, all of you coming to see me."

Moore smiled. "And Catrin's comment about a job. DCI Sayer is empire building and doesn't have enough Welsh people on her team, I just discovered."

She turned serious. "Superintendent Williams and I were talking earlier. Whatever is behind this is bigger than you and Catrin thought. Much bigger than the Rel-Comm operation. Bigger even than I anticipated, and I am sorry that I didn't foresee this possibility and act to prevent it. I feel bad about that.

"But we will not stop looking for the two men who did this to you and, equally importantly, the people who sent them to do it. I promise you that."

Alec Williams drove Sayer and Moore from the hospital to headquarters himself. Moore had been quiet, lost in thought, sitting next to the Cardiff officer. He had been conversing with Catrin a little.

Moore suddenly said, "I have a request, Alec. Your people are doing the first interview with Olowe later today, you said."

Williams contained a smile. "So that is what brought you down, really. I should have guessed. Do you want to observe?"

Where are we going now, thought Catrin, not for the first time with Karen Moore.

Moore said, "We have currently three points of investigation. First, the students from Rel-Comm, who are currently saying nothing. Holsworth's team will follow up with them again. Second, me; I'm waiting to hear from the assistant commissioner about complaints specifically levelled at me, or similar crap, which is the reason they wanted my name, I suspect. Those compaints will have the names of influential people attached we can follow up with. Finally, we have Olowe, an armed man, linked somehow to these two who hurt Shand."

Williams was nodding, in agreement with the analysis.

She asked, "Who have you got doing the interview?"

"A DI Ian West is now in charge of the investigation into the attack on Shand. Farr is too close for that, so West also takes over the Olowe file. He is experienced, very competent."

Moore added, "Alec, I want you to let Sayer prep the interview with West. If they decide to do it together, go with it."

Williams looked at Moore hard then his eyes returned to watch the road. "Shand is one of ours, Karen. And we have people well capable of interviewing the man. The arrest of Olowe and its investigation is ours, too. We will share what we get, I promise you."

Moore was staring at him hard. "Just the prep, Eric. See what comes out of that. We are supposed to be breaking down the barriers between police services. It's my commissioner's mantra. Olowe is key. He knows who sent him and gave him a gun. We need that information. Besides, it struck me by Shand's bed. How would he know Sayer wasn't with your lot?"

"I thought you said 'prep', not participate?"

"I did. Catrin, if DCS Williams kindly offers you the chance to work with DI West on this, help out during the interview of Peter Olowe, what would you say?"

Catrin responded, "In English ma'am, I would say I would very much like to do that. In Welsh –."

As stream of Welsh words came out of her. Williams eyes widened.

"That's not translatable, Karen, without getting your officer into a lot of trouble," he said. He paused a moment.

"I'll talk with West, give him the choice."

DI Ian West was of comparable age to Catrin. He was from Pembroke, she found out. They spoke in Welsh together as Moore and Williams took other calls. West told her that they didn't have a DCI as young as Catrin.

"Your DI, Andy Collard, said hold back on the gun, Derek Farr said. You agreed with that, ma'am, as I recall."

Catrin responded, "I did, then. Now I want you to use it. You say you have only twenty minutes with him back at the hospital and need to be careful that it doesn't get foreshortened. He could claim he is stressed. I think you should want him left as worried as possible, dreading the thought of the next interview."

West looked thoughtful, then spoke to Williams and Moore, as they settled. "Okay, I will go with DCI Sayer's suggestion. I'll need to take someone other than DS Helms in with me. To field strip the weapon, it needs a firearms officer."

Moore spoke up. "Why not take Catrin in with you? It's her idea. If it goes wrong, it can blow up in her face. Not the gun, of course. She's Welsh, Olowe would never know she wasn't one of yours. She's an authorised fire-arms officer."

Catrin looked at her. "I've never handled a Ruger .22."

"They are all the same, really, aren't they, Alec?"

Seeing the skeptical look on William's face, Moore added, lamely, "Practice a bit with it."

She turned to Williams. "Alec, she was Sandra Hunt's security aide for two years."

Williams was looking at Sayer. "Sandra; really? Sayer, you turn out to be more interesting all the time. Did you ever think of joining us?"

"I applied to South Wales Police after Aber, same time

as I applied to the Met. The Met offered me a job."

"Ian, take DCI Sayer in with you. You lead the interview but let her do the gun bit. After seeing Shand, I am more than happy to think of Mr. Olowe having sleepless nights awaiting his next interview. Make sure the gun is unloaded. From something said in the car, I wouldn't put it past these two Londoners to connive so that Sayer accidentally shoots the man somewhere delicate."

17 OLOWE

Peter Olowe was sitting up in his hospital bed, with a short, dark-haired woman, a solicitor called Rowena Paston, standing near him.

She said, "You have twenty minutes, I understand."

West responded. "Mr. Olowe, I am DI West, with the South Wales Police. I have some questions, not many. We won't be long."

He pulled out a pocket recorder and switched it on. "I'll record this rather than take notes, but anything we cover here we will go through again later in a formal interview, on record."

He deliberately avoided introducing Sayer, who held back and looked a little bored, apparently taking in the room and the hospital equipment.

West began with, "Why were you in the Marriott Hotel?"

"For business reasons."

"The man you approached was a police officer. We have a recording of your comments to him; he wore a wire. Why did you present yourself as a representative of a Reverend Fisher?"

"No comment."

Olowe knew he was probably going to be charged with involvement in an internet fraud. They had briefed his solicitor accordingly.

West nodded. "Well, we can't waste our twenty minutes on 'no comments' can we? Do you have any continuing contacts with Rel-Comm in London? You worked there before moving to Birmingham, we understand, while you were a student."

"I know one or two people there still, that's all."

"You said you were in the Marriott for business. Do you have business dealings with Rel-Comm?"

"No."

"How about with specific individuals within Rel-Comm, not the firm?"

Olowe paused. "No comment."

"What do you do at Serval Enterprises, in Birmingham?"

"I'm a business analyst. I look at the background and financial prospects of companies, for investment purposes."

West said smoothly, "So why would a business analyst visiting Cardiff be carrying a Ruger automatic, an illegal weapon?"

Olowe's face changed. It wasn't a complete surprise to him. They had briefed the solicitor on the scope of their questions.

"It's not mine. I know nothing about it."

Farr looked at Sayer. It was her turn.

She looked at his chest, partly covered by the hospital gown, then back at his face. "I see the tip of Anansi there. When did you get the tattoo?"

His eyes widened. "None of your damn business!"

The solicitor gave him a look and interjected to Sayer. "Relevant questions, please."

"It's relevant alright. Anansi, the god of trickery. Others at Rel-Comm have them, I am told. Is it a club badge of some sort?"

"It's a common tattoo where I come from."

Sayer switched the topic. "You have never touched the weapon found in your raincoat pocket. You are sticking with that?"

"Answered. I have no further comment."

Sayer reached into the briefcase she had brought with her and took out a small plastic evidence bag.

As she opened and extracted the weapon, she continued, "I am showing Mr. Olowe the Ruger 22LR automatic pistol retrieved from his raincoat pocket. Unloaded, of course."

On seeing it, Olowe looked more alarmed. "I know nothing about that gun. If you say it's mine, you fixed it. If you say there are fingerprints, you did it while I was unconscious. This is discrimination, the police trying to pick on me."

Sayer looked unperturbed. "For the record, you say that this weapon was never in your possession. Is that correct?"

"Yes. And I have no more to say."

He looked at his solicitor, whose expression seemed to convey that Olowe had said too much, anyway.

Sayer continued. "Mr. Olowe; watch me. You like tricks, try this one. I am going to field strip this Ruger, as any owner or user would do it."

She first removed the empty ammunition clip and checked that the weapon was empty, then drew back and removed the top cover, the slide, placing it on the bedside table. That revealed the length of the bright stainless-steel barrel beneath. She removed the recoil spring, resting on a pin beneath and parallel with the barrel, placing the pieces side by side.

"After cleaning, the weapons would be reassembled like this."

She placed the recoil spring on its pin again, parallel to the barrel.

"See this point, here, as the user holds the spring under the barrel before replacing the slide over the end, the finger often touches the tip of the barrel, on the underside. That is where the forensic people found a partial print of your left index finger, and with it, your DNA. The outside of the weapon was clean of prints. But we have proof that you dissembled and reassembled a weapon you state you have never seen before. Some trick, eh? A fingerprint on the inside of the weapon. I deserve one of your tattoos."

She looked at him, seeing the facial changes. "First denial, then we give you proof. What now? No smile and a new story?"

She waited. He worked at keeping his face neutral, but his eyes showed his fear as she reassembled the weapon and placed it in the bag.

Olowe said, impulsively, "You people could have done that while I was unconscious, too. Taken my fingerprint."

He looked away, then swallowed hard. His confidence was ebbing away.

The solicitor looked at the clock. Their time was almost up. They had five minutes left.

DI West stood and charged Peter Olowe with the possession of an unregistered and illegal firearm and the storage of a firearm in an unsafe condition. He indicated that further charges were under consideration related to fraud. They would be opposing any bail request.

As he stood, so did Sayer. She said, "Your solicitor said we can't speak Welsh in your presence during an interview and she is quite right. Let me just say there is more on the gun to talk with you about, that you can probably guess. 'Tan y tro nesa'. That means 'until the next time', and there will be a next time."

West switched off his recorder. They left without another word.

Outside, Ian West said, "They expect to release him from hospital in a day or so. We will hold him pending his bail hearing. The gun possession will keep him on remand, at least for this round. You got him running at the end."

Sayer responded, "He will be waking up worrying about it. The faster you move on him, the sooner you get to the two who hurt Emmie."

"We'll interview him once he is moved and settled. The silencer markings, I can get someone to do that."

That was the threat Sayer made before they left. The Ruger model had been fitted with a barrel that allowed a sliencer to be used.

He was assessing her. "Unless you want to traipse back here to do that yourself? You are busy, I am sure, ma'am."

Catrin gave him a stare. "You heard Commander Moore. And I have people on my team who met Emmie. They would kick my arse if I didn't do all I could to help. Yes, we are busy, but thank you for the offer, I will be back. By car, not a helicopter. Let me know when."

At Cardiff airport, before the flight back, once alone, Sayer caught up on the developments from her DI's. It was Sarah Wills who mentioned that Superintendent

Lauder had returned from his holiday that morning, two days early than planned.

"How is he?"

Wills paused. "A little stressed, it seems to me."

"Not a good holiday, then?"

Wills didn't answer that one. She just said, "See you tomorrow, Catrin. I'm in with CPS this afternoon."

As she closed the call, she overheard Karen Moore sitting nearby, say, "Look Gerry, we can talk about it when I get back. Both investigations are in good shape, Ken told me. No. Tomorrow. Check with Barbara for a time. I'm up to my eyes."

Moore closed the call without further comment. Catrin looked at her.

"Your boss is back. Not happy at all that I hijacked you into this case. I'll talk to him tomorrow but, if he comes at you on it, you were doing as you were told – and still are. Got that?"

Catrin nodded. "From what I just heard from Sarah, the holiday hasn't relaxed him at all."

"You could say that."

Moore saw the hand signal and stood, leading the way out behind the airport ground attendant. Back to London.

~~

A little more than an hour later, Catrin found out for herself. After dropping off her coat and bag and dealing with a couple of questions from team members, she went to Lauder's office. His door was open, and he was on the phone but beckoned her inside, pointing at a seat.

As he finished, he said, "A day trip to Cardiff, I hear. I can't say I'm too pleased about this, Catrin."

She waited for a moment. "How was the holiday? You

are back early."

He wrinkled his nose. "Good to begin with, then it went off the rails."

He paused, clearly deciding whether to press on with his concern about the new case or answer her question.

"My youngest son is a nurse."

"Neil. Yes, you've mentioned him."

"He failed a random drug test at work three days ago. Fortunately, in a sense, he hadn't been supplying his needs from drug cabinets. If so, he would be out. But they have put him straight into a residential program for drug addicts. One time, once chance or goodbye. He's been at that hospital six years. Our daughter-in-law called us. You can imagine…"

She leaned in, focusing on him. "Boss, I don't need to imagine. I know. My mother went through the same thing with alcohol when I was in my teens. In her case it was an arrest. I know how hard it hits."

He looked surprised. "You told me. I'd totally forgotten. It's similar, that's right."

She added, "It'll work out. Support them both. How's Elsa handling it?"

Lauder's wife.

"She went to pieces the first night, just wanted to get back home. Now, now I think she is doing better than me. It's easier to come back into work, frankly."

You need to be home, she thought, but said nothing. Perhaps this was the real reason for Lauder's crankiness.

He sat up straight. "I know Karen has a bee in her bonnet on this Rel-Comm case. Ken brought me up to speed earlier. But it is not Undertow work. We plan, implement and act, focused on the top people, not respond like a borough team. I've told her that and will tell her again tomorrow. So, be prepared to walk away from this one."

Catrin paused a moment, working out a response.

"I do as I am directed, boss. Let me know tomorrow, after meeting with her. Currently I am planning, in fact, South Wales is expecting me to participate in interviews with a suspect. There is a police officer seriously injured and the commander is convinced that there are bigger elements to this than a scam team operating locally."

She stood up. "I should get caught up. Sarah is with CPS now. We all meet tomorrow morning to review the Warminster prosecution final details. And one of the women freed from Stefan Kriel has additional inform-ation she will share with 'someone senior', but wants a guarantee to stay here in the UK. Hills and I are meeting her tomorrow afternoon, with someone from Immigrat-ion."

Talking about progress on a case he had assigned seemed to placate him. As she left his office, she hoped he would tell Moore about his family issues. In his current mood and Karen's conviction that the activity in Wales and Lewisham would lead her to this man, Akanni, it was a temperamental mix.

18 BRIBE

"He came back subdued, and he's not in the best mood."

Ken Osborne's comment was made the following day while catching up on developments with Catrin. They were both in New Scotland Yard, in the cafeteria at lunch. Catrin was between her meeting with CPS and one of the Solvenian women abducted by Stefan Kriel.

Osborne had been in a review meeting, one on an Undertow officer's performance. DC Lyle had at best an average record so far with the team. Now he had screwed up badly during his last assignment, one of Osborne's cases. He and Lauder would handle Lyle's transfer back to borough work. His departure would be the first transfer out of Undertow for poor performance since the team was established.

Catrin gave a grimace. "Gerry talked to you?"

She kept it open, not mentioning the specific subject.

"About his son? Yes. He said only you and I know."

"I hope he told Karen. She would be supportive, but they were at loggerheads yesterday over the Shand issue."

Osborne nodded. "He feels strongly that Karen is usurping the Undertow role, and particularly you, dragging you into it."

Catrin shrugged. "It has taken on a life of its own, true, since Shand's injury. But I'm glad to help. I feel a bit guilty, as I was the one who put her in the front line, making the call to Rel-Comm. It's not logical, even the South Wales people said so, but..."

Osborne checked his watch. "I'd better be on my way."

Catrin responded, "Well, good luck with that. It had to happen, a person not making the grade. I've had a morning of joys reviewing our ability to support the Warminster charges with Jarrold."

That made Ken Osborne smile. "He's one of the best at CPS for having illuminating hindsight. 'If you had–' is his mantra."

"I received an earful of that."

She saw the text message from Gerry Lauder after leaving the cafeteria and called him.

"Catrin, I met with Commander Moore earlier today. The outcome is this; you will continue to support her on this fraud case linked to Rel-Comm, directly support her but keep me informed. I don't agree with the case involving Undertow, and the commander knows that. If you need help with line management of Team A while this one is running, let me know. I have already spoken to Ken. Between him and me, we will handle whatever is needed. Neither Karen nor I want you in a cleft stick on this matter. Is that clear?"

"Yes, boss. And thank you. That will make things easier."

"I understand. Hopefully, by the time the Warminster

case wraps up and a new Undertow assignment is identified, this issue will be behind us. And on that note, I should let you know you will be going back to Cardiff, to do the follow up interview of this man Olowe. Karen spoke further with Chief Superintendent Williams there. They were impressed with your support at the hospital. Why does that not surprise me? Give the commander a call later. She wanted that passed on."

It all sounded good. Yet after the call, Catrin was sure that something had changed between Gerry Lauder and Karen Moore. She had known them, worked with them on and off for years. Gerry had been the voice of experience and stabilising influence for some of Moore's more innovative, some would say, wild investigative decisions. They had been a close team.

Hopefully, they still were, but Catrin was not so sure.

They met Inga Kaminski at 2.30 p.m. DC Loretta Hills and an Immigration officer brought her over, showed her the famous sign outside the Scotland Yard building and Loretta reinforced that she was meeting here at headquarters with the head of the team which, according to Inga, saved her from 'that evil man'.

"He bragged after he slept with me and told me I would be his girlfriend so I would be in a good job here. But I knew he said that to other women. I just wanted to get here in a nice job, live a bit in London. It's exciting."

Inga was head-turning attractive, nineteen and treated everything in life as a negotiation, it seemed. If she had a romantic spark in her it was either not yet ignited or long quashed by harsh reality. She was more irate about Kiel's lies, it seemed, than the prospect of paid sex in hotel bedrooms.

"I thought it was a job which I could tell my mother

about, make her proud."

Catrin gained the impression that work her mother wouldn't be proud of would be fine, too, but at a higher pay rate. But she didn't pursue that.

Inga had made a thing about Catrin being the Senior Investigating Officer, as she told her story. She had repeated 'Detective Chief Inspector', to herself on introduction, assessing its weight, finding it satisfactory.

Catrin rode with it. Inga's excellent recall of times and people, her attention to detail and her openness would help the prosecution of Stefan Kriel and assist in further arrests by the authorities in Germany.

"You will be called as a witness at Kriel's trial, you know that?"

"That's fine. I want the court to see me as a good person, so I can stay here, to get my visa. I will spit on him in court."

Loretta jumped in, "No, be nice in court, very polite. We talked about that."

Her private exchange of looks with Catrin said it all.

Catrin continued. "Kriel will be held in jail until his trial, so he can't get at you or threaten you."

Inga seemed naively unafraid. She pouted. "If he sends anyone after me, they get stabbed with a knitting needle, I tell you."

Loretta leapt into the affray yet again. "No, you call us or get help or run, I told you. No violence. But be careful when you answer the door or phone."

Inga and the other woman, Maria, wanted to share a small apartment, rented for them, not be kept at the detention centre. It was part of the deal.

To lighten the discussion, Catrin asked. "Do you knit?"

"No. But I have my grandmother's old knitting

needles. Good steel, not crap like they sell today."

Loretta looked up, praying for inspiration. All this was being recorded.

Catrin smiled. "Do you have any wool?"

"No." Inga paused. "Good idea, I will buy some. It will show I have knitting needles for proper use, if I need to jab some bastard in the eye."

"No violence, Inga. We said that. Any sign of a problem, you call the number we gave you. Understand?"

"Yes. Understood, Detective Chief Inspector."

From her expression, the knitting needles wouldn't be far away.

Catrin had promised she would get the letter of support for the Immigration officials. She carefully pointed out it was supportive, not directly instrumental in any decision. Loretta Hills said encouraging things to Inga, too, and, on wrap-up, took her to the Immigration officer who would transfer her back to the detention centre until a decision was reached and arrangements could be made.

As she left, Inga said, "Thank you. That was the best cup of coffee I had since I arrived here. You treat me good."

Catrin had sent out for Starbucks for everyone at the beginning of the interview. "People who know good coffee, they need good coffee," she had said seriously to Inga.

Loretta contained her smile. Her boss was famous in Undertow for leaving most of every cup of coffee to get cold.

~~

Catrin had put Mair to bed and was sitting down with

some tea, reviewing her day, when she received a call from DI West on her work mobile.

"Ma'am, we are bringing Olowe in for questioning in three days, in the afternoon. Apparently, they want twenty-four to thirty-six hours on his arrival at HMP Cardiff for settling in; it is his first time in prison. I want us to interview him at the police station, not there, to give him a taste of the outside, so he will see what he is missing by not co-operating with us."

Catrin thought for a moment. "I'll make time for that. I was just thinking about it as you called. You are running checks on the weapon, I know. Has any prior use come up yet?"

"Not so far. Nothing in the UK. We have filed an Interpol request, seeing as he is a foreign national."

They both knew that would take some time.

Catrin asked, "Would you mind if I do some checking myself with some contacts, if you send us the ballistic file? No promises, other than anything that comes up we will route the information back to you before doing anything else."

"It can't hurt, providing I don't have to pay any bills. Are you thinking about Africa specifically?"

"Yes. I am wondering if the gun came from there, rather than picked up locally here. It may not necessarily have been brought in by Olowe. But it is not new; it's been around."

West was agreeable. It couldn't hurt them to try.

He asked, "Do you want us to fix a hotel for the evening, if the interview goes on?"

"No. I'll go and visit my mum and dad, stay there, anyway. Ponty is only half an hour away."

The following morning, she had a plan worked out as

the Undertow day started up at Lavernder Hill. She called DC Pauline Stillwell into her office.

"Stillwell, I have a job for you tied to the Rel-Comm case."

Pauline gave a her a look. "Is that still active?"

"Yes. I want you to contact David Kingman in Ballistics with a file that came in overnight, the gun found on this man Olowe, a Ruger .22LR. I want help from police ballistic experts in Nigeria and any neighbouring countries."

Stillwell was already looking askance, as if this would be going nowhere.

"Direct? Not through Interpol?"

"Yes. Commiserate with him that I am still a pushy slavedriver, but I remembered him spouting on about a trip he took to Africa. Tell him that I'm sure, as a ballistic science expert of great renown, he has contacts there. I want the rifling marks checked out by the time I go to Wales for the Olowe interview, preferably, two days from now."

Stillwell stayed silent, writing down the instructions. She could but try. But her team lead was asking the earth, for an answer that fast.

When she finished, Catrin said, "And tell him there is another vase for Natalie, that's his wife, if he comes up trumps. Nothing for trying, only for any quick possibles for the use of this Ruger. Not hand on heart, court-ready stuff, just a possible fit."

Stillwell looked surprised. "One of yours?"

Catrin nodded. "She has one already, from a silent auction, a few years ago."

Stillwell was nodding, now more energized. "I'll get on it. It's probably gone up in the ranking from 'no chance' to 'faint hope' with that offer."

Catrin watched her leave and checked her computer for contact lists in the Foreign and Commonwealth Office. Fixing on one, she picked up the phone.

Within a half-hour, she had a lunch appointment with Madeleine Turner-Jones (Malaysian desk). Madeleine had drawn in a colleague, Murray Cheetham (West Africa desk), who Catrin didn't know.

Turner-Jones was delighted to help the woman who saved her life in Kuala Lumpur, particularly now Sayer had achieved the exalted rank of detective chief inspector. She knew just the place to eat.

First thing in the morning, two days later, Stillwell took her boss a file. It was not thick, but certainly not empty. Sayer was leaving at 10.30, to head to Cardiff. She found her with DI Franklin.

Seeing her, Sayer indicated that she wanted to hear the results.

As Stillwell finished summarizing them briefly, she said, "I am just surprised that Kingman came back with so much, so quickly."

"Well, it gives me something to play with in Cardiff, doesn't it? That and my lunch with people at FCO. Now Pauline, call DI West, give him the same summary and tell him I'm bringing him a copy of the file."

Stillwell looked at her, at Franklin, deciding what to say. In the end, she said, "Kingman must really want that vase for his wife."

Franklin put on a surprised expression. "Did I hear DC Stillwell infer that there was a bribe involved? One of your vases?"

Catrin looked innocent. "Not at all. His wife has one of mine already. We met at a Christmas event. She's from South Wales, too, we had a lovely talk. She bought my vase in the silent auction after that. It was for a good cause. I'm sure she would like another."

Franklin nodded, understanding. "Not bribery, Pauline. Not DCI Sayer. It's blackmail. She would have a little chat with David Kingman's wife about the missed opportunity to get another vase, for free."

Catrin looked at Stillwell. "See what happens when you get promoted? How Ed's mind has warped, turned to the dark side? Be careful. This job gets to you."

19 EXTRADITION

By 3.00 p.m., after driving through rain all the way, Catrin was back in Cardiff Dock police station.

In the interview room, Olowe was talking with his solicitor, Paston. They had already briefed the woman about the purpose of the interview.

Once the recording started, Olowe spoke up first. "My solicitor tells me you are talking about extradition. Are you dropping the charges?"

DI West said, "We are looking at all options with CPS, but we have laid the weapon possession charges; they stand."

Olowe flashed his anger, directing his next question to Sayer. "You are from London, she says. I thought you were with him."

Catrin ignored the implied question and looked at West. He was to lead, at first.

West began with "Mr. Olowe, I think you are a confidence trickster. That's part of the charge. Here's the first reason."

He played the recording of the start of the meeting at

the Marriott Hotel.

"After denying in your earlier statement that you had any reason to speak to the officer substituting for Gareth Harris, the evidence shows otherwise. Were you part of a scheme to defraud Harris?"

Olowe sat still, looked at his solicitor and said, "No comment."

"Can you confirm you know Jason Umar?"

Olowe responded, "I worked at Rel-Comm at the same period as others, including Jason, yes."

West said, "Jason flew home yesterday. Charges were dropped."

Olowe seemed surprised. "He talked to you?" That clearly worried him.

West responded, "Not to me, to the Met."

Olowe gave a half-sneer but said nothing.

West said, "I'm just showing you we hold to a deal if we reach one. Jason told us you were going to either persuade Harris to keep funding the orphanage scam or scare him into silence. That was purpose of the gun. You would show him that a complaint to the police would bring him future problems. Is that correct?"

He wasn't mentioning that the deal with Umar gave them only Peter Olowe; he would not speak about Rel-Comm or Amitra Montaigne.

"No comment."

"Have you ever used that weapon to intimidate others?"

"No comment."

"Have you ever killed someone, here or elsewhere, to conceal a scam operation?"

"You are crazy, man, asking that question. Do I look stupid enough to answer if I had? But no, I never shot anyone."

Ian West, looking not so crazy, just raised his eyebrows. "DCI Sayer?"

"Mr. Olowe, do you still deny any knowledge of the Ruger SR22 found in your raincoat pocket?"

"That gun has nothing to do with me."

"Let's examine the weapon again. This time, it's not about the fingerprint."

She delved into the folder and brought out the Ruger. Again, she stripped it down to reveal the barrel freed from the concealing slide cover. As he looked at her, her hand pointed to the tip of the barrel.

"This pistol has a recess slot on either side. Do you know it's purpose?"

"No idea, ask a gun expert."

She responded. "It's for fitting a suppressor, a silencer. And the markings in the grooves here would indicate that a suppressor has been fitted, and used, on more than one occasion."

Olowe shrugged, looking increasingly angry.

"I know nothing about any gun or silencer."

"As DI West stated, we believe you were planning to meet with Gareth Harris to convince him to continue funding the scam about an orphanage in Africa. He had already expressed his concern about the non-repayment of a loan, as he saw it to be. If this new solution by 'Reverend Fisher' turned out to be a lie, that he had realised he was being cheated, you were going to deal with it, either talk him through it, threaten him or possibly kill him."

Oli's eyes were wide with a mix of fear and astonishment.

Sayer ground on. "DI West will now add to the charges of possession of a prohibited weapon, a firearm, a new charge of intent to injure others. Your solicitor will advise you that, on conviction, there are mandatory minimum sentences in place for the more serious charge. You are looking at five years plus, I think."

West read out the charge sheet, including the prior charge of intent to defraud and the more serious charge. He gave a copy to the solicitor.

"We'll give you a few minutes to discuss the new charge."

He then stated that the interview was suspended.

The officers watched and waited in the viewing room until the solicitor looked at the camera and beckoned.

"I have explained to my client that, as far as we are aware, although you have evidence of possession of a weapon, your decision to charge him with intent to injure is an extrapolation. He wants to know if you are hiding anything, have additional evidence at this time."

"I'm glad he asked," Catrin responded.

She looked at Olowe intently. "We have two elements that support the elevation of the charge beyond simple possession. First, the vicious attack on a police officer engaged in this investigation has indicated that the group you are involved with has the capacity for serious violence, not simply fraud and deception. Secondly, we have as of yesterday afternoon, ballistic evidence indicating this weapon was used in crimes elsewhere."

She pulled two sheets of paper from her file. Checking one, she turned it around and placed it between the Olowe and the solicitor.

"For the record, I am showing preliminary ballistic fingerprint data. These are possible, more like probable, links to this specific weapon. One of the best ballistic scientists in the UK has reviewed them. To him, they are sufficient to warrant a full analysis. Understood?"

The solicitor, Rowena Paston, nodded.

"This first report links the weapon to a shooting in Nigeria eighteen months ago, a serious injury to a member of an organized crime gang. One bullet to the head resulted in paralysis and loss of faculties, but not death."

She placed the second sheet alongside it.

"This one links it to the death of a town official in Bamenda, a city in Cameroon, seven years ago. Again, shots to the head at close range, multiple this time. So, we know the weapon is probably tied to a killer, or to one or more killers."

Olowe shouted out. "That's nothing to do with me! No way you are going to tie me into those!"

He was angry now. He went on, "I got rights. Procedures. You can't do that. They can't do that, can they?"

The last part, the question, was to his lawyer.

Rowena Paston looked directly at Sayer.

"What's your intent?"

"To maintain the local charges for now. If we have a request for extradition from either country linked to these murders, CPS and the Foreign Office will be involved, as they are far more serious charges."

"Do you have any additional evidence that would directly link my client to that charge?"

Catrin responded carefully. "This information is very recent. We have feedback from ballistic experts for both countries but have no formal contact with the police authorities in either. We will be in contact with them. They will want to verify the preliminary links but, if they are sound, they may choose to follow up."

She took back the two sheets.

"How likely that is, we can't say, and it is not our

concern."

Olowe was lost in thought, his eyes moving between the different pieces of paper. He looked frightened now.

"You can't send me back. It's unfair. I did nothing like that."

He looked at his solicitor. "There are UN sanctions. You need to look into this for me..."

Catrin spoke up again. "CPS will be faced with the choice of prioritising the fraud and possession charge over any extradition request, if it goes that far."

The solicitor asked, "I'm not an extradition expert, but surely the transfer of my client to prisons in Africa has human rights implications? I need time to look into this aspect and brief him."

Catrin responded. "Of course. But let me explain the bigger picture, because I have looked into it with relevent people at the Foreign Office."

She directed her comments to Olowe.

"The major element you need to understand is that you have no right of asylum here at this minute. You are here legitimately on a business visa. You are not here illegally or claiming refugee status. You could try to claim asylum with the UK or any other country at their embassy or consulate, but you now have criminal charges here, serious charges that would go against you.

"Basically, that's it. There has been a judicial ruling that extradition between the UK and Cameroon is in breach of human rights legislation due to the state of their prisons; overcrowding, violence and so forth."

Paston nodded her head. "Now you mention it, I recall the report. That's correct."

Olowe sounded relieved. "See, I'm right."

Catrin continued. "However, there is an exception to that ruling involving any crime tied to international drug trafficking. I gather that the shooting in Nigeria was tied to an official involved in fighting drug crime and the person assassinated in Cameroon was deeply involved in illegal drug distribution there. I don't have the details. It would rest with Immigration and the Foreign and Commonwealth Office to resolve."

Olowe interjected, snapping at Paston. "Well, I want to claim asylum now. You sort that for me."

Rowena Paston sighed, struggling to stay professional, faced with her client's rudeness. "We have discussed that earlier. I explained that asylum is generally claimed at border entry or an immigration office unless you are going to ask a foreign embassy for it. There are ways of claiming it for urgent and compelling reasons. I don't see any, at present."

West spoke up. "South Wales Police want to track down the people who injured our officer and instigated both that attack and what we believe to be a potentially violent threat to Gareth Harris."

He left it there, watching him carefully. Olowe would get to the decision point soon, he thought. He looked at Catrin. "I think that's about it?"

She looked at her watch. "I'm not hanging around on this. I need to get back to London. I'm open to co-operation, Mr. Olowe, and, as DI West said regarding Jason Umar, we honor our commitments. If you want some leeway on the charges or the issue of extradition, it is in your hands."

She stood, pulled the chair back, got behind it and pushed it forward, holding the top rail.

Ian West stood also. "It's decision time, Mr. Olowe. Tell us about the gun, its purpose, and the people you work for. You will get charged with possession alone and processed here. You will serve time in a British jail. That gives your solicitor or whoever acts for you plenty of time to fight any subsequent extradition charges if they arise.

Olowe couldn't resist trying to negotiate. "How about the fraud alone?"

West spoke up. "No. I'm clear on that. Possession of the Ruger is the minimum. Prison time for it. Sentencing conditions near the low end if, and only if, the information you give us secures arrests of key people. That's a given. And you testify at their trial or trials. Break those terms at any time and extradition is back on the table."

"No way."

Olowe sat back. West looked at Catrin.

She said, "Fine. We are done. We will leave you to talk with your solicitor. Think it through. And get real. You aren't doing a Julian Assange-thing, a drawn-out process. Fail to secure asylum and the first you will hear about it is a van taking you to Bristol or Birmingham Airport, putting you on a connecting flight through Germany or Spain. You won't get much chance to apply for asylum in transit. Then you will be in Lagos or Yaounde, in handcuffs."

She picked up her folder and they walked out the door.

Catrin returned to the viewing room after dealing with some texts and voicemails. She asked West and others watching, "How are they doing? What do you all think? Any recommendations?"

Olowe and his solicitor had been in discussion for twenty minutes.

West responded, "He's active; thinking about it, not sitting there, bored."

One of the officers viewing the interview said, "The

solicitor looks finished. She just signalled."

West looked at Catrin. "Let's go back in."

"Mr. Olowe. Do you have anything to say?"

Paston answered. "My client will cooperate but wants to be assured of his safety once he does so."

West nodded. "I want it from him, in his own words, scoping out what he will give me. Not the detail, the scope. Then we will talk about protection measures, if warranted."

Olowe said, "I'll give you the names of two people who may have been the ones to hurt your officer. Then if you show me pictures, you know, mixed in with others, I will pick them out."

"And?"

"I'll confess to involvement in the fraud and that Jason asked me to do the contact with Harris. No-one else. I won't fight the possession charge, but the more serious charge, intent to injure, gets dropped. And I want protection, that still has to be on the table."

Paston butted in. "To be clear, that is all he will give. You find a way to bring in DS Shand's attackers. He doesn't testify. He doesn't give you anyone else. My client is convinced that he simply wouldn't survive. Go with that and we both win something."

Sayer looked at West, It was where they thought this might end up. West responded, "South Wales Police will go with that. DCI Sayer, for the Met?"

He was letting her twist Olowe's arm a little more.

She said, "You have almost got yourself a deal. Ian, stop the recording, please."

When he did so, she said, "You are deep into this, Peter, far more than you are prepared to admit. I think in Cameroon or Nigeria, you could go down, if they found any more information to link you to either hit, that's my gut feel about you. So, I think you know the name of the top person. Off the record, just a name."

He looked scared now, in anguish as they waited on his decision.

"I never talked to the man. He's too high up and you won't have anything on him. My boss doesn't even report to him directly. She reports to another man."

"Still, a name, once only in this room and never repeated as coming from you. It's not on record, but even so, I am a police officer, and your solicitor is here. If I break that promise she would rightly go after me."

Catrin paused, then said softly, "It's almost there. You want the prospect of a flight to Cameroon popping up out of nowhere right off the table, and the minimal time in prison, I know that."

"You will put the agreement in writing?"

West responded. "Yes, it will be in writing."

Olowe took a deep breath.

"My boss works for someone everyone thinks is the top dog, that he runs the scam operation in Rel-Comm. But she and I got drunk together once, and she let it out that the top person is someone else, a Nigerian who lives here. He is Amaechi Akanni, the head of Serval Enterprises, the company where I work.

"The day after, she told me to forget it; she had messed up. Forget the link or – I got the impression that it is in my best interest not to find out more. To me, he is just the head of Serval, a successful businessman."

He looked at her, his expression somewhere between defeated and expectant; he had met her wishes.

Catrin said, "Start the recording again."

West did so. He said, "For the record, DCI Sayer has confirmed that the Met agrees to the terms. Mrs. Paston, we will draw up a letter for your review right now. We are more than interested in taking into custody the people who injured DS Shand. We will get that letter finished and resume the interview."

Catrin excused herself for a few moments. As much as she wanted to find the people who smashed Emmie's hand, she wanted a direct call to Commander Moore, however busy she was. Her obstinacy on this one was vindicated

Olowe's boss was a woman. He would have information on her activities. And she had a boss, and above him, they had as a target his man Akanni, at the top. She wondered what Lauder, Moore and senior managers would decide to do.

20 SERVAL

Eight days after South Wales Police charged Peter Olowe with the possession of a firearm and co-conspiracy in the fraud of a man called Gareth Harris from Maesteg, a BBC Wales current affairs snippet featured the progress in the recovery of a Cardiff police officer, DS Emmie Shand.

It was a short piece, not dwelling on the crime but focusing on the challenges after an officer was injured. The video clip showed her both at home and walking in Plasnewydd with her children, her hand still bandaged and splinted.

"My family and my fellow officers have been tremendous," proved to be the most memorable quote. "Once a police officer is hurt, he or she is a victim, just like any other member of the public. It's so important to have the support, to rebuild your confidence to do simple things, like walking in the street at night."

It mentioned that, in several weeks, she would undergo a second surgery linked to the extent of the damage inflicted. 'Some parts must heal before other damage can be addressed' was the lay explanation.

The last scene showed the journalist standing where Shand was attacked, with the words, "If you see a black Mercedes with a dent below the left tail-light, report it. Time has passed, but it may well be the one used on this attack."

The following day, a team from West Midlands Police arrested a John Bennett and a Rodney Thomas at their homes in Solihull without any serious incident, other than having to pepper spray a dog and charge Rodney's sister with a related assault. She had set the Alsatian to attack one of the police officers.

The sister received bail the following morning. Neither Bennett nor Thomas qualified for bail. A charge of malicious wounding of a police officer does not get you back on the streets very easily.

The media broke the news of the arrests. A retired police officer viewing the article on Shand had coincidently spotted the vehicle in question the same day, a ten-year-old Mercedes C-class sedan.

Inside the car, which Rodney neglected to clean out properly during his ownership, forensic officers found a sachet of peppercorns beneath the driver's seat. The missing item from Shand's shopping trip had not been made public. Recorded on the Asda receipt, it had not been found in her belongings scattered at the scene.

In identity parades, Shand picked out John Bennett, as he had confronted her in the street and posed the questions. She couldn't do the same with Rodney, the driver, who used the hammer. Pain and injury in an incident do that, even to a trained police officer.

A hammer consistent with the injury to Shand's hand was found at Rodney's home. It had his fingerprints but, for some reason, had been thoroughly cleaned recently. It was a highlight of the interview when Rodney placed on record that he liked to keep his tools clean. The photograph of the toolbox he owned showed it was a mess and some of the tools, including a set of drill bits, were filthy.

The cleanest items in Rodney's possession were a new curved screen gaming monitor and Xbox, to let him play at being a hero. Those items, the cash in his wallet and an envelope of fifty-pound notes found in his bedroom amounted to nearly £3000. By sheer coincidence, solicitors later argued, John Bennett paid a similar sum in cash into his bank account the day after the attack on Shand. He would not reveal the source of his financial windfall.

"His lawyer says that the evidence is all circumstantial against Rodney," said his mother, "but it looks pretty convincing to me, I'm sad to say."

She was talking to the tall police officer from London with the West Indian lilt beneath her London accent. Hilda Thomas had been a bit nervous when contacted, but the officer, a DC Hills, had been friendly. Within minutes it turned into a social chat.

"We aren't directly involved in the investigation, Mrs. Thomas; that's with the Welsh police. Our little task force in London is looking into why so many young people seem to be going off the rails these days. It consumes a lot of police time, hurts people and sends young men like Rodney down paths that often lead to long-term prison sentences. Neither John nor Rodney have any previous conviction, so it was a surprise to everyone when they turned up as allegedly involved."

"Allegedly, that's the word they all use these days," pontificated Hilda.

Loretta Hills brought the conversation back to details

in Rodney's life. Hilda went into chapter and verse on her son's life, his friends and what, in her opinion, went wrong. Loretta took notes and sounded supportive.

~~

It was Superintendent Lauder who, with Commander Moore, had to put the case to Assistant Commissioner Sleiman. DCI Sayer and DCI Osborne were there and had input, but they were primarily looking for a decision on Undertow's priorities.

"South Wales Police have pretty much wrapped it up. They have Olowe for the Harris fraud and the pair that injured DS Shand. They appreciated Sayer's involvement and assistance, but they are closing the files. We have closed out on Rel-Comm, even if CPS is still mulling over the chances of success in prosecuting Montaigne. The question now is, do we want to allocate priorities and resources to investigate the ringleader, Akanni?"

He paused. "Commander Moore would like to, but admits she has a bias."

He looked at Moore. As per plan, she laid out the groundwork.

"Akanni and Darius Ward, the professor at USL who was so vocal about the Rel-Comm raid, go way back. They have been in trouble only once, both aged twenty-three. I was the arresting officer, working in Lewisham. In brief, Akanni was the leader. The pair were reported as defrauding their employer, but he quickly withdrew the complaint and rashly destroyed the evidence before we could proceed.

"Akanni had a relationship with a local woman, Anne Krell, who knew what happened and it played on her conscience, I could tell. If I look back, I should have done some things a little differently, listened to Vic Holsworth a little more closely, but I didn't."

For Moore, she sounded unusually contrite. Assistant Commissioner Slieman said, "No point in beating yourself up about the past, Karen. We all have ghosts like that."

She nodded. "Anyway, I have a bias against Akanni, and it is in the open. There was something about him then, and about this scam, the gun, the assault on Shand, that makes me want to go after the man. I think he killed Krell to shut her up, but there is no evidence, no body."

Sleiman nodded but looked at Lauder. Move on, was the message.

He did. "DI Sarah Wills has done some analysis of Akanni's business; it is in the report. In summary, Amaechi Akanni currently is a successful businessman, owner of Serval Enterprises Incorporated based in Canary Wharf, in the same block as Citibank. He lives in Iver, as he uses Heathrow a lot.

"Serval has divisions involved in a number of business partnerships with others. They are in diverse areas; entertainment, I mean the corporate catering and hospitality type entertainment, not the shows themselves. Another division imports and sells Nigerian art and textiles through distributors. The third division is called 'Management Services' but seems to be a contractor service to handle company downsizing, the expertise for layoff and firing employees."

"Serval is the name of an African wildcat, one which hunts by itself, not in a pack, and is active both day and night. It is apt. Looking at the business development, Sarah says that Akanni has grown his business in a sharp, cutthroat manner, not by building warm relationships. That, in itself, is no issue, of course. There isn't a hint that these businesses are rogue in any way."

He pointed at a chart on page five of the report, and Sleiman followed on his own copy.

"Olowe, who was involved in the Maesteg scam, worked in the Management Services Division as a junior executive trainee. They have now let him go with a severance package after he was charged, on the grounds of company reputation.

His finger moved.

"Armita Montaigne from Rel-Comm formerly worked in the company, importing art and textiles. She moved to Rel-Comm at startup, a logical career move. Serval became a partner with several others in the startup company but, on paper, seems to be a minor player.

"Rodney Thomas and John Bennett, who attacked DS Shand, are not employees of Serval at all. Both are occasional contract staff in the entertainment division, part of the team doing the lifting and setup work for conferences. The Danes are interested in Bennett based on fingerprints; it is related to a case where a person was badly beaten in a town called Karlslunde. The person's daughter, like the Maesteg couple, claims her father was the victim of an online fraud, but he denies it. South Wales Police are handling that link."

"The picture emerging is that a network of criminals linked to Serval are tied to online fraud scams. Some involved are embedded in legitimate jobs in the Serval organisation. We have no idea yet how extensive that is. Serval has nearly two hundred employees."

Sleiman butted in. "And probably most of those are just ordinary employees."

Lauder nodded his agreement. "There is also an international dimension to it, with Nigeria and Denmark, at least, unexplored by us as yet. Sayer?"

He looked at Catrin, who spoke up.

"We don't have a handle on the total financial scale of these frauds. The Welsh one was about £40,000. What Sarah concludes, though, is that they can't bring in anything like the legitimate business activities of Serval. It makes no sense to jeopardise the standing of the company with the taint of criminal activities. But Commander Moore wants to address that also."

Moore said, "Akanni is a trickster, a scam artist. He enjoys the process as much as the result. He is hiding his illegal pleasure in his legitimate business activities."

Sleiman asked, "So what are your thoughts on the path forward. Any recommendations? I don't see them."

He was about to reach a decision, Catrin saw.

Lauder responded, "We have considered the possible ways to penetrate the organisation but feel that the network within the businesses is very tight and we may make little headway, unless an opportunity shows itself."

Sleiman pulled a face, not liking it.

Lauder hesitated. "Akanni's weak link may be his friendship with Professor Ward. He surfaced in support of Rel-Comm, and we could have the borough go after him. But the university will be all over it, both their lawyers and the faculty members who are already against us. It could get very messy. The best we can do is get an undercover officer close to Ward, get him or her to see if they can be drawn into the mix, but that could take a long time."

Sleiman pondered the message, stretching his neck out, literally, and adjusting the knot on his tie. "We don't need that, but we don't drop cases because they are uncomfortable. And Undertow isn't short of other work; to me, higher priority work, with more potential for engagement."

He looked at Moore, who looked sombre on receiving that message.

"I'm not making light of what seems to be a sizeable fraud operation. But it needs a stronger case, something linked directly to Akanni that is potentially prosecutable. That would loosen some of the bricks and we could make progress.

"Freeze it, don't drop it. If new developments make it more workable, bring it back. But we can't spend a fortune chasing this, from what you said so far.

"Now, on your list you have two other possibles for Undertow. Let's discuss those."

PART 2. HONOUR

21 MADELEINE

"I'm smiling like baby Daniel," said Lili, sitting in Jean's lap in the workshop area of the Cwmbran Kiln, in Spitalfields.

The weekend weather in mid-September promised a fine Saturday with pleasant temperatures and sunshine. Catrin had risen early, got herself and Mair ready. This afternoon, with Chris, they were taking Mair and Lili to a children's art festival at the Tate Modern. It would be a riot of colour and shapes, hopefully non-permanent, even if the girls would be in old play clothes.

First, she was joining Jean and family in a call with Jian Li, while she decorated two pieces of the Sayer-Hughes ceramics.

Lili had squeezed her eyes to slits, looking into the screen at the baby in Hong Kong. Jian Li Yeung sat laughing, with her son in her lap. They were at home.

Mair, not to be outdone, shouted, "I smile like Lee-Lee." Her eyes squeezed closed, too. Lili was Lili, Jian Li was 'Lee-Lee'.

Catrin was laughing now. Jean said, "It means you

smile all the time, Li."

"I wish. Not these days."

They had been talking about the recent developments in Hong Kong. Melanie, Liliwen's birth mother and wife of Jean, had been getting Mair ready to go out. She was taking the girls to the local park, to give Jean and Catrin some time together with their art. It helped pay the bills.

Catrin returned to the workbench a little further back, in camera view, as Mair went to get ready with Melanie. She picked up the piece, a long, narrow flatware dish, and a brush. The shouts of "Lili, come!" from Mair repeated until the older girl snaked off Jean's lap and joined her friend. Within a minute, peace reigned in the studio.

"How bad is it?" asked Catrin.

Jian Li responded, "Things are becoming more difficult here, with the demonstrations and the government responses. Our society is polarising, and that can't be good.

"Most of us just get on with the usual things, but the constant tension worsens as China's grip inevitably gets stronger. After a year in Sweden, it feels even more of a contrast for me, the speed of the change."

Li was now on maternity leave from her work at LinTan Shipping, a large maritime organisation based in Hong Kong. She had recently completed a one year assignment in Stockholm, a transition step in her career from a role as a corporate lawyer to a business executive. James, her husband, who worked in Hong Kong, had visited Stockholm regularly. When Li announced her pregnancy towards the end of the assignment, it brought ribald comments from Melanie about cold winters and warm Scandinavian bedrooms.

Daniel, Catrin's godson, sat quietly, staring at the

screen. Li said, "I'm not sure if he is entranced with Jean or with watching your brush applying the design. Which reminds me. Miele."

Catrin finished her brushstroke and looked up, hearing the name.

"Her grandmother's health is failing now. They have all accepted it. She's comfortable and they are controlling the pain, but it won't be too long. I had lunch with Miele recently and when Mrs. Yau dies, she is considering leaving Hong Kong. She and her business partner may take up the chance to move to the UK and set up there."

Jean responded, "That will be hard for her. She has quite an extended family and her grandparents and aunts and uncles raised her."

She paused a moment. "And to set up her studio here. It's a big decision."

Catrin could see that Li was looking directly at her when she said, "True, but, given the changes, others in the family are considering the same decisions; not to the UK necessarily, but other places in Asia."

Only Li and Catrin knew that Miele's family were involved in gang life, a Chinese triad, and Miele had grown up in that world. Through her artistic interest in ceramics and her grandfather's stake money, she had set out on her own, away from the world of triads. It sounded as if Hong Kong was getting too uncomfortable for the gangs, as well.

She looked at the screen. "I can't wait to meet Daniel and hold him. I'm not sure when, but we must get together sometime. We need to plan on it."

Li agreed.

Plans were one thing. Life was another.

Like most other police officers, Catrin accepted that

life was a mix of what you planned and worked for and the sudden, sharp dislocations that came out of nowhere. She had delivered her share of the dreaded home visits; the long moments waiting for a person to open the front door and take in a police uniform, seeing the faces change and the tears flow.

Personally, she had planned to be a police officer and an artist. After meeting Chris, they had planned their wedding together. Despite the misfortune of two miscarriages and a precarious third pregnancy, they had planned to have a child. They were all big decisions in her life.

In the 'out of nowhere' category for her, saving the life of Jian Li, then a student in Bangor, was a big one. Through that case she had gained a friend from a different world.

The scar on her cheek was a constant reminder of another unexpected event, the arrest in Glasgow of a gang enforcer. Despite the damage, it had brought her to the attention of more senior staff and her career had developed accordingly.

The biggest 'out of the blue' event in Catrin's life had taken place in Kuala Lumpur, not London, Scotland, or Wales. Covering for a colleague at a recognition event there after the recovery of a lost painting, she had been on a visit to the Petronas Twin Towers in the company of a Malaysian police officer, Sergeant Jared Farra. He had been attacked and shot by an assailant. Using Farra's weapon, she had returned fire, killing the young man, Lon Ghee. That event, more than anything else, led to two years as a security aide to Assistant Commissioner Sandra Hunt.

In saving Farra, she had saved others; another Malaysian police officer, a Foreign and Commonwealth

Office staffer, Madeleine Turner-Jones, and herself.

~~

The following week, when the phone screen showed Madeleine Turner-Jones's name, Catrin first thought she was probably after a catch-up lunch. The FCO bureaucrat would foot the bill, no doubt, but there would be some catch in it. But she answered anyway.

"Catrin, I have a follow-up to the query you made a couple of months ago, the fraud case you mentioned. I need your help at rather short notice."

Turner-Jones sounded energized, getting straight to the point and missing out the preliminary pleasantries. That caught Catrin's attention as much as the content, as it was unlike her.

"I'm off work this afternoon, Madeleine. I left early to take Mair to another toddler's birthday party. We have just emerged, deafened."

Again, the bureaucrat skipped out on her normal 'how is she doing?' politesse. "That's nice, but this is urgent, I am afraid. Something has come up in my area, Malaysia, on this same fraud, not in West Africa. At least, that's the information I have."

She plunged straight on. "Two RMP visitors are arriving soon, an Inspector Syed and a Sergeant Yusoff. They are asking to meet you, at least one of them is. And no, it is definitely not a 'shake the hand' meeting of the woman who saved Jared Farra."

Catrin responded, "The Royal Malaysian Police contacted FCO?"

It surprised her. They would contact the Met if it concerned a police issue in London.

Turner-Jones sighed. "No, one of my contacts at the

High Commission there found out the police officers were already on a plane heading here, without any flag to us. It is best discussed in person.

"Apparently, as the dust settles on why the Malaysians are in an operation in the UK, the officers have been instructed to contact me and you, no-one else. I gather it is Chief Superintendent Baksh's doing, scrambling after the event to quell the contretemp between his staff and our people over there."

Superintendent Baksh, now Chief Superintendent she just learned, had been the senior RMP officer handling the aftermath of the attack in Kuala Lumpur.

Catrin thought it through. Two Malaysian police officers were on their way to do something in the UK without at least making a courtesy call to the Met. She could see why the Foreign Office and the British High Commission staff were in a snit.

"How about tomorrow, late morning or at lunch?" It didn't sound like work, more like smoothing diplomatic feathers.

Madeleine responded. "Can you do early this evening? It sounds urgent."

"I am looking after Mair and Chris is at work, something he can't leave. If it is that urgent, come round to my flat; no, wait. Come round to the shop where I do my ceramic art, the Cwmbran Kiln, in Spitalfields Market. My friends are stocktaking this evening and have their own daughter with them. They will look after Mair for a short while. But I don't want this to be a long meeting. If it is later, it will have to be at my place, after Mair is asleep. Hopefully, Chris will be home by then and we can go out somewhere to talk."

"Early, at the Cwmbran Kiln, then."

"You can find your way to the East End, I take it?"

Catrin quipped.

Turner-Jones was a Central London and Knightsbridge woman. The Metropolis stopped somewhere near Holborn. Anything east of there was a wasteland.

"Of course, I have used City Airport on occasion. It's vaguely near there. If I get lost, I'll ask a police officer."

"Thanks, I won't be too long."

Catrin's parting words behind her, as she closed the door to the Kiln were meant to be for Madeleine and the visitors as well as her friends. She had opened the shop door as they approached.

Madeleine was a tall, big-framed woman, carrying some weight now, but always moving with a ballet dancer's poise. The older man was smaller than her, but the younger Malaysian was a match in height and was physically fit.

After handshakes and introductions, she led them across to a patio bar, busy with market customers. Madeleine ordered wine, for one, and soft drinks for the others, knowing Catrin did not drink alcohol. Neither did the visitors, both being Muslim, Catrin deduced.

Inspector Syed had passed on best wishes from Chief Superintendent Baksh, giving the impression that this was a condoned activity, contrary to the earlier information from Turner-Jones. He was trying to save face; his bosses must have reached him in transit. Syed had commented that Sayer was a name spoken highly of in RMP headquarters, where Sergeant Farra still worked.

Catrin thanked him. As they sat down, she said gently, "Your ID's please. On the table."

Both officers looked surprised, but did so, pulling out the black wallets with their police identity cards. Catrin did likewise, showing her own to them. Her examination wasn't cursory. She checked full names, validity dates and the photo versus each man.

"CCID. Not D14?"

They were part of Commercial Crime Investigation, not the Organized Crime Division.

Inspector Syed responded, "Fraud and cybercrime investigation reside in CCID. We liaise closely with D14."

She took that to mean their boss scrambled for support from Chief Superintendent Baksh once the issue arose. She put her own ID away and they followed suite. Sergeant Yusoff gave his boss a telltale glance, as they did so.

Catrin said, "I watched you enter, and this is my ground. No one followed you in, so checking ID isn't an issue."

She wanted him to know she could read him, that she was streetwise also, and was aware of the sergeant's thoughts about the risk of disclosure of police identity badges in public. She focused on Inspector Syed.

"Farra and I stay in touch, not regularly, but I know he is doing well. His son just started university. But how can I help?"

The inspector was older than his colleague by a few years, but both looked younger than her, which made Madeleine the oldest person at the table. Once they had started talking, the FCO officer had left it to the Malaysians to explain the issue.

"We are here, ma'am, because a colleague, in an undercover role, will be meeting with an Englishman. Well, a Scottish person. She is placed within a gang based in KL led by a man called Omar Kaur and was suddenly told by him to be here. We caught an earlier flight, via Singapore. She will arrive tomorrow morning. The meeting is tomorrow afternoon and is routine."

He stopped, deciding what to say next.

Catrin looked at the sergeant. "Are you her contact, her liaison?"

Yusoff nodded but looked impassive. If they had been Met personnel, she would have asked him to answer. Catrin got the impression that while the Inspector was making the most of the situation, his sergeant was resenting the need to involve the Met. Tough, he needs to get used to it. She gave him a cold stare.

Inspector Syed continued his explanation. "We have an operation in Kuala Lumpur to arrest a group currently perpetrating a number of frauds. Most are focused on wealthy individuals across Malaysia. Sizeable sums are involved. Our country is a major target for internet fraud, but we also have criminal elements heavily involved in perpetrating them.

"A new player has emerged, tied to one of our targets; at least, new to us. He is a a British citizen with a home address in Coventry."

The words 'Coventry' and 'internet fraud' came together in Catrin's mind as Inspector Syed finished his sentence. The memory of the interview with Peter Olowe came back. He was into internet fraud and based in Coventry.

"The person is a businessman called Roland McEwen. My officer has met him previously, with Omar Kaur, in KL."

Sergeant Yussof interrupted. "They are transferring a scam operation to KL, one that the Met recently closed down in London. We thought McEwen would come over to KL again, but Kaur suddenly told our officer to come here, in his stead. She has a brief from him and instructions to call him if the negotiation goes outside that, but it means she is penetrating further into the organisation. I'd prefer her to just hold the meeting and get back to KL."

He glanced at his boss and Madeleine did the same to Catrin.

Syed, however, continued with his diplomacy. "But we are instructed to contact you both. We have done that. We are in your jurisdiction and are looking for any support that you may feel to be appropriate, should the need arise, not that we expect any problem."

He waited for an answer. Instead, he got a question. "Have you yet advised anyone in the UK of the transfer of the fraud operation? The Met or the West Midlands Police, perhaps?"

"No. Events are still unfolding. We are telling you, ma'am, right now."

Catrin wondered if they hadn't been flagged, whether the first time they would hear about this would be after the Malaysians made their arrests. Sergeant Yusoff face revealed that he hoped that Catrin would tell them simply to get on with it.

Catrin gave Turner-Jones a glance. She appeared impassive. "Madeleine?"

There were procedures in place through the Foreign and Commonwealth Office, but Turner-Jones had not mentioned those. She should have. Other people in the Met would be more appropriate contacts and Madeleine knew that.

Turner-Jones said, "There's more."

Her look to the visitors encouraged Sergeant Yusoff to speak up, reluctantly. "My officer has heard the name Amaechi Akanni, an African, mentioned by McEwen. Mrs. Turner-Jones insisted on this meeting now."

Catrin asked, "Are you recording the meeting between McEwen and your person in some way?"

Sergeant Yusoff gave her a dismissive look. "No, we

are not taking the risk. Too much is at stake in terms of our officer's placement to ruin it with a microphone. Besides, the location is an apartment belonging to McEwen."

"Where and when?"

"A place called Nine Elms, by the river. Tomorrow afternoon."

Catrin came back at him. "Nine Elms, ma'am or Chief Inspector, if you please. And if you continue to act in front of me in the manner you are doing at present, Sergeant Yusoff, I will text Chief Superintendent Baksh directly with a formal complaint, with you sitting here. This is like getting blood from a stone. Now, what contingency arrangements do you have in the event of problems? What is already set up here?"

The sergeant had, from his eyes, been shocked at her reprimand, "Nothing, ma'am, other than us. We plan to be close by in a car. It's simply McEwen and a trained police officer. If she calls me, we can handle it."

"You say. You hope. But not in my city."

She closed her eyes and counted to three. When she opened them, she focused her attention on Inspector Syed.

"We can provide a laser microphone, hopefully to monitor the window of the apartment if the location is suitable, to try to track the meeting and record the conversation. It would be undetectable. And we will have experienced local officers in support, in the event of problems. One moment."

She stood and walked away a few paces. In the background, Inspector Syed was quietly remonstrating with his sergeant in Malay. If Turner-Jones had not revealed yet her fluency in the language, she was probably taking it all in.

Her first call was to Lauder. His response was, "There's no real time on the clock to review this thoroughly, is there? But the name Akanni coming up; Karen would hate to miss out. Go for it."

She had outlined her proposal.

Her next call was to Andy Collard.

Ten minutes after she stepped away, she returned to the table.

"Inspector Andrew Collard and DS Ian Underhill from my team will meet you tomorrow early to provide advice and support. I have given Collard Mrs. Turner-Jones's mobile number. We are busy with our own operations, but we want to be seen to support our colleagues. Madeleine, please make sure Chief Superintendent Baksh hears that through channels.

"In my people, you have two of my most experienced officers in undercover surveillance in support, for the preparation and duration of the meeting of your officer with McEwen."

Sergeant Yusoff was now looking a little contrite. "Thank you, ma'am."

Madeleine was smiling, looking pleased with the outcome of the meeting. "I do appreciate it, Catrin. Thank you. Gentlemen, do you want to shop or eat, or head back to your hotel? Let's leave DCI Sayer to retrieve her daughter."

Inspector Syed expressed his appreciation and said, "I noticed in the pottery shop window a poster about Sayer-Hughes ceramics. Mrs. Turner-Jones told us you are also a ceramic artist."

Catrin smiled. "When I get the time."

"We should look in the shop, see if something of yours would be a present we could take home."

"You are very welcome to look around, if you wish,

but at another time. They are closed at present, stock-taking. The works you mentioned are only sold through a gallery near Harrods. Mrs. Turner-Jones know it."

He looked down, a little abashed. "Under the circumstances, it might be best for us to leave any shopping here until the work is completed. We are, as you can imagine, a little tense about the meeting to come."

At last, some honesty, she thought. The sergeant was wound up tight, that was obvious.

"I can see that. Sergeant Yusoff, I do understand these tensions. Take care, and I hope the meeting is useful to your team."

For the first time the younger officer smiled and said 'thank you' as if he meant it. Even then it was transitory, as if he still struggled with the involvement of others.

Catrin called Lauder after she put Mair to bed and gave him an update.

"It sounds like you did what was necessary. They can't fault us for lack of cooperation, at least. The distance listening was a nice touch."

"Yes, we'll hear first-hand whatever the Malaysians get, I thought. The sergeant was clearly unhappy about that."

Lauder sighed. "Handlers are very protective of their people in place. We know that. By the way, I have tomorrow off. Ros and I are going to see Neil and the family, now he is out of his treatment centre, to spend time with the kids. He is back at work."

"I'm glad to hear that. I'm sure they can all do with the support."

22 BINTI

It was mid-morning on the following day when Andy Collard went to see Catrin in her office. She had just returned from another meeting.

"I have put Rita Tully and Terry Jameson with the Malaysians for their meeting later this afternoon. The location is only fifteen minutes from here, at that set of apartment blocks along the river. I'll monitor from here."

Catrin knew the location of the apartments at Nine Elms. They were expensive units, in a series of parallel towers overlooking the Thames.

He continued. "Cassie Miller will do the audio. Jameson has sweet-talked access to an empty apartment on a higher floor in the next block over, with a good angle. The security head for the complex has a son in cadet training and he bent over backwards."

She smiled. "That was an easy one then."

Collard turned serious. "I think the Malaysians are fish out of water. They may know what works in KL, but... here? Ian is a bit concerned."

If Ian Underhill showed concern, Catrin thought she

should, too. "With what?"

"Access time. It takes two minutes to get from the listening post to the McEwen apartment, down the one block and up the other. The Malaysians are absolutely against any police presence in the building itself. They don't want the risk of exposing their officer's cover if McEwan spots an undercover officer. To them, this is a routine business meeting."

"And?"

She could read his face.

"This Commercial Crime group, their unit. It sounds closer to the Fraud Squad than our work. We aren't comfortable about a 'business meeting' approach. If something gives and McEwan is capable, then the business meeting may turn into mayhem. She would be at risk."

"What do you recommend?"

"Terry and Rita are both AFO. At the very least, I would prefer them armed at the listening post with Cassie and the Malaysians."

She nodded. "Go with it. I'll authorise the weapons. I'm thinking about the extreme violence used with Shand."

"So was Ian."

She added, "And give Armed Response a call. We will pick up one hour of standby costs for a team to be available around the meeting time, and I'll get the charges forwarded to FCO. They can swallow this one."

She sighed. "Other than pack them all off home on a plane, that's the best we can do at short notice."

As he left her office, she called out, "Keep me informed."

~~

"The sound is as clean as I can get it. I wish the movers' van would sod off. They emptied it ten minutes ago."

Cassie Miller, the audio engineer, was fiddling with the control unit linked to the laser microphone, now positioned behind a potted plant hastily acquired for the balcony of the unit they were using.

As per her briefing, the undercover officer, known to them simply as 'binti', had made enough noise in the apartment. She had turned the television on and, a minute later after checking channels, turned it off. She boiled a kettle and hummed to herself alongside a tune from the radio in the kitchen area. Cassie had worked away, building the filters in the raw feed from the microphone. She needed the voices of the people present clear above routine background noise.

She asked, "This other person, a man, is he a bass or a tenor voice, d'you know?"

Sergeant Yusoff thought a moment. "A very bouncy man, full of it, his voice is a higher pitch."

Rita Tully was unhappy that they had no other observation in place than their own view of the apartment, albeit that the windows were reflective; they couldn't see inside unless someone opened the sliding patio door to the balcony.

But she did as she was told. DS Terry Jameson just sat it out. He had more important things to do on assignment for Ken Osborne after this. He would be at it now if he hadn't been pulled in to babysit the visitors.

It was a waiting game.

Suddenly they heard the trill of the entry doorbell on the phone in the apartment and binti, short for Laura binti Assad, answer it.

"Binti means 'daughter of', in this case, Assad," explained Inspector Syed, at one point in the silence, as the officers and audio engineer waited. Now they heard her clearly.

"Roland, it's your apartment, I assumed you would come straight up. Well, thank you; that is very polite of you."

In less than a couple of minutes, they heard the door open and binti spoke up. *"It's so nice to see you again"*

"And you also, Laura."

Cassie smiled. His voice was clear.

Binti Assad continued speaking. *"I brought you a present from duty-free, a bottle of that favourite whisky you mentioned in KL. See, I didn't forget. Who is your friend? Welcome also."*

Tully looked across at Sergeant Yusoff, who had frowned. The briefing had mentioned that McEwen would arrive alone.

"Call him Fizz. That's what he goes by."

Binti made the right noises of welcome. They could hear movement within the room.

Rita spoke into her radio, linked to the operations room in Undertow. Andy Collard and a DC Haines were there, monitoring the feed.

"Can you do a search for a nickname of 'Fizz', boss; male, possibly from the Midlands area, perhaps with a link to this McEwen?"

Collard responded. "We are just doing that, Rita. I don't like this."

Tully asked Inspector Syed. "Sir, is he known to you?"

Focused on listening to the feed, both Malaysians just shook their heads. Syed said, "He must be local, working with McEwen. See how she plays it."

Binti's voice was steady, sounding friendly, but with an edge. *"I thought it was going to be just us, Roland. Is 'Fizz' a colleague? Is he in on our arrangement?"*

"You could say he is, Laura. You could say that, yes. Let's open that bottle you brought me. We will all have a drink."

Binti Assad gave a small laugh. *"You know I don't drink alcohol, Roland; but it is for you. However, I think I will need clearance from back home to talk about any business with another person here. If you don't mind?"*

"Go ahead. Call Omar Kaur, he will explain it."

They could not hear anything for a moment, other than binti, talking into her phone. *"Mr. Kaur, it's Laura. I'm with Mr. McEwen. He has a colleague with him, a Mr. Fizz, but that's a nickname of some sort. Can I proceed?"*

Rita expected the officer to say something based on the response she heard. It would give a status update to them. But the silence went on.

The next thing they heard was binti Assad saying brightly, *"That's OK then. I saw there were crystal glasses in the cupboard, I'll get them for you. The whisky is special."*

Within seconds they heard three gunshots, a single, followed by two shots close together. There were angry noises from two men and chilling screams from the woman, shortly followed by a door slamming.

Andy Collard said firmly, "I'm sending Armed Response. Rita, Terry both of you get over there, get access. Use your own discretion. No stupidity, please!"

Rita replied, "We are already on our way."

Rita and Terry were running, closely followed by the Malaysian officers, racing down the staircase, not waiting for the lift.

Alone in the observation area, Cassie was the only person to hear Laura binti Assad's voice. There was no-one she could check with, and she was totally focused on capturing her words. The voice became fainter, speaking in a foreign language, coming in fits and starts, through pain. There was a new background noise outside, a diesel taxi. Miller worked at altering the parameters and adjusting sensitivities to ensure as much as possible from the officer was recorded.

The taxi roared away just after the voice stopped.

She waited, hearing the door being slammed open and first Tully then Jameson shouting 'clear' as they worked their way into the apartment.

Jameson's voice came across much louder in the room. "Oh my God, what a mess."

Then the audio engineer heard DC Tully say. "Cassie, stop the recording, if you are still there."

It was later in the day that the police technician was told that she had recorded the final words of a police officer bleeding to death. And like any undercover officer, Laura binti Assad had conveyed as much as she could in the time available, sentences that contained words that were important indeed.

23 WRECKAGE

Inside the apartment, after Terry's exclamation, the Undertow officers found two people and a lot of blood.

Leaning across the breakfast bar was a Malaysian woman in her late twenties, apparently unconscious, with a large knife wound to her chest, a single blow that seemed to spread up from the entry point beneath her sternum, following the rib line to exit at the armpit.

Behind her lay a large Caucasian on the floor, unconscious, on his back in a pool of blood. He still held a knife in one hand.

Terry pointed to the woman as he approached the man, his weapon focused on him until he could reach down to disarm him. He checked him for other weapons, finding none.

Rita reached across the breakfast bar and checked the Malaysian's pulse, looking at the eyes. Binti Assad wasn't unconscious, she was dead. When Rita moved to the other side of the breakfast bar, she was shocked by the volume of blood under the woman, running down her front to the pool formed on the floor. The knife must have severed one or more large arteries.

As she stepped back, she thought about the noises heard on the sound recording, as she saw the gun in the sink. It had fallen, she concluded, from the woman's hand.

"Cassie, it's Rita. Stop the recording if you are still there."

She looked behind her. Terry crouched by the man. "He's breathing and regaining consciousness."

Rita turned towards the door where the Malaysian police officers now stood, transfixed. Inspector Syed stared in shock at binti Assad. Sergeant Yusoff focused on the man on the floor.

Rita said, "She was armed, wasn't she? You knew that?"

She spoke as much to vocalise her thoughts as to ask the question, recalling their evasions about support tied to their officer. She was armed and meeting with only one man.

Neither responded.

DS Terry Jameson took control, focusing on them, standing up.

"Please. Stay there or go outside and wait. I order you to do so. I know it is your colleague, and I'm sorry, but stay out of the crime scene. There is nothing you can do. You have to leave it to us."

He didn't listen to the response as he was now on his phone, concurrently briefing Collard.

Inspector Syed nodded at Rita. His face had turned ashen. "We'll wait outside, in the lobby; I will have to report to my superiors. I suppose this one is Fizz."

If looks could kill, the man would be as dead as his undercover officer.

In moving the knife out of Fizz's grasp, the man had

groaned and stirred slightly. He was obviously in severe pain, panting, cursing under his breath and keeping his eyes on Jameson.

Terry finished his brief update to Collard. "McEwen has made a run for it. Should one of us pursue?"

Whatever Collard told him he shook his head at Rita. "Right, we wait here. Protect the scene."

Tully nodded, her face white with anger and worry She was trying to come to terms with being part of an operation resulting in a dead police officer, seeing the woman she knew only as 'binti' lying there, and thinking about her own job, possibly seeing herself in the future.

"An ambulance is coming," Terry told the man Fizz, swallowing back the wish that it would arrive too late.

He looked around. There had been three shots. Two, at least were in or through the man, lower down, from entry wounds near his hip and navel. The smell of ruptured intestines and bowels was growing, filling the room. He could see where another round had gone into the wall across from the dining area.

Ignoring the man's groans, he checked the entrance hall. There were no signs of blood there. Then he saw the splintering at the edge of the cabinet door close to binti Assad. He walked over, avoiding the blood and, using his pen, reached across the Malaysian to flip the door open. The mess showed the gun had been hastily pulled from inside the cabinet.

He updated Collard that it appeared that McEwen not only ran for it but was unhurt.

As he closed the call, he said to Tully. "Andy is in with the boss now. We just wait and secure the scene. Go find our two friends outside, tell them that a car is coming for them. They can talk, but they are on their way back to the station, Sayer says. We are to detain them if they don't cooperate. Tell them that, too and if need be, arrest them."

Left alone, he looked down at the mess around Fizz. The man moved his free arm slightly. He needed help, but Terry ignored him. He moved back to the door to await the arrival of the paramedics and the team who would conduct a murder investigation.

From Andy's face, Sayer could see immediately that a major problem had occurred. As he briefed her with the main points, she focused on procedure.

"Superintendent Lauder is away. I am I/C as of -."

She checked the time. "Five thirteen. Andy, note that. You take three others and head to the scene, take charge there and report to me directly. I will take over the liaison with Armed Response. I'll also alert Commander Moore and try to reach Lauder and the borough. You contain what you can on site and have Syed and Yussoff brought back immediately to Lavender Hill, but not into our shop. They can talk to who they want to, but I want them off-scene and back here before the media get a sniff of this."

Catrin was assuming the role of Incident Commander. By rights, if an Undertow officer was injured or killed, initially it should be Lauder, as the senior officer. As Ken Osborne was also out for the day, it was her job.

Collard turned in the doorway. "And if the Malaysians insist on doing their own thing? It is their officer who is dead?"

"It's our crime scene. They do not get the choice. Detain them if necessary. Go!"

She picked up her own mobile and moved out to the operations area, calling out for several officers to assist her.

Karen Moore sounded calm. When nothing was

happening, she sounded energized; when the world went to hell in a handbasket, she sounded calm. Catrin had briefed her twenty minutes ago. Now she was calling back.

Her first words were, "How are Tully and Jameson doing?"

"Keeping it together. Collard is in charge there now. They have the apartment isolated and there are uniforms on scene. SOCOs are on their way. We just had confirmation that McEwen's car is in the parking, in his assigned slot, so he can't be far. Armed Response and other units are looking for him and his photo is circulated. The borough people are checking CCTV."

"Catrin, Superintendent Kevin Tooley has just been assigned to lead the investigation into the fatality. He's Homicide and very experienced; you know that. Tooley is on his way now to Nine Elms, with members of his team. When he gets there, he assumes control and will call you. You then sign off as Incident Commander and assist him as required. You have the Malaysians at the station now?"

"Not yet, ma'am, but they are on their way. And a representative from their High Commission will be coming, to speak with them. We have given them a room to talk. And Ken Osborne has just got back. He is with me now."

"Keep them there until told otherwise by Tooley. He is liaising with FCO about a foreign police officer undercover here apparently being armed without authorisation. We hope the weapon came through other sources available to them, not through the High Commission, but if that were the source, they would deny it anyway. It's as much a hot button for FCO as the death of the RMP officer. I won't keep you, as I can hear the phones ringing."

"One thing, ma'am. They found a bag presumably belonging to 'Fizz'. He's a Thomas Fitzgerald. It's a torture kit. And we have the first read of the final bit of the recording, not official, just a verbatim translation for me from Turner-Jones, over the phone. We think the undercover officer's cover was blown in KL. The meeting was to extract information and presumably kill her."

Moore sighed. "From bad to worse."

She rang off.

Ken Osborne looked at her. "What can I do?". He could see that Sayer had been in tears at some point, although she sounded in control on the phone.

"Take over everything else but listen to this first and here is the translation. When we get Tully and Jameson back here, can you deal with them first?"

He looked at the text as the voice played. It wasn't long, but he felt the impact. "They'll need support. Yes. I'll handle that. You focus on Tooley and first, take a break."

She smiled. "That's a polite way of telling me to fix my face. Thanks."

As she moved to do that, DC Stone waved at her, holding a phone. "A DI Khan, ma'am, with a Superintendent Tooley. They are just arriving at Nine Elms. The superintendent wants to speak to you."

Later, she called Chris. "It's finally happened, an officer killed in the line of duty. Not mine, but I had some involvement. I don't know when I'll get back."

On her mind was her comment made earlier to Collard about the alternative of packing the Malaysians on a plane and closing the operation down. 'How I wish–' she thought.

She and Chris had talked about this possible scenario

some weeks after her promotion. What happens if an undercover officer gets injured or killed? Catrin had a large frontline team to manage now.

She had responded, "There's a procedure laid out. I will have to be there, night or day if it is an Undertow officer, even if Lauder assumes the lead."

Chris had just arrived home and didn't know any details, but his wife was about to go through the experience.

It was later, after feeding and bathing Mair, when he asked their daughter, "Bedtime story?"

Momentarily, she looked confused. Whenever Catrin was home from work in time, she read the bedtime stories. But mummy wasn't here now. Then she smiled. "Cocodile!"

"The Enormous Crocodile it is, then."

24 RAIN MAN

It was eleven-thirty p.m. when Catrin arrived home exhausted. By six thirty a.m., she left again, showered and changed, heading this time to New Scotland Yard. Morning news coverage included an item on shots fired at an apartment block overlooking the Thames, and a swarm of armed police searching the area. Two people, unidentified, were either dead or injured.

"We expect an update from the Met this morning. So far, we know of two victims. Another resident saw an Asian visitor enter the apartment yesterday. It is leased to a Roland McEwen, who is now in custody. We understand that police arrested him nearby.

"McEwen is from Glasgow, a business manager. His primary residence is in Coventry."

At New Scotland Yard, all the seats around the meeting table were occupied. Several senior officers stood, refusing offers of a seat during the opening update.

Lauder, Sayer, Osborne and Collard were representing Undertow, each feeling vulnerable. Commander Moore took charge, looking sombre.

"Right, the update. Let's get started. We have arranged that DCI Sayer will give the background first and Superintendent Tooley will brief us on the progress in the formal investigation. Then we can finalise the next press release and briefing."

Catrin moved to stand by Moore and spoke to the room, conscious that Assistant Commissioner Tom Sleiman sat in her direct sight.

As she began, the far set of doors opened and Commissioner Worthington came in, alone. DI Collard gave her his seat.

"Shortly after 5.10 p.m. yesterday, an operation at Nine Elms went seriously wrong. In hindsight, the goal, to support a meeting between undercover officer from the Royal Malaysian Police and a British target, was unachievable. The officer's cover had been broken before she left Malaysia.

"The joint operation received authorisation at short notice. We had little advance warning. Undertow Team A was assigned to support the Malaysian team, a DI Syed and a DS Yusoff. According to them, this meeting followed one in Kuala Lumpur between the individuals, a planning session to move a scamming operation from the UK to Malaysia, one that the Met shut down in Lewisham months ago.

"McEwen chose his London apartment for the meeting venue. The officer, under the cover name Laura binti Assad, had the use of it during her visit. She planned to stay there overnight before flying back to Kuala Lumpur.

"DC Rita Tully and DS Terry Jameson accompanied the Malaysian team to the listening post set up in an adjacent block. The agreed procedure used a laser microphone focused on the main glass wall, to circumvent any problems if McEwen routinely checked for electronic surveillance in the apartment.

"We had no visual sighting of the meeting. When McEwen arrived, a man he referred to as 'Fizz' accompanied him. He is now identified as a Thomas Fitzgerald, from Wolverhampton. DC Tully requested DI Collard to check the databases for this 'Fizz' but the incident occurred before the response came through."

Collard watched his boss. As she went on with the timeline of events, he thought that she was struggling to remain impassive, but was in control. She looked down again at a set of notes she was holding as she refocused on the group.

"At 5.12 p.m., just after introductions, binti Assad called a number in Kuala Lumpur, a call to her gang boss, requesting approval to discuss the business issues in front of a third party. What was said to the officer wasn't recorded, but evidently, as I will show in a moment, she was informed it was a set-up, that the gang leader had discovered she was an undercover police officer.

"Within seconds, three shots were heard, and screams. We later found out from our Malaysian colleagues that binti Assad had been armed at the meeting, a weapon provided to her here in the UK. That was not authorised by us, I might add. We had both DC Tully and DS Jameson armed and a tactical unit on standby, as per procedure."

She took a breath, paused.

"Tully, Jameson and the Malaysian officers raced from their building across to the neighboring block, entered the apartment, which was open, with standard precautions. They found Fitzgerald on the floor with gunshot wounds to the abdomen. A knife was in his hand. Binti Assad was dead, with a knife wound to her chest that was traumatic;

Fitzgerald had opened her up. Initial assessment is that she retrieved a hidden weapon from a drawer or cupboard and fired, the first shot missing, before two rounds wounded Fitzgerald as got to her with his knife.

"Audio analysis revealed McEwen fled at that time. Fitzgerald was cursing and screaming before passing out, reviving when Jameson removed his weapon. Officer binti Assad, however, knowing she was being recorded, spoke in Malay until she became unconscious. We have that translated and it is easier to read than to listen to, I assure you."

She pointed at Osborne, who switched the slide on the screen.

"Kaur told me he knew I was working for the police… his man saw me meet Ladi and checked him out. They let me come here. They want everything I know… I missed, first shot and… I'm sorry. McEwen ran. I'm not going to make it, I think. Tell Ray and my family I love them all, I'm sorry to leave and Ray must pray for understanding. Don't let Kaur get…"

Catrin kept her voice even. "Omar Kaur is the head of the group she infiltrated. He apparently answered her call on his mobile. McEwen had said she could call him, by name. The RMP are following up on that. Binti Assad's real name is Sofia binti Awang. Ray is short for Rayyan. Rayyan bin Ahmad is her husband, who is also an RMP police officer."

She paused, taking a deep breath.

"It is apparent that, earlier in KL, a routine briefing meeting between binti Awang and her liaison, DS Ladi Yussof, became known to the Kaur gang. Fitzgerald had a small toolbag with him containing pliers, tinsnips and a butane blowtorch, among other things; a kit for torturing her to extract information before presumably killing her – and to do that far away from Malaysia. From her messages, they wanted everything that the RMP knew about both the Kaur and McEwen operations. At least she was spared that horror."

She spoke faster now, more controlled. "DI Collard, supervising the surveillance operation, reported to me and I sent him there as on-scene commander. I assumed the role of Incident Commander and stayed at Lavender Hill.

"The Malaysian officers were brought to Lavender Hill and assisted our enquiries. Inspector Syed needed medical attention at one point, a stress reaction as a result of his operation unravelling and losing a team member. Both men are now back at their High Commission. I handed over to Superintendent Tooley at five forty-seven p.m. and worked with him to coordinate communications with FCO, Commander Moore, the Malaysian Embassy and at one point, in direct contact with the RMP in Kuala Lumpur. Superintendent Tooley will brief us on the investigation."

She moved away as Tooley moved forward but was stopped by a voice.

"Before he does that, a question."

The voice was loud, firm. She looked at Commander Reed, Karen's opposite number in Homicide. "You mentioned Rel-Comm, but not by name. Is Undertow's involvement in this incident tied to the investigation into Akanni?"

He held Catrin's eye, wanting a response from her.

"It's too early to say, sir. If we had recorded the interview, as planned, and it provided more information about McEwen's activity that linked him to Rel-Comm, it could have re-opened that line of enquiry. But -."

He cut her off, fixing his gaze on Moore. "I thought,

Karen, two months ago, given the discussions at the SCLC, that one was scotched. Why are you re-opening it?"

He was hostile.

Moore, normally an able combatant in any affray, swallowed and hesitated. "As Sayer said, John, we were following a new lead. It's too early to say."

Reed gave a look somewhere between annoyance and disbelief, inferring to all it was a ploy to re-open the Akanni investigation. Moore glared back but said nothing.

He's showcasing, thought Catrin, because the Commissioner has dropped in. From her time as Sandra Hunt's aide, she knew that was a waste of time. It didn't impress the Met executives.

She spoke up. "I was going to say, sir, our entire focus now is on the events that unfolded; on the death of a fellow officer, Sofia binti Awang."

Suck on that bitter pill, she thought.

"Quite. But one more question." It was Commissioner Worthington speaking now, so everybody else became quiet.

"You spoke directly to a senior officer of the Royal Malaysian Police at one point, I understand. Who authorised that?"

She was not sounding critical, but wanted to understand, it seemed.

Catrin blushed. "No-one, ma'am. He was connected to me through the Malaysian desk at FCO, Mrs. Turner-Jones. He didn't call direct. We both knew Chief Superintendent Baksh from another incident."

Assistant Comminssioner Sleiman spoke up. "DCI Sayer is the officer who accompanied Turner-Jones to Kuala Lumpur. She defended an officer there during an attack—"

The Commissioner broke in. "Ah! I recall the brief, now you mention it. Thanks, Tom." She was still focused on Sayer. "What did you tell him?"

"The relevant facts as we knew them, ma'am. He had spoken to Inspector Syed and wanted to understand it from my perspective."

The commissioner looked thoughtful. "Thank you. That's all from me."

"Status of Fitzgerald, DCI Sayer?"

The question came from one of the communication people. Catrin looked at Superintendent Tooley. He responded as he moved to the front.

"Currently he in intensive care in the Royal Brompton Hospital after major surgery. He'll be in hospital a while, having received serious abdominal injuries. He required a colostomy, probably permanent, and he has some spinal injury. But it looks currently as he will live, for arrest and trial. DS Innis is waiting to charge him with the murder of Sofia binti Awang as soon as cleared to do so.

"Fitzgerald is under armed guard. He has a prior record and we have contacted the West Midlands people for any insights not recorded. If he is a torturer for hire, he probably has a track record in that part of the world. His toolbox was unused here, but it is undergoing forensic testing now."

"Roland McEwen was arrested without incident walking along Jeffreys Road and is in custody. His suit trousers have small blood splatters near the bottom, currently being analysed, enough at least to hold him and charge him with conspiracy to murder.

"I will be overseeing the second interview of Roland McEwen at Lavender Hill after leaving this briefing. Last night he was totally uncooperative.

"Later, I will be meeting with the RMP officers to

interview them further. We already have the statements of the Undertow officers involved."

"I will be charging both Fitzgerald and McEwen with first degree murder, despite the weapon fired at Fitzgerald. It is not self-defense when you plan to torture and kill another person.

"We will also prepare an international warrant for the arrest of Omar Kaur in Malaysia, on the same charge, but will take that through FCO. However, I suspect, with the information we have already provided to our colleagues in Malaysia, they may have their own charges to lay in that direction. I will be surprised if they pass him over to us. Now, the facts for inclusion in the press briefing..."

Again, the Commissioner spoke up and people listened. "Superintendent, the information provided to the Malaysians; I have a similar question to the one to DCI Sayer earlier. What has been provided formally, as evidence, not as a status update?"

Tooley looked at her, his face showing that he well understood the import of the question. "I will re-check to confirm, ma'am. My understanding is that everything was provided in telephone calls. A copy of the doctor's confirmation of death of the officer and photo of her face, taken at the hospital, were faxed directly to Chief Superintendent Baksh, to allow them to proceed formally there. No on-scene evidence has been sent. Nothing else has been sent by email or text, fax or courier."

With the second question from the Commissioner on the same subject, Catrin wondered what the issue was. Reading her face, Lauder leaned over slightly and whispered, 'death penalty' in her ear.

She hadn't thought of that at all yesterday. As Incident Commander, everything had been by phone. The speed of developments and the communication requirements allowed for nothing else. Then a memory from a training course returned, regarding the provision of evidence to other countries with the death penalty in their statutes. It had largely focused on UK/USA communications, but was equally applicable to Malaysia. The country had the death penalty in its penal code.

Catrin walked back to the rear wall as Tooley continued. She was still tired. As the routine elements of the press brief for the murder investigation were discussed, the Commissioner stood, signalling to Sayer to take her seat. Catrin shook her head, but Worthington insisted. As she walked across and mouthed a 'thank you', the Commissioner whispered, "You need it more than me!"

Worthington gently patted Sayer's shoulder as she sat down, before leaving the room herself.

After the briefing, Catrin regrouped with Moore, Osborne and Lauder. Andy Collard hesitated; he was part of the team, but unsure if he should participate in the review with the senior team. Catrin brought him in with a wave.

Moore said truculently, "I'm glad you spoke up when you did, Catrin. John Reed is getting right up my nose these days. I swallowed it once, but… you brought it back into focus."

Catrin gave a small smile of appreciation. "I'm not sure the Commissioner was happy with me talking to Chief Superintendent Baksh."

"You did nothing wrong. What are you going to do? The man knows you and he's just lost an officer."

She paused. "You said, 'the facts'; over the phone that's nothing to get us into trouble."

Catrin looked at Lauder. Gerry said quietly, "She kept

to those. But he has seen her under stress before. She told him Turner-Jones already translated the audio cut of the officer's last message for her, then she played it to him. She cried as she expressed her condolences about losing a brave and dedicated officer."

Moore looked serious, then her mouth contorted slightly. "Nothing wrong with that. Nothing at all. I could have done the same thing in that situation."

She must have caught Andy's reaction. "I do, you know, cry at times. Besides tearing people's heads off for breakfast."

He looked alarmed, but she ignored it.

"If Commissioner Worthington has a problem, we'll hear about, in confidence, not like Commander Reed did it. And if she doesn't, then we won't. But she'll remember. That woman has a memory like... like the Rain Man."

She looked at Collard's blank expression. "Rain Man. Dustin Hoffman. The movie. What was the character called?"

"Something Babbit, ma'am," said Lauder seriously, his eyes twinkling at Catrin, who had broken out in a smile.

Moore continued to focus on Andy. "What the hell sort of movies do you watch these days, not knowing Rain Man?"

Andy said, "It was context, ma'am. Now you mention it, I see what you mean, I think. Although the Commissioner addressed us with greater eloquence, I recall, during her visit."

Catrin was openly laughing now. Police officers needed to vent. Humour was a better outlet than tears, at times.

25 RESPECT

The following day, Catrin found it hard to concentrate. She had difficulty getting to sleep last night and, when the alarm sounded, in getting up. During the morning briefing at Lavender Hill, she, Lauder and Osborne acknowledged the disruption and emotional impact of the last few days, but focused on getting people busy again, back to assigned tasks, some now rescheduled.

By midday it had gained a semblance of normality. By the end of the day, for those whose work didn't take them into the wee small hours, they awaited snippets of news on the investigation into the Malaysian's death, but their primary focus was on their own cases.

Catrin left early, returned home and spent time with Mair. For a change, she prepared dinner. Normal things. That night she slept soundly.

However, the day after, the sudden, unannounced appearance of Assistant Commissioner Sleiman and Karen Moore heading into Lauder's office mid-morning made a ripple around the Undertow unit.

Five minutes later, Lauder called in Sayer and asked DI Collard to have himself, Tully and Jameson available on standby. People got on with assigned tasks, but with one eye on Lauder's office door, wondering what was going on.

They were in session for half an hour.

After calling Osborne into the room, Collard, Tully and Jameson were pulled into the discussion. DC Haywood made the cryptic remark that it must be standing room only.

Ten minutes later, everyone came out and Moore and Sleiman left, with only a nod and odd comment to people they passed on the way out. It took a further ten minutes for Lauder to call a group meeting.

"There are some developments you need to be aware of that will mean changes in assignments for the next few days. DCI Sayer, DI Collard and DC Tully will be with Foreign Office and Malaysian High Commission staff travelling to Kuala Lumpur tomorrow, on a commercial flight taking the body of Sofia binti Awang home. They will be in dress uniform at the funeral, which takes place the same day as they arrive, local time, according to custom."

A ripple moved around the area, with people looking at each other in surprise. Forestalling the potential quest-ions, Lauder continued speaking. "Discussions between the FCO and Malaysia are white-hot at present, as you can imagine. This, at least, gives us at Undertow the representation to show our respect. Some of you may know that DCI Sayer has been to Kuala Lumpur previously. In an incident there, she shot the assailant, saving several lives. The Royal Malaysian Police requested her presence and invited other officers to attend. AC

Sleiman and the FCO agreed to leave it to us to decide.

"And no, before you ask, it's not coming out of our budget. Catrin?"

She spoke up. "Commander Moore thought that the officers closest to the events should be invited first. Andy and Rita agreed to go. Terry will act for Andy in his absence. Ken and the boss will cover for me. Terry?"

She looked at Jameson. He spoke up. "I hate flying, so it makes more sense. But I was glad to be asked. I'm leaving it to Rita, as we were the closest when it happened. I know she will do us proud."

Tully looked as if she was somewhere between shock and tears.

Sayer continued, "It's a long flight, about thirteen hours each way. But it is an opportunity for us to show our respect for a fallen officer, as the boss said. It's worth it. After the ceremonies at the airport and the funeral, the RMP will look after us for a couple of days before our return."

It was DS Wong who asked. "Any news on people arrested? Are DI Syed and DS Yusoff going back with you?"

Catrin looked at Lauder, who motioned for her to speak.

"The Malaysian officers are currently on their way home, so they will already be there. The RMP have arrested Omar Kaur. The link between his phone and the call made by Sofia is solid. They don't have what he said, but they have a link."

She heard someone say, "Great. Got him!"

"But there is a complication. The FCO have informed the Malaysians that under Commonwealth Mutual Use of Evidence provisions, any information supplied from here used in the prosecution of Kaur requires their agreement that a death penalty sentence is waived. It is British policy. That is not going down too well in KL. As visitors, we have to tread carefully."

In the assembled faces, she could read those for and against the decision.

DC Loretta Hills said, "It's a long way, but it's good we are represented and that Rita is going. We'll all do whatever is needed to cover here. Will you get the chance to look around a bit?"

Sayer was formulating her answer when Lauder spoke. "Andy and Rita will. DI Sayer has another job there; to interview Kaur."

DS Underhill said, "That sound like one of Commander Moore's good ideas."

The team knew Karen Moore and her ways.

Lauder said, "Not 'good', Ian. AC Sleiman called it a 'brilliant' idea, didn't he?"

Catrin saw the annoyance on Lauder's face. She thought, we shouldn't be discussing this in the large group. Before she could speak, there was a collective groan from several officers, getting the drift.

Catrin responded. "Yes, I have my work cut out for me. So, your job is to make it easier by ensuring all goes well here. Now, Andy, Rita and I are out of here, getting our uniforms sorted out. We are to be in full dress at the ceremony, including shoulder lanyards and white gloves. Now, back to work, everyone."

As they broke up, DS Wong said, "Full dress, in that heat and humidity. Rather you than me."

Rita Tully looked surprised. "I hadn't thought about that."

Wong smiled at her. "When you get there, you will understand. It will be as if you are wearing an overcoat in a sauna, when you are outside."

In the meeting earlier, Karen Moore had said, "I have been talking several times in the last twenty-four hours with Chief Superintendent Baksh. We put on out thinking caps. He came up with a 'saving grace' for the RMP, to help with the FCO fiasco, telling the Malaysians how they can use our evidence. Apparently, it was as much the way the person from the High Commission did it, a man called Gilbertson, I gather. He was almost lecturing them. Baksh agrees with me that you should interview Kaur, see what we can get out of him."

Sleiman spoke up. "This is innovative, Sayer. Brilliant, in fact, if you can pull it off."

Catrin kept her face impassive, although her mind was already rebelling.

Moore continued, her voice firm. "Omar Kaur was taking on part of the scam operation based in Rel-Comm. Some cronies of his were taking part of it into Thailand. So there have been prior discussions, arrangements made, and I don't believe all of that has been handled by McEwen. I want to know if Akanni was involved. I think the link we have is Olowe in Wales, through some woman to be identified, to McEwen and up to Akanni."

Catrin butted in, "Has McEwen said anything? Useful, I mean?"

"No, he is tighter than a drumhead. So, this is conjecture. If we can get Kaur to realise that the UK end screwed up badly, he may be more disposed to swap McEwen's boss for his own life."

"But you just said that the FCO have already told the Malaysians about the evidence. If so, Kaur's lawyer will already be aware."

Moore replied softly, "Within these walls only. Tooley is also planning to arrest Kaur's brother-in-law, Hatar

Jebat. He is sure he was involved. He is in Southampton and Tooley is preparing the case. Timing will be adjusted to fit this interview unless he makes a move to fly home sooner."

Catrin looked from Moore to Sleiman to Lauder. "Basically, you want me to get the man Kaur to give us information that will lead to the arrest of Amaechi Akanni?"

Sleiman spoke up. "As I said, brilliant. It gives us what we want and gives the RMP a valid justification for taking a death sentence off the table; they are helping catch another senior crime figure associated with the death of binti Awang."

Moore added., "You and Sergeant Farra are going to convince him that if he doesn't, the information will be provided informally to the RMP, creating hell for the FCO and their Malaysian counterparts about the legitimacy of its use in court. It could, in principle, give them the opportunity to send Jebat to the hangman, if we let him go back there."

She smiled. "I have every confidence in you."

Lauder had looked unhappy with the whole set of events. He just said, "I think you can take it that the Commissioner has no issue with your discussion with Chief Superintendent Baksh."

26 FUNERAL

Catrin had travelled first class on Malaysia Airlines before, with a dreamlike memory. Years earlier, she had been returning to the UK after the incident at the Petronas Twin Towers in the company of her friend Jian Li. At the time, she thought it was Li who paid for the upgrade from business class. In fact, the Malaysians organized it, as she had saved the life of one of their police officers.

Her memory was of exhaustion and relief at going home, of a long sleep and a freshly prepared dish with scallops and salad whose flavours she had never quite found again. It revived her, in a sense.

This time, on the way from London to Kuala Lumpur, she was similarly pampered. The Malaysia Airlines Airbus A350 had only four first-class seats, each in a private cubicle, but they reserved the entire First and Business Class sections for the delegation. Turner-Jones briefed them hurriedly at the airport before the 10.30 a.m. departure.

"Catrin, you will be in First Class, as delegation head.

DI Collard, DC Tully and I will be in business class. The service there on board will be formal and quiet, to keep the respect needed. The curtains to the back of the aircraft will be closed and cabin attendants will not allow other passengers to come forward during the flight.

"There will be two officers in full uniform sitting in the back row of business class as we board, a man and a woman. The complete row in front of them will be left empty. Both are close colleagues of binti Awang. They flew here on the outbound flight from KL to escort her home. The officers were part of the honour guard during the loading of the transport casket, and they will stay in dress uniform for the flight home. There, they will join the full honour guard on arrival.

"There are mourning implications. I suspect they will be left largely to themselves, with one or more of the delegation members talking with them. For us, I will check, but at present we err on the side of silence and respect on board. So, until we hear anything different, nod and acknowledge the two police officers, but don't approach them or begin a conversation with them. If they speak to you as fellow officers, that is a different matter."

"The expectation is that you will change into dress uniform before arrival. It's a long trip and we don't want you half in, half out of uniform while travelling.

"Please don't worry about your roles in the day ahead. People will guide you and we have no real part to play other than to be there. It will be a Muslim funeral, with a significant police presence, at all ranks. The funeral cortege will go from the airport to downtown, past the RMP headquarters and on to the mosque. Later, there will be the funeral ceremony there."

She glanced again at a document.

"As you, Catrin and Rita, will be wearing your uniform

hats on arrival, the most important thing to note is that you must not remove them, despite the heat, particularly in the mosque. There, out of respect for your uniform, you will not be required to wear any other head covering. Some female officers will wear a hijab beneath their own uniform hat, others will not. All is acceptable, providing you do not bare your head.

I will be wearing a tudung, a Malaysian headscarf, in colours appropriate for mourning. You two and I will be with a female group; DI Collard will be with a colleague of mine with the men.

"Remember, while you will mainly hear Malay spoken, everyone speaks English. Mind what you say to each other, don't smile, and be constantly aware how you deport yourself. From the time the plane door opens in KL airport, we will be on parade, on show."

"Sleep on the plane, it's a long trip and an even longer day on arrival."

They were over the Black Sea, the lunch service just cleared away, and Catrin was drifting off while watching the landscape below. Food, quiet and the flight came together to remind her she had been through three hectic days. But sleep could wait. She had been on this route before. Heading constantly south-east, dusk would come early, body time, giving a night of sleep onboard before dawn, close to their 7.15 a.m. arrival into Kuala Lumpur airport and the long day ahead.

She wished privately that they were not being met on arrival. They could then head to the hotel, get sorted out and dress appropriately for the funeral in greater comfort.

When Collard suddenly came forward and tapped gently on her cubicle partition to talk confidentially with her, she took in his expression and said quietly, "What's up?".

"It's Rita. She went to the washroom, changed, and is now in full uniform sitting in her seat. We are only a little over two hours into it, hardly started."

Catrin thought a moment. It had been borderline, the decision to bring Tully, given how upset she was after the discovery of the body. She whispered, "Let's not make a fuss. Do you know why?"

"No. But I think it is probably the two officers at the back, in uniform. She took a long look at them coming on board and has been obviously mulling over something ever since. Then she just got up, took her garment bag out of the overhead and went to the washroom to change. Shall I ask her about it, or tell her to see you?"

"No. Ask Madeleine to come forward, please. You sit back down and keep an eye on Tully. But leave it be."

It was ten minutes later, after a brief discussion between Turner-Jones and one member of the Malaysian delegation, that the FCO staffer beckoned to Tully. "With me, please, Officer Tully."

In a well-practiced sweep, Turner-Jones moved a long silk scarf from her neck so that her head was covered as she walked to the back of business class, to the row where the two uniformed officers sat alone in the centre pair of seats. They stood as the two British women approached, taking in the younger woman in her dress uniform as Turner-Jones spoke to them softly in Malay.

Tully listened uncomprehendingly, a little amazed at the capability of the FCO official. When the female RMP officer replied equally softly, it was only the tonal change which would give away that it was a different speaker.

Turner-Jones turned to address Tully. "Sergeant Lee and Officer Zanab are colleagues of Officer binti Awang.

I told them about your role at the incident. They invite you to join them on their row if you would like to do that?"

"It would be a privilege to do so. Thank you."

The female officer said, "You are in uniform already."

She hadn't asked why, just observed.

Rita said, "It feels... I just felt I should."

The two Malays nodded, understanding, and gestured to her. The middle pair of seats were given to the two females, the male sergeant took the empty window seat on one side in the same row. A flight attendant fussed about, moving things, getting them settled. Turner-Jones returned to her seat.

It was about twenty minutes later when Catrin stood, moving to the galley area; not to pick up anything from the trays on display, but to take in the cabin. At the very back, before the closed curtains, Tully was talking quietly with the female RMP officer. Catching Sayer's eye, Madeleine stood and moved forward.

Catrin commented, "It seemed to work out."

Turner-Jones said very quietly. "I watched the thumbs on phones as I sat down afterwards. I suspect by now a lot of RMP officers and others will be in the know that a Met constable chose to perform her own honour guard on the flight over. It may do something to ameliorate the tension created by my colleagues in KL."

Catrin nodded. It may do something to help Rita get through the aftermath of Nine Elms, she hoped. That was why she had suggested it.

Some time in the quasi-night, Catrin went to the first-class washroom and, as she came out, saw the Malaysian Deputy High Commissioner near the window, close to the exit door, talking quietly with the flight attendant. He smiled at Catrin, and she went across the aisle.

He said very quietly, "Our flight attendant tells me that we are at the point I like, on other flight schedules, to be awake and look outside. We have both been on this route many times. It is when we can sometimes see the start of the Himalayas on our port side. It always makes me think, whatever we face, it is dawn, and we have a new day, a good day."

The flight attendant smiled. "I enjoy that sight, too, Your Exellency."

Catrin said, "Dawn for us will be closer to arrival. I will see Malaysia in it again, from the air."

The Deputy HC responded, "And that too, will be a good day; a hard one, with sadness and honour, but still, a good day."

He paused. "Your colleague did very well, with her gesture. I could see it was heartfelt."

The flight attendant smiled. "She is lovely. I can always tell when it is a person's first big flight."

Catrin replied, "As hard as it is, I am glad she came with us. It will be an experience for her to be in KL."

"And hopefully an easier one for you than your first time." He said something quietly in rapid-fire Malay to the flight attendant. Her eyes widened.

"This is a special flight, indeed. May I get either of you anything?"

As the aircraft began its descent, all the Met officers were in uniform. Others in the delegation had freshened up, preparing themselves for the solemn ceremonies about to begin.

First would be the wait in a private lounge area, for the aircraft to empty of regular passengers. The delegation would rapidly clear immigration formalities there. They would be taken to the area where they would watch as RMP officers, including the escort from the aircraft, provide an honour guard as binti Awang's casket was transferred to the hearse.

From there, the British contingent would be meeting briefly with British High Commission personnel, transferred to the hotel, allowed time to shower and freshen up before joining the ceremonies later.

Turner-Jones spoke to them as they clustered after immigration and customs formalities. "I remind you that the only no-go area of conversation, and they won't raise it, is binti Awang being armed. The UK news releases deliberately muddied the waters on the origin of the gunshots. FCO are being carefully myopic about the breach, given the other sensitivities about the use of our evidence."

Catrin responded, "I know. We are glad to have Fitzgerald out of circulation. For you only, I just heard that they found the DNA of two other people on his bag of tools, only one of whom has been identified so far. Superintendent Tooley has a serial killer under lock and key, and I am to convey that news orally to Chief Superintendent Baksh, as a positive outcome for us arising from the tragedy."

As on the last time Catrin flew to Kuala Lumpur, Turner-Jones was welcomed by Malaysian officials as an old friend. This time, the RMP contingent in the airport welcomed Sayer not as a young officer sent to give a five-minute talk, but as an esteemed comrade. In uniform, she felt as if she fitted in.

The morning arrival allowed more than enough time for the formal events to occur and the funeral and burial to take place. Conscious of their uniforms standing out in array of RMP officers and formally dressed mourners, the Met officers were guided by Turner-Jones and others in what to do and where to sit. Catrin's time as Sandra Hunt's aide came back, the days when, every minute, you were visibly on show.

She was also reminded of other funerals of police officers killed in the line of duty, in London; of other gatherings, the mass of uniforms, the set faces, the patient wait without signs of frustration, sometimes for no more than a glimpse of a hearse.

She recalled specifically the comment from people on other occasions like this. "There always seem to be too many police officers, like masses more than would ever know the person."

She answered that the same way each time. "It's a colleague who died doing the job we do. It reminds us. It helps us start a new shift, on a new day, taking the same risk, sometimes. We don't need to have known him or her. It lets us show respect for the officer and reminds us of who we are."

It was of note that, as the ceremonies proceeded, it was only Rita Tully who stayed dry-eyed throughout. Catrin caught Andy Collard wiping an eye surreptitiously and gave no indication she saw it. It had been the face of binti Awang's young niece looking bereft that set Catrin's tears flowing.

As Terry Jameson predicted, Tully represented Undertow well; in fact, she excelled.

During the formalities held after the funeral, the three officers were briefly presented together to the family group, face to face with the parents and husband as other mourners waited to offer condolences. Turner-Jones kept them in sight and earshot. It was one of the planned but sensitive moments.

Madeleine heard Sofia's father say he heard of Sayer previously and thanked her for attending. Collard passed by simply with the expression of his condolences. As Rita offered her own condolences, Sofia's mother asked her, "I understand that you were the first to see Sofia after the attack. How did she die?"

It was not totally unexpected that the British visitors would be asked about this. But it was a straight question, and a waffly answer wouldn't work. They had no idea what Inspector Syed or Sergeant Yusoff had said.

'Bravely and very quickly', was the appropriate response, Madeleine had briefed them. No detail. No mention of the recording or Sofia's last message, particularly. Leave that to the RMP and the Malaysian officials, as they saw appropriate.

Rita didn't hesitate. "Savagely. It was fast, but she fought her assailant to the end. Hero is used too easily these days, but Sofia is a hero to me. I honour her memory."

She looked down and swallowed, then looked back silently at the woman.

"Thank you." It was in the mother's eyes, besides the sorrow, the pride in her daughter. The father just nodded his appreciation. The husband, now widower, Rayyan, was tight-lipped, controlling his face as best as he could.

As Rita Tully, young as she was, moved on, eyes dry and face now impassive again, Madeleine wondered whether she would be interested in a job in the Foreign Office. Sending her out to replace Stephen Gilbertson in the British High Commission would be a good start. The police officer would be the talk of the RMP by tomorrow.

Sayer and Tully had more going for them than bloody Terry Graham, the British Deputy High Commissioner, and his pet toad Gilbertson ever would. But that battle was for tomorrow.

27 TWILIGHT

In Iver, Buckinghamshire, Hasanna Akanni, Joan Lucas and Frances Coombs were having dinner at the Coverley Golf Club restaurant.

It was at short notice, a change of plans for Hasanna's thirty-fifth birthday. Amaechi had suddenly cancelled arrangements for her to fly out to Athens, to join him for her birthday and two days of sightseeing, as urgent issues in Thailand now demanded his attention.

Frances and Joan decided a 'girl's dinner' would be the best short-term substitute, rather than involving Simon and John, forcing Hasanna to be the odd one out at her own birthday celebration.

Hasanna said, "This time it is too much; he could have sent one of his people, surely?"

Joan and Frances exchanged glances. Joan gave a slight shake of the head. A birthday is not the time to discuss Hasanna's excessive dependency on Amaechi.

Frances was the activist there, Joan the moderator. She repeatedly told Frances it wasn't their role to interfere. Hasanna and Amaechi grew up in a different culture.

They handle their marriage as they see fit. If Hasanna asked for help, that would be different. Interventions were destined for trouble and bitterness.

Instead, they got one of the club staff to sit with them briefly, to talk about their golf training for beginners, usually the children or partners of an avid member. When Hasanna agreed to a trial lesson, they announced that the beginner's course was their joint present.

After he left and Hasanna appeared taken by the idea of trying to learn, her mind went back to her husband.

"I don't understand it. For some business sectors, Amaechi is content to let his line managers take responsibility and he acts as the CEO. For others, he micromanages everything. If he were to take a standard approach, I am sure we could spend much more time together."

They heard the pop of a champagne cork and looked in the direction of the sound, at the waiter. It wasn't their order. But it was. The server explained, "From Mr. Akanni, ladies. He sent a text. This is to go with your dinner, and he has a car reserved to take you home, so enjoy it."

Ostentatious and irritating, thought Frances, who drove them to the club and deliberately stayed off the wine, as the designated driver. As the waiter poured champagne into the flutes, she decided to take a token sip to Hasanna's health. Damn the man, she was still driving home.

~~

In Kuala Lumpur, the Met officers were hiding in the air-conditioning of their hotel rooms, exhausted, their uniforms hanging limply in their wardrobes. The RMP used a dry-cleaning service familiar with uniforms and theirs would be collected tomorrow morning, cleaned and pressed, then returned the same day.

Andy hadn't slept well on the flight out. With the early start that morning to get to Heathrow, he worked out that he had been awake for nearly thirty hours. He talked to his wife and kids and, local time be damned, after his shower he closed the blinds and went to bed.

Catrin and Turner-Jones met by prearrangement in the executive lounge, an hour after they got back; showered, tired, but needing to compare notes.

"It went well, your team's participation, Catrin. That's the feedback I am getting."

"Thank you. I am glad we are through it, but pleased we were able to represent the Met here."

Madeleine agreed. "Rita Tully was outstanding. First time here, first long flight and... her sense of the occasion. I am very impressed. You don't want to transfer her to FCO, by any chance?"

She smiled impudently.

"I'm not that heartless; I'll keep her."

They went through the agenda plans and issues arising for the following day before heading to their rooms. For Madeleine, she was eight hours ahead of the people in Whitehall. They were starting their day there and she had calls to make well away from the rooms of the High Commission.

Catrin talked on her iPad to Chris and Mair as soon as she got to her room, as they were preparing for their normal activities in London. When she returned after her meeting with Madeleine she decided to sleep for an hour, then go for a swim in the pool or for a walk, have something light to eat and try for a full night's sleep.

When the alarm woke her, she checked her phone and in the array of other work messages, there was a text from Rita, sent ten minutes ago. Could they meet or talk, as she had a question?

She called her on the hotel room phone.

"I'm glad you called, boss. Thanks. I had a call from Ana, Officer Zanab, from the Honour Guard. She is asking me if I would like to meet up and see a bit of KL? Is that alright?"

"Go for it, if you have the energy," Catrin replied. "Are you starting with a cold or, what?"

"I napped for a bit and woke up. I was crying my eyes out when Ana called. It has all overwhelmed me, keeping it together today. It's easier in my room and having had a good cry. I don't know if it is jet lag or Sofia or tiredness... but I am feeling better for it."

"Well, that's good; it's natural. When you go out, remember it's a Muslim country. Here, at least, you can drink alcohol in places where it is allowed, but not in general. Be careful."

"The thing is, she and her husband said they would pick me up at seven... Would you come, just for an hour, say? I'm not comfortable and Andy said he was crashing. If it's good, then you can grab a taxi, or if its not, we can make excuses. Is it rude to ask you?"

Catrin smiled. "Well, it's good of you to ask. Let's meet up at six-fifty in the lobby, prepared for anything."

As she closed the call, she decided that she wouldn't tell Madeleine that the new bright star of interest to Foreign Affairs sounded like a teenage girl talking to her mum before a big date.

As they entered the large lobby of the hotel, a couple

came towards them. It took Rita a moment to recognise Ana Zanab out of uniform.

After they did the introductions, there was a momentary lull, in which Ana said, "I wanted very much to see the missing member from our honour guard before she went home. And you, Chief Inspector, also, of course."

"Right!" replied Catrin, giving her a mock look of disbelief.

"No, really, it is true. I wanted to tell you something. The coverage of the funeral on the TV showed you three from the Metropolitan Police together several times. It was quite something."

Catrin responded, "Well, to be on television! Rita, you are becoming quite a star."

Ana's husband, Malik, said quietly, "As are you all. DCI Sayer, you were wearing the ribbon of Meritorious Conduct of the Federal Territory of Kuala Lumpur. That caught my eye."

The small ribbon on Catrin's tunic. Rita didn't know the details, but there had been a fuss at the tailors, the official uniform outfitters, about whether the boss wore it and where it should be placed.

Malik added, "I served in the army. Malaysian awards are as complex as our titles, but we need to know them. I would think that a lot of people will have noticed an English police officer with a Malaysian decoration."

Ana said, "It is for DCI Sayer's role in an incident at the Twin Towers. She saved Sergeant Farra; he had been shot. Your colleague, Mrs. Turner-Jones was there, also, we know. It is one of the RMP stories we learn. Our guests are special indeed."

Malik seemed impressed but also perturbed. "That was going to be our first stop. For the magic time, as the sun sets. As the Towers go from a dark silhouette in the sunset to the brightest light of night. But I am not sure we should, if it is distressing, ma'am?"

Catrin thought for a moment. "It's Catrin, not boss, or ma'am tonight. And if we can go there for the magic you mentioned, Malik, and not talk at all about my last visit, I think it might be good for me."

In the growing twilight, Ana and Malik carefully left the two visitors to wander individually, to take in the Twin Towers as the light changed and to take photographs. At one point, Malik saw a teenage couple looking for a tourist to drag into whatever scam they wanted to try, and they had Rita in their sights. He wandered over. One look was enough to make them move on.

As the sky went dark and the lights on the towers grew in intensity, Sayer sat on a low wall and stared at the sight. Ana thought at one point DCI Sayer's head was bowed. Perhaps she was praying, she thought.

They waited.

It was eight minutes later that Catrin approached them and, in doing so, it jolted Rita into doing the same. As they talked, Sayer said, glancing at Rita, "With your permission and my thanks, I am going to head back. I will grab a taxi, but you three should enjoy this evening."

Rita smiled. She was OK now.

Ana said they should drive her back and Catrin declined. Malik insisted he walk with her and be sure of the taxi. As he did so and they approached a cab, Catrin thanked him again for his hospitality.

He gave her a smile and then said, "The gratitude is all mine, I assure you. Ana is inspired by you both. That is the correct word, I think. My wife is exhausted by the events and the great responsibility of being part of Sofia's honor guard, but between Rita and yourself, she has met police officers who have simply inspired her, she said. I will get DC Tully back to the hotel, I assure you."

As the taxi pulled away, Catrin took a last look at the Towers in their lights. She thought they were an incredibly beautiful sight. Somehow, earlier on, alone, closer to them in the twilight, came the moment she finally let go of her regret at having killed a young man, Loh Ghee, only yards away.

28 HIGH COMMISSION

The following morning, Andy Collard sounded refreshed. "I slept like one of my kids; all night until four a.m. then bounced up, wide awake. The workout in the fitness centre was great, and I had a swim. I could take to the life of one of these travel executives, I tell you."

Rita smiled. She still felt tired, but the evening had been special. She felt sure she had new friends, ones who even at a distance she would keep.

Both officers' agenda was comparatively light today; to observe the interview with this man Omar Kaur, followed by a separate, 'get to know you' for the two of them with a few people arranged at RMP headquarters, a meeting to discuss approaches to gang crime; and finally, a dinner at the British High Commission.

They knew that the dinner would be the stodgiest part. Rita joked about watching Catrin carefully to see which cutlery to use when. Two years of being in the company of an Assistant Commissioner would give her boss the experience at banquets.

When Turner-Jones and DCI Sayer joined them, they

just listened. The FCO staffer appeared ready for action, they saw. She, with Sayer, had a meeting at the High Commission before the big interview at the RMP Headquarters.

They would all meet up there.

Turner-Jones said, "I wanted to thank you for your efforts yesterday. I spoke to Catrin, and you both need to hear it, too. You did well, all of you.

"Tonight, at the High Commission, they will discuss the events of yesterday. There will also be guests from other embassies or High Commissions. People will be analytical, just as you must be in your own job. But what you did yesterday, being here, will have immeasurable benefits for our relationship with Malaysia at this sensitive time, I assure you. When it gets boring or asinine tonight, remember that."

Later, as they parted, Turner-Jones went to collect her briefcase and borrow two umbrellas from the concierge. Andy asked his boss a question that was on both his and Rita's minds.

"We wonder, with your task this morning, how do you feel about the death penalty? You will be threatening a man with it, really."

Catrin could see that both her officers wanted to know.

"Let me guess, Andy is against and you, at least in this case, are for it, Rita. Am I right?"

Rita replied, "Yes. I never thought I would say it, but after the last week, yes."

Catrin smiled, less from humour than sympathy.

She paused. "I killed a young man in this city, shot him, a number of times. You can say that is different, self-defence, that it was necessary, but... it weighed on me a lot. Still did a bit, now I am back, until last night. At one time, with my psychologist, I said it would be easier if he hadn't been so young, or instead of being the kid sent to shoot Sergeant Farra, it was his uncle who gave the order that I killed. That the young man had no chance to learn of his errors in life. It was Dr. Herrington who asked me why I kept carrying the load, the weight of it.

"When I looked at him with my, 'I don't get it, look', he said, "You took an oath to uphold the law. You are a police officer; that's what you did when you shot the man, you upheld the law. It's the same now. Whatever I say to Omar Kaur, I am a police officer. I don't get the choice on the question of the death penalty. Think on that."

As she left to collect her things and join Turner-Jones, to leave for the High Commission, Rita looked at Andy, who was looking intrigued.

Rita suddenly pulled out her phone and looked something up. "Asinine means stupid or foolish."

"I know," responded Collard. "That answer makes me feel a bit asinine."

As they saw Turner-Jones and Sayer enter their taxi, Rita said, "It's obvious their meeting this morning will air the disagreements about the plan, but with the boss and Madeleine, I don't think this man Graham is in for an easy time."

Catrin and Turner-Jones left the hotel in a downpour. The taxi windshield wipers moved at high speed and seemed to do little to help visibility, but the driver seemed happy enough.

Turner-Jones said, "It will clear by the time we leave the High Commission."

The British High Commission was downtown, on level

two of an office tower block, Menara Binjai, across from the Intercontinental Hotel. Staying there would have proven convenient but in their wisdom, the High Commission had reserved rooms at the Hotel Majestic, sumptuous and with a colonial past. By the time they arrived, despite folding umbrellas, they were dripped on and splashed.

"Terry Graham doesn't like the Intercontinental, which I do. It's got Americans, he says, as if anywhere doesn't; and it has a faux-British pub, which I like, as it's a friendly place. It's just too damn convenient for visitors, is the real reason; we could arrive unexpectedly and catch him asleep at his desk."

From that, and other comments, Catrin got the impression no love was lost between the two bureaucrats, but Madeleine had been perfectly behaved yesterday.

As the meeting began, with Deputy High Commissioner Graham at its head, Turner-Jones was now unreadable.

Graham began, after introductions, by asking Stephen Gilbertson, seated by the master's right hand, to give an update. Gilbertson was prepared.

"Let's begin with the RMP. There are four officers; the two who went to the UK and their immediate line command. The one in charge who authorised the trip to the UK has already been transferred; to Sarawak, probably, given some godforsaken job and told never to visit Peninsula Malaya again. Their unit is being reorganized. Inspector Syed is on medical leave. He had another stress attack during the funeral and was whisked away quietly to the hospital."

Sayer frowned. These were police officers that this bureaucrat was so blithely talking about. She didn't take kindly to that.

"Baksh is placing a lot on the agreement that we don't create hell with them over binti Awang's weapon, and on the outcome of the meeting today. Their Foreign Affairs people consider that a brokered deal for the negative fallout the government will take once the news is out that none of binti Awang's killers can go to the gallows. That's it, in summary, Terry."

Graham focused on Sayer. "And, DCI Sayer, you don't know any of this when you do your tête-à-tête with Baksh later. He is influential and likes us; well, he and I get along well. Let's keep it that way."

Catrin said nothing, although clearly, he expected a tug of the forelock. Turner-Jones said stiffly, "DCI Sayer is well-prepared."

Graham continued with, "We have come out of this not too badly, considering."

"Considering what?" interjected Turner-Jones, her annoyance now obvious by her tone of voice.

"The Malaysians are touchy as hell about the death penalty. They tore a strip off poor Stephen when he broke it to them, told it the way it has to be, with our evidence."

He looked at Gilbertson, who piously nodded in agreement.

Turner-Jones responded firmly, "It is their country, their laws. It's your job and your staff's job, to handle matters sensitively."

Terry Graham looked astonished and was about to respond to the FCO desk officer when she added. "Sir Anthony wanted that conveyed to you in person, Mr. Graham, and in this meeting."

Catrin thought, whoever Sir Anthony was, he wasn't too happy with the situation and now Madeleine, sitting on the message like a hen on her eggs, had just broken all the shells in a bigger venue than a private meeting in Terry Graham's office.

Graham paused, giving Turner-Jones a hard look. Somehow, if it were to quell her in some way, it had no effect. She just stared back.

Turning defense into attack, he focused again on Catrin.

"Now, in your interview with this Omar Kaur, make sure it doesn't send us downhill on this issue of hanging. I don't agree with this approach at all, let me be clear. I have put that on record with Whitehall and been told it is not my choice. I gather London has done the preparations and we have dutifully done our part here. We don't want this haunting us. You, at least, get to go home tomorrow evening."

Turner-Jones now looked as if she would have sent Terry Graham home the day he first interviewed with the Foreign Service.

He's full of it, thought Catrin. A lot of power locally and a liking for flexing his muscles.

She spoke up. "I know my job, sir. And I will do it as well as I can."

It was an older female staff member sitting near the bottom of the table who spoke.

"Terry, Sayer would have to do a hell of a lot to screw things up; she has considerable standing here, and not just with the RMP. Ahmat Budi came back from London and his comments about her are glowing."

Catrin showed her surprise. "Their former deputy high commissioner?"

The woman replied, "Yes, he is in a senior Foreign Affairs role now."

Terry Graham glowered at the woman, who appeared

unconcerned.

"Thank you, Roberta," said Turner-Jones.

Well, I know whose side this Roberta is on, thought Catrin, and it is not her boss in KL.

The second agenda item, 'Feedback plan and review of actions after the Kaur interview' seemed to take no time at all. Not the fifteen minutes allocated. Deputy Commissioner Graham announced he wanted to finish this meeting as soon as possible, as he had 'additional engagements to fit in'.

On the short drive to RMP Headquarters, Madeleine thought the additional items may involve some calls back to London or to cronies stationed elsewhere, to rally the troops and shift some of the blame.

"We still hang people in FCO, you know? It is somewhat more metaphorical, but they feel the pain as the noose tightens. Look, I told you, it's now sunshine and steam. The day will be nice, later on."

29 KAUR

Constable Danish Tuah was young, powerfully fit and handsome, many would say. Only eighteen months out of cadet college, he enjoyed the work within Sergeant Farra's team but yearned for a role out on the streets and the goal of becoming a seasoned plainclothes officer.

His boss was an enigma; soft-spoken, measured and quiet. That he once served as a formidable gang crime officer and had incurred major injuries in the job only added to the mystique. The eyes, as much as the lines on his face and the hair going grey, revealed his experience to Danish. Farra's face was as composed and unreadable as the young man's was expressive.

Danish was surprised by the morning's assignment to assist during an interview. It wasn't a regular role for him, but it was recognition of sorts. He would be the uniformed officer ensuring the prisoner behaved.

Unusually, he was told to stand in full view of the prisoner, not to one side.

Sergeant Farra explained that a British police officer, a woman, would sit opposite the prisoner. Sergeant Farra would face the defense solicitor. Danish hadn't realised that interviews were so orchestrated.

Farra's last words during the briefing intrigued Danish. "You will hear things than may upset you; that's OK, we are all human. If you need to restrain the prisoner, you must do so at once, not wait for a command. Above all, protect the woman, but in doing so, no matter how you feel, you must not injure the prisoner at all. Use absolutely minimum force to restrain the man, if required."

That surprised Danish. Omar Kaur's reputation suggested he was brutal, but others did the dirty work. This interview didn't sound routine at all. But it was linked to the tragic death of Officer binti Awang. That would lead to emotions running high, of course. He would watch Kaur carefully.

Jared Farra hid his thoughts that Danish's facial responses would also be seen by Omar Kaur.

~~

Chief Superintendent Baksh appeared less formal in the privacy of his office at the RMP Headquarters. A DI called bin Othman and Sergeant Jared Farra were with him when an aide led Catrin into his office.

They began with comments on the events of the previous day before moving on to the morning ahead.

"I knew you would rise in the ranks, Sayer, and not simply because you saved this man." He reached out and touched Farra on the shoulder.

"We still keep him busy, but we don't let him get into the troubles he used to cause."

Farra raised his eyebrows; that and a smile through pursed lips provided his only reaction to the senior officer's jovial comment. They knew that, while healthy, his fitness rating would keep him off the streets for the rest of his career.

"While you, I understand from Commander Moore, are in it a lot deeper these days. Deeper than art crime, at least."

Catrin smiled. "But I don't cause trouble, sir. That just seems to materialize out of thin air for all of us, doesn't it?"

Baksh laughed. "True enough. And where is Mrs. Turner-Jones?"

Catrin looked innocent. "She developed a diplomatic headache and has momentarily needed to rest. She presents her apologies. She thought we may need some time to talk undisturbed but will be along in a while, to see how it goes and what she needs to do to – what's the word – 'assist' the High Commission afterwards."

He smiled. "You know, I thought she was a little formal, might I say, bureaucratic, in the past. But I think highly of her now. She loves Malaysia, knows our history, is an avid linguist."

She couldn't resist it. "You probably think of her a little better than Deputy High Commissioner Graham and his collegue, Gilbertson, I suspect?"

Baksh looked at her and rolled his eyes. "I'm not touching that one."

He glanced at Inspector bin Othman and then at the clock. His face turned serious. "To matters at hand. Sergeant Farra, are you ready to incur the wrath of Mr. Kaur's solicitor?"

He looked at Catrin, "He'll remember him, I am sure."

Farra said, "More than ready, sir."

Baksh looked at his watch. "They have had half-an-hour together. Off you go, you two. I'm looking forward to the feedback. Sayer, your two officers are already in the viewing room, as you requested."

If this went to pieces, she wanted the feedback to Lauder and Moore from her own people. That was Tully and Collard's main job for the day.

As they entered the interview room, Catrin took in the two men seated at the table and the young officer standing against the wall. The solicitor, Leo Chawdri, in a suit, was grey-haired and about sixty. His client, in casual clothes, was large, in his forties, dark-haired, with his bearded face presenting a neutral mask, other than the eyes. They looked angry, then suspicious, at seeing the officers who entered.

The lawyer seemed surprised. "Where is Inspector bin Othman? He called for this interview. I thought he would be here. You, I remember. It is Sergeant Farra, if I am right?"

As they seated theselves, Farra said, "You have a good memory, Mr. Chawdri. We have met before in similar circumstances, but with different clients."

"So why are you here now, not Inspector bin Othman? I have had no briefing on that aspect."

Farra ignored the question and looked at Kaur as he pressed the recording switch.

"Interview commencing at 10.03 a.m. Present are Sergeant Jared Farra–."

Catrin spoke up. "Detective Chief Inspector Catrin Sayer, Metropolitan Police, London."

Farra pointed across the table. "Omar Kaur."

"Leo Chawdri, solicitor for Mr Kaur."

Farra began with, "Mr. Kaur, you have been charged under Section 120A of the Penal Code of Malaysia with criminal conspiracy, that you did conspire with a Roland McEwen and a Thomas Fitzgerald to assault and murder

Sofia binti Awang, an undercover police officer known to you by the name Laura binti Assad."

Chawdri spoke. "To which Mr. Kaur will plead not guilty. He had no knowledge of events previously related to us by Inspector bin Othman, occurring thousands of miles away. Again, why are we here now?"

Farrar ignored the question again and focused on Kaur. "Do you know a man called Roland McEwen, Mr. Kaur?"

Kaur looked at him, clearly unwilling to speak. They sat in silence for ten to fifteen seconds, the only noise coming from Danish Tuah, who gave a nervous cough, causing Kaur to glance at him

Farra continued, "No response, I see. And do you know a Thomas Fitzgerald?"

Again, Kaur said nothing in response to the question, but he sat upright suddenly, sufficient to make Tuah move a little, in the event of trouble.

Kaur said to Farra, "You. I remember the face now. I thought you were dead or pensioned off."

He looked at Catrin. "And you. Why am I being interviewed by a British police officer?"

Catrin stared back, her face unreadable.

Farra continued as if the prisoner had never spoken.

"I repeat, do you know either of these men?"

Farrar waited an interminable thirty seconds this time before saying, "No answer again. DCI Sayer, if you please?"

Danish saw the British police officer pull a tape recorder from her pocket and say, before she switched it on, "The last words of Officer Sofia binti Awang."

The voice filled the room, the dying words. Catrin followed the cadence as the others listened, her eyes glued to Kaur's face, seeing his attempts to cover his reaction, anger being the predominant emotion. She switched the recorder off.

Danish, standing out of the way, found his eyes blurring with tears at the rawness of it, a young police officer's last message. It was stark and hit him hard. He concentrated on managing his own feelings, glad he was a bystander.

Then he saw the face of the prisoner; he was looking at him now, staring past this police officer from the United Kingdom, with her musical voice.

Chawdri spoke up, sensitively but firmly. "As sad as the event related to the recording may be, we will object to its use in any subsequent proceedings here."

Farra shook his head. "The call between the phone that Sofia used just prior to the attack was linked directly to your clients' phone, Mr. Chawdri. We have the timings on record. We also have new information to share also."

He looked at Sayer and she said, "The UK end of the phone call made two minutes before Officer binti Awang was attacked by Thomas Fitzgerald." She started the playback again. After a second, Sofia's voice filled the room, in English.

"However, I think I will need clearance from back home to talk about any business with another person here. If you don't mind?"

A Scottish male voice responded. *"Go ahead. Call Omar Kaur."*

"That is Roland McEwen. A slip up, and a big one." Farra's comment partly filled the silence on the recording during which no-one else in the interview room spoke. Then binti Awang's voice came back.

"Mr. Kaur, it's Laura. I'm with Mr. McEwen. He has a colleague with him, a Mr. Fizz, but that's a nickname of some sort. Can I proceed?"

Catrin switched the recorder off.

Chawdri said quickly, "Same thing. There is no direct evidence that my client was involved."

Farrar asked Kaur. "What do you have to say to that, Omar? You recognize Roland McEwen's voice saying to call you, surely?"

Kaur glanced at his lawyer, then pursed his lips and shrugged his shoulders. Again, he refused to speak.

In the silence, Chawdri looked at his wristwatch.

Farra looked at Catrin and waited.

Danish realised that DCI Sayer was about to take over the lead role in the interview.

"Mr. Kaur, I am empowered to lay a charge of murder against you, under British law. For us, involvement in the crime is the same charge for perpetrator and accomplice. Mr. Chawdri will explain to you the international aspects regarding criminal charges and prosecution. I have with me the first set of evidence, including these recordings and the certified transcripts of what we just heard, to provide formally to the Royal Malaysian Police."

Danish noticed that she had opened her file folder and brought out a printed document, a large, unsealed envelope and a smaller sealed letter bearing the British High Commission crest. Kaur was starting to look bored, dismissive of some foreign criminal charge.

Catrin continued, "The normal process now is a resolution between states, between their ministries and criminal prosecution systems, about who should do what. It's called territoriality, the decision on who charges the accused and who prosecutes them."

Kaur was looking even more bored, whereas Chawdri was watching her intently.

Suddenly Omar Kaur spoke, for the first time. "He says that means the death penalty is off the table."

He nodded at Chawdri, then stared back at Sayer.

She replied, "With my formal transfer of files is this letter provided by the High Commissioner here. It makes clear that any use of UK evidence in a prosecution must include a veto on a sentence of death, as the UK does not have the death penalty in law."

She paused. "Once I pass over this package, and it is accepted and used, the possibility of execution for your involvement in the death of Sofia binti Awang is off the table."

Kaur looked at her afresh. He couldn't read her. But this woman was telling him that, to some degree, she had power of life or death in her hands. He could relate to that.

Danish tried to control his face. This was a double blow; that the UK's involvement impeded the Malaysian courts.

Then Danish heard the UK officer say, "But I may not do that. I may not charge you. I may choose to pass this information over to Sergeant Farra, colleague to colleague, police officer to police officer, and tear up the High Commission letter, to see what will happen here. Perhaps it could take you to the gallows. I haven't decided yet, but I am thinking about it."

Danish couldn't believe it. A senior police officer was saying that she would disobey instructions, on record, in front of a hostile defense solicitor.

30 JEBAT

In the silence that followed, Catrin pulled a second file set out of her folder. "This is the comparable information on your brother-in-law, Hatar Jebat. He is now in custody in Southampton."

She saw the surprise on his face and Kaur couldn't stop himself speaking. "Hatar's's daughter lives there. He was visiting her."

Catrin grimaced. "Not true. It may be a convenient cover, but he was there to take part in the questioning of binti Awang. Not to conduct it, but to pose the questions and bring back her answers.

"It struck the investigating team within the first few hours that, if McEwen were entering a new business with you, how would he know enough to question binti Awang and assess the information extracted from her? The officer who led the investigation is very experienced. With help from the authorities here, we found out Jebat Hatar was in the UK and pinpointed his location."

"What we have so far is here." She patted the file and deliberately checked her wristwatch.

"We will charge him with first degree murder in about eight hours. Your brother-in-law is not as sharp as you, I suspect. He even wrote on his computer the questions you wanted answered.

"Arriving at McEwen's apartment when he thought Sofia was restrained and ready, he saw the police cars and made his taxi take him back to his hotel so he could scoot off down to Southampton. We have a statement from the taxi driver, some video identification from CCTV and, guess what? They retrieved a list of questions on a computer he owns. He thinks a delete button deletes things. How silly of him."

She looked at Omar Kaur. "What happens next depends on you."

Chawdri spoke. "What precisely do you mean by that?"

"I am clarifying that I have three options. To pass information on both you and Hatar Jebat directly to the RMP is one, although it won't do my career any good. I can follow my instructions about you, save your skin, and still give the Malaysian authorities a chance to use the death penalty against your brother-in-law. As he hasn't been charged yet, at worst, that decision would get me a rap on the knuckles. But I get to watch at a distance how the prosecution and the defense argue over the coming months on the legality of the evidence."

She leaned forward, "Or I can place all the information in this envelope and give it under the High Commission transmission letter. Malaysia would honour the commitment. It would remove the death penalty option for both of you."

Chawdri said, "Mr Jebat is in detention in the UK. Authorities there will charge him and try him."

It was Jared Farra who spoke. "Territoriality is an

unpredictable thing, as you know. It may prove more appropriate to have Hatar and Omar tried together, here."

Chawdri said clearly, for the record, for his client's benefit, "Detective Chief Inspector Sayer, you are saying that you are considering proactively the transfer of information to the RMP contrary to your government's express intent, solely to ensure that the death penalty is an option for my client and perhaps also for his brother?"

Catrin avoided the question. "Mr. Jebat will be charged with a crime in the UK, sir. That's all I know for certain at present. As I said, I am considering my options."

Chawdri asked carefully, "You are British, a police officer. Surely you must see the moral need to provide the information under the terms set by your government, if required?"

Catrin responded, "Now that's a good question. Let's first talk about what else I have here."

She held up another printed report. "This man Thomas Fitzgerald. I am assuming McEwen chose him, Mr. Kaur, not you, giving you the benefit of the doubt at present. He's a strange one, currently playing games with the officers interviewing him, even from his hospital bed."

"He claims he is a 'service provider' for 'information retrieval' but won't go further as to what that means. Ask him, he just smiles and switches off. He will be charged with a second crime, a cold case, a mutilated body of a convicted drug dealer from Leeds. The DNA was found in the ferrule of a chisel in the tools Fitzgerald brought to the apartment in Nine Elms. In the same tool bag are a pair of tinsnips, apparently clean, but with some different DNA trapped in the hinge section, once the parts of the tool were dismantled."

"As Officer binti Awang said in her final message, you wanted to know what the RMP knew about your criminal activity through their undercover operation. McEwen hired a professional torturer to extract it. That news is not out there yet, but it will be, soon. There and here."

She heard what could have been a muffled cough concealing another noise directly behind her, but she didn't look. Kaur did. Whatever emotions were going through the young officer's face were reflected in the sudden expression of fear on his.

Sergeant Farra spoke up. "And this is just beginning. Fitzgerald is trying to play mind games with his interviewing officers and, Mr. Chawdri, you know where that goes, slip-up by slip-up."

He looked at Sayer. "At this stage, we have given Mr. Kaur and his solicitor enough to consider; let's take a short break to allow them to discuss matters in private. Mr. Chawdri, you know your way around here. Officer Tuah, if Omar Kaur needs the facilities, you are to escort him there and back directly. Another officer will be waiting outside to assist."

As Danish watched the two police officers pick up their files, he tried to ensure he looked professional and detached. He wanted to be seen to be a capable, experienced officer for his boss.

As they walked out, he saw that the woman was watching him, and she had a scar on her left cheek. It made him wonder.

By the time they resumed, Danish felt he was back in control of himself. He had been very professional when taking the prisoner to use the washrooms, courteous even. He didn't feel that way, of course, now. But he was sure he was being professional. For some reason, Kaur seemed to be more relaxed when the other officer assigned, an older woman, came to speak to them in the corridor.

As the recording resumed, DCI Sayer said, "I'm sure by now you want to know what I am going to do. As Mr. Chawdri asked about 'the moral need', I'm going to digress a little. I am not the investigating officer. I was sent here in part because a unit within my command provided the surveillance support to the team monitoring the meeting between McEwen and Ms. binti Awang. I was one of the first people to hear that recording and when a Malay speaker translated it for me, I cried, I admit it."

Danish was shocked; that this woman led a front-line team also admitted to her emotional response. In front of the accused and his solicitor, too.

"The other reason I was sent, is that I have been here before. I was with Sergeant Farra when he was injured by a gunman at the Twin Towers."

Farra spoke up. "If Sergeant Sayer, as she was then, had not taken my weapon as I fell, I would be dead."

Sayer added, "And if he hadn't had the strength and clarity of thinking to pass his weapon to me, so would I. We have both been there, at the point Sofia was at as she spoke to you.

"Mr Kaur, do you have any doubts about what I will say about my understanding on the availability of the evidence against your brother-in-law, if I pass it over now outside that envelope? Or if I go the whole way and include you, and place my job on the line? I will say I provided the information freely, one police officer to another, during an investigation. I will fly back here to testify to that in court, if necessary."

Danish could see the lawyer hesitate, thinking what to say. DCI Sayer had, with her unusual lilting accent, made abundantly clear her intent.

Looking at the faces across from him, you would think the temperature had dropped in the room.

Then she said. "The only thing that will get me to put these documents in the envelope covered by the High Commission letter, is if you give me information I want. Now."

Chawdri was immediately on it. "What sort of inform-ation? My client won't -."

She didn't let the lawyer finish, she focused on Kaur. "Charles Kingdom Akanni. Amaechi Akanni, to you. McEwen's boss. You know him. You and he arranged the transfer of the fraud business from London to KL and I want him. Give me enough to satisfy me and that gets you the coverage for you and your sister's husband."

Kaur let out a big sigh. "So that's what this is about! I'm not sure I'll make it to trial anywhere if I give Akanni to you. No."

Catrin responded, "Don't be bloody naïve. I'm not looking for you as a witness, although that would be great if you suddenly felt compelled to confess."

Kaur sneered at that.

"Still no. You are bluffing. You won't throw away your job."

Jared Farra spoke up. "I am hoping she will take the middle road, that DCI Sayer chooses to obey her instruct-ions regarding you, but not include your brother-in-law's file in the envelope. By tomorrow, I will make sure that your family knows that in the months ahead, while people argue where Hatar should be tried and what the limit-ations on use of evidence will be, the death penalty will hang over her brother. And that you turned down the one opportunity to eliminate that risk. That should lead to family harmony, I'm sure."

That hit home, they could see.

Jarra continued, "And you saved yourself, but not her brother. How's that going to look with people in prison?"

He pointed at the file before Sayer.

"Evidence of Hatar's arrival at the scene. Evidence of the questions to be put to a young woman about to have her body defiled under torture, one of my colleagues. You can bet that, if your neck is safe, we will go after your brother-in-law with every legal means available. I promise you that we will make every effort to get him back over here and place a noose around his neck."

His outburst led to an awkward silence.

After a moment, Catrin continued firmly but quietly. "I'm not going to rush in and arrest Akanni citing your name. I want things that you know, things that will put him away. You will have to trust that I use the information so that his arrest comes out of nowhere. He and his people haven't exactly done you any favours in the last week or so, have they?"

She leaned forward. Kaur was now looking at the table, pensive. She moved forward enough to make him look up, into her eyes.

"Fitzgerald is going to sink McEwen, as Sergeant Jarra inferred. The question is, will McEwen break and sink you even further?"

They watched the doubts grow in Kaur, the small signs of his resolve weakening.

Kaur suddenly said, "I need another break to talk it through with my lawyer."

Sayer shook her head. "No. We have no more to tell you. I want to know if you will talk to us now, or I make my decision and walk out of here. And I swear to God, after being at Sofia's funeral yesterday, the way I feel about you right now I would be happy to see you hang."

In the ensuing long moments of silence, the only people in the room who mattered were Sayer and Kaur, eye to eye. She was looking up at him, too close for comfort for Danish Tuah. Kaur was a big man. If he chose, he could smash his forehead into Sayer. Danish was on tenterhooks, ready to move.

Kaur said, "Stop the recording."

No one else said anything. For a second Danish was lost, unsure what was happening. As the recorder button clicked off loudly without the session closing properly, Danish looked at his boss. His face was neutral, but the eyes showed success. The visitor from the UK had done it. Omar Kaur was going to speak off the record.

It was forty minutes later when they formally went back on record.

Danish Tuah saw DCI Sayer stand and move immediately behind Omar Kaur. She was now going to charge him. He wondered if it was a police practice to place a hand on the arm of the accused, a sign of formal arrest as the charge was laid.

As she spoke, she focused on the now impassive face of Sergeant Farra. "Omar Kaur, I charge you with the crime of murder, in that, with others, you did plan the grievous assault and unlawful death of Sofia binti Awang, contrary to British law."

She reached into her folder and withdrew the envelope, now sealed, containing the files on Kaur and his brother-in-law. She passed it and the letter from the High Commission over to Sergeant Farra. As she did so, Leo Chawdri released his breath, unaware he had been holding it. Kaur simply sat there looking across Sayer's empty chair, past Tuah, into infinity.

Danish Tuah had watched this British officer pick up on every point, drain the detail on each piece of information that Kaur offered. It hadn't been recorded, but she had pulled out a notebook, writing constantly. Only Catrin and Jared Farra were aware that Collard was recording every word anyway.

Danish caught a fleeting break in DCI Sayer's own impassivity, a halt in her arrest charge, at the microsecond she said, 'death of'. He looked away momentarily, sensing that like every other RMP officer he knew, Sayer was hurting now, at the prospect of any sort of opportunity for leniency for this man.

All he could hope for was that both Kaur and his brother-in-law were found guilty and imprisoned, for all if not the larger part of their remaining lives. He wondered whether Hatar Jebat would be tried in the UK or sent back here to stand trial. This was far more confusing than he expected.

As the interviewing officers left, two other uniformed officers entered, to take charge of Omar Kaur. Farra beckoned Tuah to come with them.

Outside, he was formal. "Thank you, Tuah, for your assistance. Interviews are not easy things, sometimes. We knew this one was going to be one of those and you did well."

The senior British officer was watching him. She said, "Yes, thank you. I'm not sure everyone, or anyone here particularly, will be thanking me for my actions just now. Sergeant Farra says you want to get into detective work. It is hard at times; rewarding, but it takes its toll. Be aware of that."

"Thank you, ma'am."

He was momentarily lost for something more meaningful to say and then added. "To have met the person who saved the life of Sergeant Farra is a great honour. No-one will speak badly about you. I will not allow it."

Farra smiled at his intensity. "You, Tuah, will respect the absolute confidentiality of the interview room. Please remember that."

Tuah responded earnestly, "I won't ever break that, Sergeant. But they will know that no-one can speak a word against DCI Sayer in my presence."

Catrin smiled. "You do have an expressive face, Constable Tuah. I can see how that would play out. Thank you."

31 HIJACK

At the cocktails before dinner, Rita and Andy stayed close to Catrin and Turner-Jones. Some Commission staff and guests from embassies moved around and talked with them while others gravitated to the Deputy High Commissioner. The reception room had two main camps, of which everyone was aware, as they portrayed blissful ignorance.

The High Commissioner, Neville Yarrow, a former banker, gave a short welcome address early on during the preliminaries, and apologised for needing to leave before dinner. Yarrow had appeared for the funeral of Sofia binti Awang, as the death occurred on British soil.

Rita felt that there ought to be black bow ties, dinner jackets and fancy gowns, with James Bond standing in the corner, but it was business suits and dressier dresses for the women and no attractive unattached male in sight.

The long table, though, when they entered the dining room, lived up to her expectations. Rita carefully assessed the array of cutlery as she scrutinised the menu. The seating had her next to a German, a cultural attaché, and his wife. Sayer was higher up the table and, for reasons unclear, Mrs. Turner-Jones was seated one position lower than the man Gilbertson. Rita thought she should have seniority and be placed higher up the table, with Catrin.

Not to embarrass her, Madeleine had given Rita a quick talk on what would happen. "Work the cutlery from the outside and watch others. Initially, divide your time equally between the people on either side of you. Later on, conversation across the table will start, as people get more comfortable with each other. Be careful about using jargon if the person next to you is not English. Above all, relax."

"What do I say?"

"Oh, nothing much. Mr. Graham will probably lead the conversation topics. To the person next to you, just tell them you are a police officer. See what happens."

"Does Andy need the same brief, do you think?"

Turner-Jones said, "I doubt it."

Rita looked surprised. "Neither of us get to attend formal events in our job."

"He has an uncle in the Foreign Office, though; and you didn't hear that from me."

In fact, Rita quite enjoyed talking to the German on one side, and a woman called Roberta on the other, from the staff. It was during the main course, salmon, with the fancy fish knife and fork, that Terry Graham raised his voice to get attention.

"As we who reside here, each at our country's service so to speak, have the pleasure of the company of several police officers from London, given the tragic events involving the death of a Malaysian police officer, I suggest we talk about law, order, and punishment a little, with our experts present."

He smiled. Rita saw where this was going, given the morning's events. From police officers, to courts, to sentences, and the death sentence. The DHC was rallying support, she guessed.

Then she saw Turner-Jones, who had been exceedingly quiet, raise her eyebrows, not at her, but at the German attaché next to her.

He spoke. "A wonderful idea, Terry, if I may say so. Ingrid and I were talking about our visitors from England. Ingrid?

His wife, who had been busy with the people on the other side of her, said, "Yes! Chief Inspector Sayer, I am to pass on to you the kind regards and best wishes of Herr Gerhardt Amstel."

She looked at Graham. "I know, Terry, I should say Catrin. You said, informal, no fancy titles tonight. I do apologise."

Then she beamed at Sayer.

Catrin smiled at the mention of the head of the German Federal Police Art Crime Unit. "Gerhardt? How nice. Herr Amstel is with the German Federal Police. I know him well."

The attache's wife smiled. "He is an older cousin. I knew your name before, from him. I called him this afternoon and told him you were here. And on television yesterday, even!"

Seeing several people looking slightly puzzled, the attache's wife said, "Gerhardt and Catrin have worked together, as police officers. They are both art detectives, famous within their field."

It is a small field, thought Catrin, thank goodness. And she was in different pastures now.

Terry Graham, for his role, needed a better handle on his facial response, with or without cocktails or wine, Rita thought. She, like everyone else, saw this was news to Graham; he had been caught flat-footed.

It was the attaché himself, Wilhelm, who said, "Of course, darling, Terry knows he has one of the top art detectives in Europe at dinner. We should take advantage and talk more about art and the people who rob the galleries. It is an interesting subject, yes?"

"Indeed," jumped in Turner-Jones. She looked at the couple from Sierra Leone. "Catrin had on her staff a wonderful detective who specialised in Islamic and African art, a Detective Obi. He saved a painting from Malaysia found in the UK. People here were very appreciative."

Rita watched Terry Graham looking to retrieve the direction of the discussion. It didn't happen.

In answer to a question a few minutes later, the Sierra Leone couple, Gabriel (call me Gabe) and Fatu, came alive as Catrin responded to a question from Fatu.

"I once saw some Hassan Bangurah works in London, but I know so little about your art. I would like to learn more. I don't get much time for art these days, I am afraid."

Fatu looked at Gabe. "She knows Hassan's work" Her face shining with joy, she looked down the table to inform the guests. "We know the artist personally."

Despite the reverence of tone and the nodding of others, Rita thought she might not be the only person present unfamiliar with the artist. Gabe looked incredibly pleased.

From that point on, art and art crime were the topics, through the dessert and coffee and liqueurs, into the wrap-up and farewells.

As they broke and made their goodbyes, Rita saw Gabe shake hands with Terry and slap his arm hard enough to merit an assault charge.

"Wonderful dinner, Terry; wonderful."

Rita thought Terry Graham's agenda had been well and truly hijacked. And she suspected that the culprit or culprits were staying at the same hotel as her.

~~

For inexplicable reasons, other than the terse and reluctant explanation from Turner-Jones that 'policy issues' were involved, the four British visitors were flying back to London on Qatar Airways in business class, through Qatar airport and connecting there with a British Airways flight.

Catrin had made it clear in the preparations that, after the High Commission dinner, she would be taking time with friends until their evening departure the following day. Turner-Jones was working. Andy and Rita had signed up for a day tour; a rock climb at the Batu Caves, followed by a visit to see the rain forest and the inevitable finish at the Petronas Twin Towers before the drop-off the hotel.

Rita had concluded that their boss was going to spend time with the Farra family.

It was Andy who pointed. "Isn't that the boss, there?"

The last stop on the tour, they had just arrived at the Petronas Twin Towers. Rita looked where he was pointing and, sure enough, it was.

She was with a Chinese couple with a baby. As Rita and Andy exited the small tour bus and Rita called out Catrin saw them.

She said, "These are my friends, Jian Li Yeung and her husband, James. And this young man is my godson,

Daniel."

As they made each other's acquaintance, Sayer looked at her colleagues. The tour bus guide was busy with the other passengers. Collard looked at her, sensing that 'this was the place', where his boss killed a man.

She looked at him. "One time only, quickly. Our car was further back than where your van is is now. Sergeant Farra was in the front seat with Constable Ashland, the driver. Madeleine and I were in the back. Loh Gee, the gunman, started there, by that red car and, as it went down, there was where he fell. Those seconds changed my life."

Rita asked, "And after?"

"I was in shock. My next clear memory was seeing Jian Li at the hotel. She had flown in. Today, we got to do some of the things we planned to do then."

Jian Li said, "It's a spectacular view from the top. We have just come down. We are heading back to our hotel, the Doubletree. Daniel is ready for a feed and a nap."

Tully asked James, "Do you live in Malaysia?"

"No, in Hong Kong. Catrin and Jian Li have been friends for a long time. We came in for today."

Tully responded, "It must still be a long way to Hong Kong, though. For a day together."

James looked at Catrin and smiled. "Not for this one. We like her. And her family."

Rita was trying to decide what to say when she saw Catrin look at Andy. Collard had broken away and pulled out his phone to read a message.

As he looked across at Sayer, she said, "No. We are off-duty, five thousand miles away. Not a thing, until the flight back. Put it away."

Sayer looked at Jian Li and smiled. "Time to go."

PART 3. COPSE

32 PIPELINE

The joke going around Undertow was posed as a question. Would DC Loretta Hills be successful in her next undercover role? She was going to pretend to be a police officer.

Unfair, she said, in response to the banter.

The following day, DC Hills would be PC Sykes, a Thames Valley constable, who was also an enthusiastic gardener.

Loretta sat cramming more information, to build on her basic knowledge of gardening. She was making a call on Hasanna Akanni, in Iver. Fortunately, they knew the Akanni garden from photographs on Hasanna Akanni's Facebook page.

Loretta had been wide-eyed when reviewing them. "She built this garden up from that mess in less than two years. Wow! In my street we don't run to ornamental gardens stretching into the distance. It is a lot to absorb."

DCI Sayer had been back from her trip to Asia for four days. Andy Collard reported sick for three of those days with a bug of some sort.

On her return, Rita appeared unusually quiet. She talked about the experience to others, one-on-one. At her first team briefing after their return, she commented how privileged she felt to have represented the Met and the Undertow team there.

In private, she said little more. Yes, DCI Sayer did interview Omar Kaur. No, she couldn't say more, but the boss and Andy had been superb throughout the entire trip.

To her closest colleagues and her family, she showed two photos passed on to her by a friend she now had in the RMP. One showed Sofia binti Awang on her graduation from the police academy. The other showed the three police officers from the British delegation, in uniform, taken after the funeral. They were standing amid an array of RMP officers, with one older man in uniform talking to Sayer.

"That's Sergeant Jared Farra. He told me that the boss saved his life on her first visit. And look, on her tunic, the ribbon. The Malaysians gave her that, but she won't talk about it, so don't ask."

It was Collard, on his return, who told people Rita had been a real hit with the RMP and why. Terry Jameson asked him, "And you, Andy?"

"I filled in as the token male. I talked about football. Rita and the boss didn't make me carry their bags."

Tully gave him a smile. "I wish I knew you wanted to do that. I'd have bought more souvenirs and clothes."

Collard said, "The way I feel now after being laid up, I can just about carry my phone and not much else."

Terry, silently adding food concerns to his fear of flying on the list of reasons not to go abroad, asked, "Did you eat something that disagreed with you?"

"Who knows? We were half-way around the world. It could have been anything. We took a tour on the last day, sightseeing and rock climbing. And we spent some time in the rain forest. What gets me is that I was being careful about what I ate. Rita and the boss tucked into everything."

Rita nodded. "It was good food. I'm looking up Malay restaurants in London now."

Sayer had taken a day off on return, to be with family. When she returned to Undertow, she had been tied up with Lauder and Moore for most of the first day back at work. The following afternoon, she met with DCI Osborne, DI Franklin and DS Wong, then acting for Collard. It was the following morning, with Collard's return, when she gathered team members she needed and went to the whiteboard.

"Team A's new assignment; Charles Kingdom Akanni, age forty-three. Born in Kos, Nigeria, a dual national. After arrival in the UK, he first lived in Lewisham. He is now a successful businessman. You know about Rel-Comm Enterprises – he is linked to that. While he runs several legal businesses and is a multimillionaire, he has established a large illegal scamming network in a number of countries."

From their expressions, she could see, other than Andy, they were not completely swayed that this was a legitimate target for Undertow. This was Fraud Squad territory.

She continued. "He lives in Iver, near the Pinewood Studios site, in a big house with a large garden he bought a few years ago. It turns out that he owns a second plot at the back, a copse of trees, undeveloped, a barrier between his garden and the road behind. The copse does the same for four other neighbouring gardens. He got the woodland cheap, by signing a non-development agreement co-signed and supported by the British Lichen Society. There are rare or special lichens there."

Ian Underhill looked askance.

"Plants, of some sort," said Wong.

"A combination of a fungus and algae," added Richard Roe. He smiled. "My 'A' level biology. I should have been a scientist."

Catrin said, "Thank you, panel members. If we could get back... Akanni apparently bought that land a lot earlier than the house, a windfall purchase as a true friend of the Lichen Society. The information, not that much better than a rumour at present, is that there is a body in there; a girlfriend that disappeared years ago in Lewisham, name of Anne Krell. It was Commander Moore's case at the time, never solved."

Realisation set in on their faces, recalling Moore's fixation with Rel-Comm.

Stillwell asked, "Shouldn't Thames Valley Homicide be sending in digging teams and cadaver dogs, and holding the man until they locate the body?"

"It's a little more complicated than that. First, we have no evidence. Second, if we are wrong, it's another media mess, like Rel-Comm. The commander and I met with Media Relations yesterday and a couple of people from Thames Valley Police. Undertow is first going to look at alternative approaches."

She settled herself against the edge of the table behind her and paused.

"There's more. The man has a real vicious streak, as Sergeant Emmie Shand discovered. Finally, information I received in KL would indicate he was the one who chose

Fitzgerald. Akanni promised Omar Kaur that quote, 'he would find someone that would get every bit of information out of Laura binti Assad'.

Sofia's work name. From their expressions now, she knew they saw this as their case, as did she. In fact, she got the impression they would fight Thames Valley tooth and nail to keep it, if needed.

"So, what's first?" asked DS Stephen Wong. "Get someone in place, close to him?"

Sayer looked at Collard. He led operational details.

"No," Andy responded. "First, we need someone to talk to his wife, Hasanna. Preferably, someone non-Caucasian who knows about gardening and can bond. And female, we think that's best."

Eyes focused on Loretta Hills.

She said, "I wish I hadn't made a thing about my tomato plants now. I know sweet FA about real gardening. Richard knows about lichens; she will love him."

Her tone, though, belied her reluctance. She wanted this assignment, they could see.

Collard looked at DI Franklin and DC Digsby. "And a discrete check of the copse, to give a cost estimate for effective surveillance coverage electronically, visual and infrared I presume, with covert and continuous operation.

"I want instrumentation specifications, insertion plan details and costs. We are going to spook Akanni into moving the remains buried there and catch him or his people in the act as they move the body."

Catrin said, "It won't be rumour then. It will be irrefutable, hard evidence."

"Is this Hasanna Akanni involved in the businesses, the legit or the illegal stuff?" It was Loretta who asked.

Catrin said, "We don't think so. I get the impression she is something of looker, a trophy wife, mad about gardening. But I don't know. I'm hoping, Loretta, that you will get a read on that, or a gut feel about her, at least. Oh, and you will need a Thames Valley constable's uniform. You are going undercover as a police officer."

In the laughter, Loretta gave Sayer a grimace. "Nice one, boss. You know how this lot will go on about that."

~~

Loretta was now inside the hallway of the home of Amaechi Akanni and his wife. It led to a reception room with large windows giving a view of the garden behind. Hasanna Akanni was in her mid-thirties, Loretta knew. Other than their dog, a large smokey gray labradoodle, she was alone. Her husband was at work.

Undertow were sure of that. They didn't want him there when Loretta called.

Hasanna Akanni was reflecting on the reason a police officer had knocked on her door.

"Shouldn't this be a job for the council, one of their people? A notice about tree-trimming? I didn't think the police would be involved."

Loretta smiled. "It is. But we get a lot of odd jobs at the Slough police station at times. The council employee who was to inform you was bitten earlier today by a dog. His stand-in objects to calling on any houses with dogs and they are starting the trimming tomorrow, so they want all people affected to know. I've got two other houses to pop in on, then I am done.

"They may be trees protecting your privacy, but the council has the right to trim them off the road if they are dangerous to traffic or pedestrians. That's why I am here."

It was three days after the briefing session. During the

tree-trimming, one or two of the workers would be doing something unusual for tree trimmers, installing night-vision cameras.

Hasanna said, "Hardly anyone uses that little road behind us, not any lorries, at least."

Loretta responded, "There will be some there in the next week or two, that's why they are trimming beforehand. It's the pipeline that needs checking. You got the notice about that earlier, you must have. In the mail?"

Hasanna looked blank. "I didn't. And I handle all the stuff to do with the house. If my husband had got it, he would have given it to me to deal with."

Loretta looked surprised. "Well, next week, they will be digging up in places at the side of the road, putting in their testing probes, or whatever. I recall from the plan they showed me, the line runs across the corner of the clump of trees behind you, the strip along by the wall."

"They are our trees! Amaechi owns the entire plot to the corner. I don't want the trees damaged. Besides, they are protected."

Loretta said, "Then something has gone wrong, if you are the landowner for whole copse. I mean, it's not the trees, the pipeline will be clear of those, I'm sure. They have been in place a lot longer. But the line looked to go under the wall somewhere around that corner, I thought. If they dig there, they are going to have to be careful; those old walls are solid, but if they disturb the foundations...

"I'm going to have to tell my husband about this. Next week, perhaps? Can we stop or delay it?"

"The next week or two. I don't know where they are starting the project. All I can do is put you in touch with the right people at the council. But I doubt it. I know we have some traffic management at the crossroads during the setup and breakdown stages. All the sub-contractors will already be booked, like us. I think you are looking at a claim after the fact, really."

Hasanna's voice took on a worried tone. "I hope I didn't miss something I should have dealt with. I hope it's not me. Amaechi will... he'll be blazing mad anyway."

Loretta could see the apprehension, the distress. She looked out of the window. "I love your garden. I'm surprised by the *Clivia* though, beautiful as they are. Outside this late in the year. You are brave!"

Hasanna Akanni suddenly smiled, a subject of pleasure. "Most people call them Natal lilies. You know your plants, I see. Those are excess from my greenhouse stock, and they don't do well in strong sunshine either, but the trellis gives just enough shade. I love to see them growing outdoors, if you know what I mean?"

Loretta nodded. "I do. I love gardening."

If the team at Lavender Hill could hear the lies, they would be proud of her.

"You like lilies?"

"Yes!" enthused Loretta. "A lot of people think of lilies just as funeral flowers, but the varieties are beautiful."

"Come see these, then."

She led the way across the reception room out into the back garden, to the side, where a new greenhouse sat. Opening the door for her, she waited as Loretta entered, feeling the heat and humidity as she entered. Ahead were different trays of seedlings on one bench but on another sat a series of plant pots. Loretta struggled through her memory and suddenly said, "Spider lilies, *Lycoris*, how gorgeous! You are so fortunate."

"Aren't they beautiful? My husband insisted on a greenhouse with lights, and temperature and humidity control. I can grow plants all year, give them to people."

Hasanna beamed at her.

After admiring them, Loretta looked at her watch, then at the garden stretching into the distance. It was beautifully maintained, despite its size.

"You have quite a garden here, Mrs. Akanni."

She added, as an apparent afterthought, looking at the trees, "If they do disturb the wall, insist that the original stone is reused for the rebuild, it will look a lot better. The letter will say, 'restore to equivalent status' or something like that.

"If you press them, the council people will object, of course, as its more cost and effort for them to use the original stone. If you don't, they will repair it with some of these 'new stone' reconstituted brick things they make nowadays. But if you or your solicitor pushes, they will probably agree. We have seen it happen a lot now with older property."

Hasanna replied, "I've seen that 'new-old' stonework around. You are right, it's not the same. That's a good tip. Thank you. Do you have time for a cup of coffee?"

Loretta pulled a face. "I shouldn't, I should get to the next house, but… a quick one?"

Hasanna led her through to the kitchen. She had found another person to talk to about plants and perhaps get more advice about how to handle this new problem associated with the pipeline.

A few minutes later she was looking glum. "Amaechi loves that copse. He bought it before he bought this house, as I said. Years ago, he just came across it and bought it at a steal of a price because he wanted to own a bit of England, I think!"

She pulled a face. "It's just as well. I don't think the people around here would have been too happy with

Nigerian neighbours back then. It's less of an issue now. I've got some good friends here, all keen gardeners."

Loretta sounded sympathetic. "Less of an issue, but not a non-issue. I get your meaning. We all have that."

She gave a final glance out the window, turning towards the door, preparing to leave. "It looks a quiet bit of woodland."

"It is, unless Amaechi is blasting away at the carrion crows and pigeons with his shotgun. He does it under a – what's it called, a license he doesn't have to apply for?"

Loretta responded, "A general license. It is restricted to certain months and specific pests, though. Do you shoot, as well?"

"I wouldn't know one end from the other. No, I just like my home and my garden, and travelling with Amaechi sometimes, on his business trips. Meeting people, seeing places. We put Ani in the kennels, though, when we do, so I don't like to be away for a long time."

The dog. Loretta asked, "Annie?"

"No 'e', a-n-i. It's short for Anansi, the god of trickery. Amaechi chose it. He's a lovely dog, nice tempered, but as a puppy he was always up to tricks."

33 PLAN

Loretta was back in Lavender Hill, still in a Thames Valley uniform.

"If Hasanna Akanni is involved in her husband's business, she is a better actor than any I have met. My read is that she looks like a celebrity but is highly insecure and in fear of her husband. The house and garden are showpieces, but she gave me glimpses of her constant anxiety and a fear of her husband becoming annoyed by events beyond her control."

Collard asked, "Do any of Amaechi's business people visit?"

"They don't. No parties or visitors. Quote, 'Amaechi doesn't bring business home. He regards it as his sanctuary from the world and his work'. So, we won't get anything from the house, I expect."

Loretta gave a grimace. "She gives you the feeling that she is his personal handmaid at times, which I found creepy. He has business contacts meet him for golf or dinner, at a place called the Coverley Golf Club.

"She goes with him to some of the business events

here and abroad but is happiest at home with her dog and her garden. She has friends, two local women, who she met through gardening, one a little older, the other quite a bit older. Two families in Notting Hill they were close to, neighbours, seem to have faded into the background as her husband doesn't visit Notting Hill with her or encourage them to visit Iver."

DS Wong chipped in, "She does sound a bit isolated, one way or another; not what you would see in a partner in crime."

Loretta went back to her notes made after the visit.

"She grew up in the same town as Akanni. Their parents know each other. Looking at her now, she must have been stunning in her late teens. Akanni returned home to visit his family, where they met. She was swept off her feet by the new jet-set business executive. Apart from the great looks, she's a keen cook, an insanely enthusiastic gardener, and she looks after their dog.

"I gave her the info on the tree trimming and I'm sure she'll pass it on to him. Other than the shotgun, there is little else to report. She's sure he has no other guns in the house."

Omar Kaur had provided several vital pieces of information. Among them, Akanni's Art Division often undervalued their import duty declarations, the reason why DI Mark Harper and DS John Obi from the Arts & Antiques Unit, Catrin's former assignment, were in the review meeting.

Kaur also revealed that Akanni had talked about his organisation's discipline. Catrin had briefed them about that.

"There are rules for poor performance; they get set back or let go. But Akanni has only one rule for betrayal, and they know that. He set that example early on, Kaur said, with someone who, 'let him down badly, a long time in the past'."

"Later, the only time Kaur had visited Iver, for a meeting held during a golf game, Akanni made a further reference. 'The first one; I walk over the grave regularly. It reminds me to be vigilant', he told him."

Moore was sure that it was Anne Krell, and she was buried in the copse.

Gerry Lauder said, half-convincingly, "We could arrest him on the shotgun. It's registered, but it sounds as if he is a bit lax on storing it properly. It's serious enough to get entry but wouldn't be enough to hold him. We need more."

It was DI Mark Harper who asked, "If any art he brought into the UK with dodgy import status is in his home, we could get in there, bring him in for questioning, spin it out, but not hold him for long. Did you see much?"

The question was to Loretta.

"I saw the entry hall and part of the main living area, and the kitchen. There is art there, some framed textile work on a wall. And two wooden statues, one about a metre high, the other smaller."

Catrin responded, "It's a big stretch from either of those items to digging up a corpse on his property."

Lauder directed his next comment to Karen Moore. "I don't see this, Karen, to play a waiting game with Akanni, just monitoring the woods, or fiddling around the edges with paintings or gun storage. He's not stupid."

She retorted, "And if we do what you say, drag him in and go digging, then find Omar Kaur lied to Sayer, we look like fools. Media Relations will have a field day. John Reed will be eviscerating me with Sleiman again."

He shrugged. "It won't be the first time. But it will settle it one way or the other."

Moore looked at Sayer. "Your view?"

Catrin hesitated. "I'd like to give him a little soak time with the message Loretta delivered, to see if we get anything from the original plan. Say forty-eight hours. We will hold off the tree-trimming a day. If he calls the council number Loretta gave Hasanna, wanting to object, that will be an indicator. We need to decide on the next step before going to the trouble of installing camera surveillance in the copse."

"And if he does nothing?"

"Have Mark and John take him at his office on the art charge, I would say. It's in our territory, not Thames Valley, for one thing. We get a warrant to search his workplaces, his home and property for art stashed away. Then we find the shotgun improperly stored, as well, and Mark brings in someone to talk to him about that. While we are doing the interviews, let cadaver dogs loose in the copse and his garden, saying we are checking for missing antiques that may have been buried or hidden. If a body turns up, we charge him. If not, pull the animals out, focus on the art in the home and the gun charge. Stay with the evidence base."

She paused. "If we do all that, he will know. He'll do something, but I don't know what; perhaps relocate abroad, fast."

Moore pulled a face. There was a lull, waiting on her decision.

Finally, she said, "My preference is to wait it out using the copse surveillance approach for longer and build the pressure on him. Catrin's plan is intermediate. Gerry's is 'hit him now'. I guess I'll go with Catrin's approach. What's Akanni's schedule again?"

DI Franklin, the Digital Intelligence team lead, said, "Two days in his office. Then the day after he is at his Newcastle location. He has another trip to Africa next week, Ghana this time."

"We act before he goes abroad. Obi, are you up to it? Kenyan on Nigerian, so to speak? If we go straight for the art, earlier than we said?"

John Obi sat back, gave DI Harper, his boss, a quick glance. In discussing the art import issue, they thought John Obi, born in the Midlands to Kenyan parents, might be a better fit to lead the interviews.

John responded, "From what I heard just now, I don't see why not. He's tricky and vocal, you say. If the art info is correct, it may be easy to spot his import duty fiddles or it could take some time. We can drag it out, but not prevent him getting bail. Any idea who his solicitor is?"

Moore said, "No, but whoever he brings in will be first class. Let's make sure Art and Antiques gives us enough time to give his place a thorough going over."

She sat up straight. "I think we have it. A couple of days to see if he bites on the news Loretta provided. After that the art issue. A phased plan with fall-back options. Good."

She looked down at some notes she had scribbled.

"When he's arrested, Obi, Catrin could sit in the interview with you if it helps, see if she still remembers anything about art stuff. If it gets interesting, perhaps I'll sit in with you, to turn his crank. He'll remember me. You won't mind that will you?"

Wonderful, thought Catrin. She had thought Karen Moore had outgrown the 'let me at him' stage. In this case clearly, she had not. It must have shown on her face. Superintendent Lauder gave her and Obi a pitying look.

'All yours', his expression conveyed.

It turned out that their detailed preparations, with 'fallback options', were irrelevant. Amaechi Arkanni came up with a plan of his own and, as usual, Gerry Lauder had read it right.

34 REALISATION

"A police officer came around today, about the road behind us."

Amaechi was sitting quietly on the patio, thinking of his visit next week to Ghana. He looked at his wife and said quietly, "About what?"

"The council are tree-trimming ahead of some pipeline inspection. The council person was bitten by a dog earlier, so she finished the notifications. She's a gardener, too. We chatted away."

Hasanna told it slowly, measuring her husband's mood, a learned behaviour.

Akanni seemed to listen intently as she explained and passed over the notice. It had fallen off the counter earlier and she crumpled the corner, retrieving it.

His response was strange, she thought. He didn't get annoyed or angry. Amaechi asked, "How about coming to Accra with me next week? I'm looking into some wonderful Kente textile opportunities?"

Her face showed her response. "I would love to, but..."

The timing was completely wrong for her to leave the gardening work. And she had accompanied him previously to Accra.

Amaechi didn't take in the response; about the flowers, the dog's check-up at the vet, things like that. Other women would scream with delight at a trip to West Africa.

As she focused on the completion of the dinner preparations, he reflected he had got what he wanted in Hasanna but, as he needed to change, she wouldn't.

He was out of time.

Months ago, with the report back from McEwen after hammering the Welsh woman, Amaechi reached an important decision. The confirmation of Karen Moore's involvement in the raid on Rel-Comm and that she now held a senior rank at the Met changed everything. He would have to make a new life, but where?

He mulled that conclusion over for some time, considering places where his legitimate businesses could be managed successfully while no arrest warrant or extradition request would be accepted. That excluded places with extradition treaties and his current scamming operations.

In the end, he settled on Vietnam. Amaechi found a small villa with a twenty-year leasehold option in the city of Thanh Hoa, about one hundred and fifty miles from Hanoi. He would have to use the three-month visa cycle at the beginning. Many foreigners lived there for years, leaving for a day or so every three months then returning with a fresh visa.

That held some additional complexities. He would need to avoid travel to a location where he could be arrested. But the issue wasn't insurmountable. And once settled, he had money and the ability to persuade people. He knew how to arrange things. Money talked.

Over the months following the Rel-Comm raid, he made financial arrangements through a bank in Hanoi, making a stopover there twice on his business travels to Asia. Final steps would be as simple as booking a flight and leaving the UK after activating some bank transfers.

But the mess involved, including dumping Hasanna, bothered him. She would never settle to that sort of life. Her family and his own in Africa would be devastated. As a scammer, he loved his anonymity and his current reputation, which would disappear if he became a fugitive. He worried about that aspect more than the risk of prison, and kept any idea of Vietnam on the back burner.

When Olowe admitted to his role in the Maesteg scam, he wondered if it was time, but still vascillated. Once Roland McEwen was charged following the Nine Elms fiasco, he knew he was looking at the inevitable.

Despite the logic of escape and flight, his excellent escape plan appealed less each day.

Strangely enough, he worried less about McEwen's arrest than the others. Roland would never speak against Amaechi. If he did, they would both never see the light of day outside a UK prison, as they knew too much about each other. But the worry at four in the morning came from his inner voice; 'everyone has his or her breaking point'.

Amaechi's first scam occurred when he was fifteen, involving a local man living near Kos. The next few years were now blurred in his memory, the small stuff he did while he also studied.

When he received the grant to be a student in London,

he was as accomplished a scammer as he was a business student and, in a sense, he had made his first kill; another scammer he knew, called Desmond. The older boy had once taught him a little but later became a pain, a hanger-on, demanding that Akanni should take him on, look after him. Amaechi's solution was simple; arrange a minor scam involving the daughter of a local gang member, leading the tracks back to Desmond. Two months later, Desmond's body turned up in a ditch.

Akanni was surprised how he felt about that; an initital satisfaction and no remorse. A problem had been re-solved. It fooled him.

In Lewisham, while he was a student, when Anne Krell had blurted out to him that she had leaked the truth to DS Moore, he had immediately been conciliatory, supportive, not angry. She knew that Amaechi and Darius were hiding something they had done, because Amaechi had not been with herat the time, as he claimed. He had asked her to lie for him and she couldn't do that. She wanted to find a way for them to deal with the problem, whatever that was.

She was astonished and grateful that he didn't want to ditch her. Amaechi took it all on his own shoulders.

"When they come, I'll tell them the truth. You'll have no problem."

Thinking he would have to do part of the dirty work himself this time, he played on his last day or so of free-dom with her. "They will send me back to Nigeria, after whatever I face here."

He had suggested a day trip to the Chiltern Hills, to see 'a bit of traditional England, have a meal in a pub with a thatched roof'. Full of guilt, she had agreed.

When they stopped at the place where Darius Ward was waiting, and she saw their expressions, she knew something was terribly wrong. By prior agreement, Darius held her, Amaechi strangled her. Moore's witness was gone.

Darius had spotted the copse on the back road near Iver on the planning trip. He argued the logic. "It's nowhere. It is ignored by the people in the homes over there, as it is not developable. The land is protected, and it looks to be too small and heavily wooded for recreational use. On one side the gardens are fenced off and it is walled on the other, at the roadside."

Amaechi had planned to bury the body in the hills, but Darius was persuasive. "These hills and tourist areas, remote as they seem, always have some walker's dog or wandering tourist who would find the body within a year."

Amaechi came up with the most apt description of the copse, one that would haunt his life. "It's like a hidden burial ground for one."

They waited it out after killing her, first in a lay-by, then in a car park. Anne Krell was buried an hour before dawn, two metres in from the wall bordering the copse.

What Amaechi never expected was the sense of loss of Anne. Not guilt, not remorse, just loss. In the year or so following, once Lewisham Police had backed away and their tiger of a detective sergeant had been moved on, promoted, he held Moore to blame. He never forgot that or let the resentment of Moore diminish. He grew to hate her.

After Anne, other women for him were temporary, they didn't last. It was on the trip home over a year later that he was attracted to Hasanna, to both their parents' pleasure.

Even as he asked her to marry him, he was sure she

would be a perfect wife. But she wouldn't be his Anne, with his last memory of her being the terrible face, eyes bulging as he choked the life out of her.

He waited years before returning to Iver. Before that, it was a relatively simple matter to buy the land. He joined the British Lichen Society, read up on the subject, talked to a few people and worked his magic. It was their network that made the thing happen; a man with money backing the need to conserve the copse, to support rather than resent a protection order.

When he did return to the area, it was with an estate agent. No mention of the copse was made to him. Amaechi was interested in property in Iver, although it was hard to come by. The man saw an aspiring immigrant, a hard worker with a good business head. He was a success story in the making and the agent told him he would help.

After a tour around, Amaechi picked four spots, none with available property currently. "If something comes up in our price range, let us know."

The man did so; repeatedly. Amaechi made the effort to follow up most times, but never said yes. Neither did he tell the man or Hasanna that only five houses were of interest to him.

When their current home came on the market, he made sure that he bargained hard for the place without revealing he would have paid the earth for it. His Anne was now with him, at the bottom of their garden.

And that was the problem now.

His thoughts were all over the place, the wins and losses. Moving to Vietnam was logical, and feasible. But he would be leaving Anne behind. He would be leaving Hasanna behind. True, he would have new opportunities, but his parents, parents-in-law and wife would be devastated. He would walk away from all the decisions and problem-solving needed for his legitimate businesses. He would never live the same way and would always be looking over his shoulder or waiting for the local police to arrive. Not having a criminal record there did not mean he would avoid being targeted by someone needing a kickback.

He see-sawed daily on the path forward. Until today, with the apparently innocous news from Hasanna about a pipeline survey.

Moore was relentless and now getting too close to him, if the visit by the police officer was what he thought it to be. He checked the time and called the council information number on the notice in the hope he was being paranoid again.

The recorded message was perfect. Exactly what he would expect from the council. Normal hours were stated, emergency numbers were given. The person's voice was that mix of 'we are here to serve you' and 'we really don't give a damn' tones. He would have done it that way himself, he thought.

But the number on the sheet left with Hasanna was not the same as the contact number he found on the council website. An earlier call on a burner phone to that number gave him the comparison.

He pressed the button to leave a message, seeing as the police would have his mobile and house phone numbers already. In slightly hesitant steps he told them he was responding to a notice left about the tree trimming. He somehow missed that there was work going on in the road behind and wanted to know if it would it affect his property at all. After leaving his call back number, he added, "I'll be away on business for a day or so. On second thoughts, leave it, don't bother to call back. I'll phone again when I get the chance."

From the back of his mind had come the idea of a new con, a totally different solution, one that two months ago he would have rejected out of hand as madness. Now, reflecting on it, he decided it was a trick he couldn't miss. It was the way out of the mess and, in doing it, he would be carrying out the best scam of his life and making everything right.

~~

The following morning, Hasanna woke to a strange sound and smell; her husband was already up and was in the kitchen, humming something. Normally she went down and prepared breakfast while he showered and prepared to leave for work. The smells were enticing, one of their weekend brunches they loved, and on a weekday, too. And he was cooking it. She smiled, concluding that Amaechi had cancelled the day in the office and perhaps even the Newcastle trip tomorrow. He would be home. He sounded like he was happy today.

She wondered whether she should text Frances, put off their plans for a visit to the garden centre they arranged for this morning.

When she went downstairs, he smiled at her and said, "I thought I would surprise you. Ani is fed, and outside."

She was smiling, focused on him, missing that her phone was still plugged into the charger, it was now switched off.

As they ate, she mentioned her plans. "Joan is coming over. We were going to plan the bulb order for us all. Shall I put her off? I'll call her."

Pleasant as this was, she wasn't sure of his plans for

the day and didn't want to ruin his mood.

"When is she arriving?"

"At ten, we agreed."

He smiled and gave a glance up towards the bedroom. "Plenty of time for us then, and afterwards, when she's here, I will do something else."

She smiled, happy with the way things were working out.

In the reception room earlier, he had opened the packet of zip ties, in preparation. He wanted her to enjoy the breakfast and the lovemaking. She deserved that.

35 HOSTAGES

As Joan Lucas parked in the short driveway, Amaechi Akanni opened the front door and went towards her, smiling.

"Hasanna is around the back, I'll walk round with you and say goodbye before heading out."

When they rounded the rear corner of the house, Joan saw Hasanna sitting on a seat pulled away from the patio set. Joan felt the blow, a slap really, to the side of her head at the same time as she realised that Hasanna was terrified, with her hands fastened together with a strap of some sort.

She recoiled from the blow, stunned. Amaechi pulled her arms together roughly, expertly working the long zip tie around the wrists and pulling it.

As he finished and Joan gasped, "Why?" he just said, "Any trouble, and I will tighten them so that you will lose your hands or fingers, they will die for lack of blood. You know about that sort of thing."

His face was different, hard, brutal, she saw. Everything she and Frances Coombs had talked about, the concerns that she had quelled in her friend, were there but magnified a hundred times, stark and frightening.

Joan stood there, confused, as Amaechi walked away, across to the wall. By the time she thought of running as best as she could with her hands bound in front of her, he was holding a shotgun. Then she heard the barking from Ani, down the garden, nearer the copse. The dog could sense their terror.

That was the only way to describer her friend's face.

"Off we go," he said, pointing the gun at the copse. "Hasanna, up!"

Hasanna stood, shaking. Without a word, she turned and walked on to the lawn, moving towards the bottom of the garden. It was his expression that made Joan follow. She saw in his eyes that he would be just as happy to kill her here.

She moved forward, to be with Hasanna, and whispered, "What's going on? Has he gone crazy?"

Hasanna was too scared to answer. She just looked in absolute anguish.

Joan glanced behind her. Amaechi was pulling out his phone, the gun now in the other hand. It made Joan think. Her own phone was in her purse, and she had dropped that when he hit her. Hasanna had nothing with her.

Ahead, they could see Ani, jumping and excited now, barking. His lead was tied to the handle of the lawn-mower, a large wide-cut heavy thing. Hasanna instinctively stopped near the dog, about ten feet away.

"Into the copse, now."

"No, please Amaechi, no!"

They were the first words out of Hasanna that Joan heard. As she turned back to reason with him, Joan saw the shotgun point at the animal and fire. Both barrels.

All she could remember was the sound, the canine yelp that was more a scream, and Hasanna's own scream rising above it. The explosive force of the animal being torn apart splattered Hasanna more than Joan, but Joan's bladder emptied. Hasanna had bent over, wretching.

It was one of the absurdities of life. Joan, a retired nurse, saw that Hasanna had breakfasted well that morning. Nurses have enough experience of patients and vomit. She looked at the dog, expecting Amaechi to have shot the animal in the head. In fact, he had shot it in the rear quarters. Awful as it was, the silent dog's eyes still moved uncomprehendingly for a second or two until Joan saw the familiar change in the pupils as it died.

He said to Joan, "Now, take her into the copse. Not far; do nothing stupid. Look after her, I have a call to make."

As she helped her friend into the undergrowth, she heard Amaechi say, "Police. I have two women as hostages. I am holding them at gunpoint."

Joan focused on Hasanna, as they only thing she could do. It was too weird. He had called 999 and asked for the police.

~~

Gerry Lauder had never been seen to run inside the Undertow suite. The speed at which he went into Catrin's office wasn't a run, but it caught everyone's attention. Not to mention his call out to DI Wills, the closest senior officer, on his way.

"I want two units, lights and sirens, ready to go in five minutes. They are heading to Iver, Buckinghamshire. Tell the armourer that DCI Sayer and probably another officer will be drawing Glocks immediately."

He entered Sayer's office without knocking, where she was meeting with Collard. Catrin stood, missing that message but aware something was amiss.

"Catrin, you need to draw a personal firearm and head out. Karen called, insisting on the weapon. She's on her way out of the Yard now, heading for Akanni's home."

"What's happened?"

"Fifteen minutes ago, he shot his dog and called the police, telling them he is holding two women as hostages in the woods behind his house. Thames Valley Police have officers securing a perimeter, and an Armed Response Unit is on its way. Locals are holding the fort while they send a negotiator from headquarters. Apparently, Akanni threatens to kill them if he doesn't get to talk to Moore."

She let out a groan. "He's on to us. But–."

Why am I going, she was going to say?

Lauder added, "He also insists on a police officer called Sayer being with her. Both of you being present are a condition of their release. One is his wife, the other is her friend, a woman called Joan Lucas."

As Catrin stood there, taking it in, Lauder continued, "Their hands are zip-tied, it seems. The officers responding to the call say there is the top half of a dog and a mess of blood in the garden ten feet from the edge of the copse. He used the shotgun. That is all we know at present. I have two cars preparing, one to clear the way, the other to get you there. Take someone with you. Your call."

Catrin's mind went to the dog. Why the back end? Anyone killing an animal would go for the head. To make it more horrible, perhaps? To set a stage?

She automatically picked up her suit jacket and reached in the cupboard for her ballistic vest. Her equipment belt and holster were in there also As she did so, she called to Andy Collard who just stood, awaiting instructions.

"Take over for the rest of the day. Pick up the meetings I am booked for. Your discretion on next steps at each one but don't put anything off."

Collard nodded. "It's a pity that we don't have cameras in those woods already."

Her eyes fell on the officers currently available in the operations area, sifting out those with AFO status. Terry Jameson, Pauline Stillwell and Richard Roe. Roe was newly qualified. The look on his face showed he knew he was at the bottom of the heap.

Whatever it was, Catrin chose not to miss the opportunity to give a junior officer some experience.

"Roe, draw a weapon. Be ready in four minutes."

She turned and left the room. Richard bounded forward, asking, "Am I driving?" but his boss was out the door.

Lauder said, "Don't be silly, Roe. We need a proper driver, one who has been north of the Thames before. Go see the armourer."

As Roe moved to the door, Terry Jameson called, "Draw the gun..."

Roe yelled behind him, "... and you draw the vest also." He was gone.

Terry looked at Lauder. "I didn't even get the time to tell him what he should have done first."

Lauder smiled briefly and went back into his office. He had calls to make, people to inform.

DC Garry Stone, the newest member of Undertow, asked, "What should he have done, then?"

"What the boss just did. Go the bathroom."

~ ~

Lauder's black humour about his comfort zone being South London wasn't lost on Roe on the drive over. Close to Heathrow, the journey from Lavender Hill to Iver took twenty-nine minutes, about half the normal time he would have expected without lights, sirens and a constant flow of information to the drivers from Traffic Control.

Along the way, they heard the updates: the news of the arrival of the Armed Response Unit and the negotiator, an Inspector Liddle. The surrounding area had been closed off, including the roads in front of and behind the home, with officers dealing with the diversions.

As they arrived, Thames Valley Police had finished the evacuations of both houses directly across from Akanni's home and the houses either side.

As they left their vehicle and donned their ballistic vests, Richard saw three civilians standing with several uniformed officers inside the barricade tape, by a police car. One, he decided, must be the husband or partner of the Lucas woman, it was all over his face. The other man and an officer were trying to calm him. The woman was watching them.

Frances Coombs saw the police cars with the different markings arrive. They were from London, the Met. From the second vehicle, two people in plain clothes got out. Both were armed. They put on protective vests that were different from the others she had already seen. These two must be specialists called in to help, she concluded. She ran across, as they were admitted inside the barrier.

"Excuse me, excuse me!" She focused on Richard. "You have to get them out. Please! They are my friends."

Her voice was rising, angry. A local unformed officer was now behind her. "Mrs. Coombs, we need to let these people get on."

Frances continued, "I should have told Hasanna, I wanted her to leave him. I didn't..."

Richard was standing still, looking at her as Coombs burst into tears. The Thames Valley officer gently took her arm to steer her back.

Almost inanely, he thought, he said, "We will do what we can to help."

As he looked for his boss's response, he found that Sayer hadn't even stopped. She was now approaching Commander Moore. He hurried after her.

36 SHIELD

Commander Moore and DI Leigh were standing with several uniformed officers and a young, stocky woman in tactical gear. Moore wore a Thames Valley ballistic vest over her coat.

The name tape on the vest of the tactical officer said 'Craigh'. She wore a helmet with an integrated headset, the microphone sitting near her chin. Catrin addressed her first.

"DCI Sayer, with DC Roe, for Commander Moore."

Constable Craigh nodded, taking in Sayer's own vest and sidearm. "We are waiting on Inspector Liddle's instruction, ma'am. One moment."

She turned away, speaking into her microphone.

Karen Moore said, "Sayer, Akanni is still in the copse with the hostages. We are under their orders; it is a Thames Valley op."

Catrin nodded, but her primary focus was on Craigh, who turned back. "Sergeant Houseman asked me to verify you are trained as an executive security officer?"

Her eyes were assessing Sayer, noting her build, her

physical ability.

"For two years. And I am still AFO."

Craigh spoke into her mike to confirm Sayer's status, then said to her, "Inspector Liddle is making his decision on whether one or both of you go forward to join him during the negotiation. If both together, Sergeant Houseman asks are you prepared to shield?"

Moore said, "I don't need–."

To be cut off by Craigh. "It's not your choice. DCI Sayer?"

"I am up to it. Yes."

Roe, being used to Moore being omnipotent, felt some where between surprised and lost.

Craigh turned away and walked off to the nearby van. Inside, he could see another technician watching two screens.

Roe had seen the drone high over the trees. The controller, in uniform, stood near them, watching it and his control station, in a folding case, set up on its own stand. A standby drone sat connected to a charger unit, to be ready, if needed. Thames Valley were equipped similarly to the Met for these situations, it seemed.

It took only a minute, a long minute, until Craigh returned with another member of her team. They heard her speaking to Houseman. "Separately. The commander first. Confirmed."

She turned. "Commander Moore, please go with this officer to the rear of the house and wait, in view, at the corner. You do not move until called. Then you walk slowly to the man in the centre, Inspector Liddle. He is alone and his vest is marked 'Negotiator'. Liddle is standing by a flowerbed about twenty yards into the garden. You must stay on his left side as you face forward. Have you got all that, ma'am?"

Moore arched her eyebrows. "To the back, visible, wait, left side. Yes."

In seconds, she walked beside the tactical officer, heading into the garden. Roe suddenly caught sight of John Leigh looking a little lost before he pulled out his mobile, to report back to the Yard, no doubt.

Craigh said to Sayer, "She is bristling to talk to the target. Liddle's not happy with that."

Neither am I, thought Catrin. But now is not the moment to train Commander Moore in hostage retrieval. She looked at Roe, who appeared ready to ask a question. She put her finger to her lips and then faced Craigh, the woman in her late-twenties, the constable who was in charge.

Rank was irrelevant in a hostage situation, Roe knew. He had just seen it demonstrated. In the command structure, the negotiator and the armed response leader were in frontline command, with clear but differentiated responsibilities. The former officer's goal is to talk the crisis to a peaceful outcome, the latter to act unilaterally at his or her discretion if the hostages or others are in risk of imminent injury or death.

After listening to something, Craigh said to Sayer, "He will get one hostage out, then show you to the target, to get the second. We need him out in the open."

Sayer nodded. "Too intermittent, I take it?"

The sighting of Akanni by the Armed Response team.

Craigh nodded. "The trees, but the breeze is also making it more difficult, yes."

Catrin asked, "What's he got? He has a registered shotgun, we found that out yesterday."

"That's it. A Westley Richards 20 gauge, a traditional double, so he has two shots without reloading. He fires birdshot shells in it, we understand. Checking the house, that's all the ammunition we see there and, from what we hear about his use of the weapon, he only blasts away at crows and pigeons. One moment."

She was listening.

Craigh picked up where she left off. "The damage to the dog fits the pattern, but why the back end, we don't know. Houseman has put the negotiator position at seventy metres from the copse, behind a raised flower-bed. No one is to be closer than that without his author-isation."

Effectively out of range of serious damage by birdshot, Roe understood. And with the flowerbed, a shield to drop behind. Not completely, but also enough to allow visual sighting and communication if people raised their voices.

Sayer asked, "How do you read him?"

"He was agitated at first, but now he has calmed down. The inspector has helped there."

"Calm as in listening to reason, or as in SBC?"

It took Roe a moment. SBC; Suicide by Cop.

Craigh shrugged. "I'm not up front. Houseman says it's the resignation on his face. We think he wants his last hurrah with your boss, and you, for some reason, Then he'll try to blow your heads off or his own. Or fake it, so we do it for him."

Roe could see her concentrate, listening.

She said into her mike, "OK. Confirmed."

Her hand went over the mike. "You will mirror what I said to the commander, but when you are called forward, walk half-way only. No further. Liddle wants to get the commander back then, with the ploy that she sees you are hesitant, and she is coming back to encourage you to go forward. When she gets within range, take her to the floor. We will move officers in front, shielding."

Sayer nodded. "It still leaves the walk back. And if he

has slugs..."

Roe realised that his boss was referring to solid ammunition for a shotgun, as opposed to the casings of pellets. The thought had not crossed his mind.

Craigh looked at Sayer with fresh eyes. "It's our main worry. We just want to take him out, for exactly that risk. Houseman will call it if he sees the gun move."

Sayer said, "Substitute me. Put me with the hostage retrieval team. I'll peel off and give you both the shield for Moore and the control of the timing. Check with him."

Now Roe was completely lost.

Craigh said nothing to her, just turned and spoke into her mike. Then she waited, silent. Fifteen seconds later, she said, "He'll go with it."

She looked around her. "Kennedy, you are up. Your hat, please. Put on this officer's jacket and vest. Wolsley, give DCI Sayer your vest."

Roe saw that Catrin was undoing her vest. She said, "Roe, you won't do. Wrong gender and dark hair, or I would use you."

As she removed her suit jacket, Craigh said to the officer called Kennedy, "Wear this. When ready and in the vest, you go stand where Inspector Liddle said, with him, DC Roe. You will be DCI Sayer. You start walking when called, but go no further than halfway to the Commander and DI Liddle. Got it? Not a step nearer."

Craigh looked at a tall, well-built officer in regular uniform, now also wearing a ballistic vest. "Hurst, take DCI Sayer with you for retrieval. You do the talking. We don't know if he would recognize Sayer's voice."

Roe now had an inkling of what was happening but wasn't at all clear how it was going to unfold. He was struck by the fact that, after hours of training and practice as an Authorised Firearms Officer, he was finally armed and in a real situation, but with people who sounded as if they had done all this for real before.

When the group went around the corner at the call from Liddle, Roe stood with PC Kennedy, now in his boss's jacket and a Met ballistic vest. His first sight was the dog, or what was left of it, near the bushes, a hundred yards away at the end of a well-kept lawn surrounded by an array of flowerbeds. Blood and death among floral beauty. It was stark.

Moore was now nearing Inpector Liddle, standing in tactical gear at the flowerbed, to join him on his left side, both about thirty yards in front of their own group.

Sayer, in the Thames Valley bowler hat with the chequered band, followed the other officer, Hurst, as they made an angle between the negotiators and a tactical officer with his weapon trained on the woods beyond. Another tactical officer, with a vest bearing the markings 'LEAD' on the back, was further forward, on the same side. That must be Sergeant Houseman, Roe thought.

Two more armed officers were in parallel positions at the other side of the garden, their rifles raised, focused on the copse.

Inspector Liddle called out as Moore arrived. "That's far enough. No further, ma'am." That was for Akanni's benefit. He switched on the megaphone.

"Amaechi, Commander Moore is here with me. You can see her. Send out Hasanna and Joan. That's what we discussed. I'm sending two police officers nearer to you, to help them back."

The voice came from the thicket. "Where's the other one, this Sayer?"

Liddle responded, "She's here, in the suit jacket, by the

house."

"Hasanna can go but Joan stays with me, until I see Sayer moving."

Moore turned, looking back at the cluster of officers by the house, suddenly seeing Roe standing by another officer in Catrin's jacket. Sayer, now wearing a uniform hat, was with another officer. Moore stared for a moment but gave nothing away.

Liddle said, "Sayer will come forward to talk only when Hasanna is safe. You can talk to both officers then."

Several moments later, a tall, slim, black woman came stumbling out of the copse, her hands tied in some fashion. Catrin and Hurst move forward rapidly, beckoning, encouraging her.

Catrin saw that Hasanna Akanni was terror-stricken, her eyes moving between them and the remains of the labradoodle, now the focus of flies and other insects. Akanni's wife gave it a wide berth as she came past, her knees visibly shaking. At some point she had vomited and not quite missed her legging below the knee, from the stain. The leggings were scratched and torn from branches or thorns. Hasanna was wearing a T-shirt, now torn open at the top. It all added to her state of fear and dejectedness. Her hands were raised, one pressing the torn cloth over her chest; a remnant of modesty in the hell she was going through. For her husband to treat her this way must be mind-numbing, Catrin thought.

"Don't look there, look at us. Come on, Hasanna, keep going. That's right. Look at me now. At me." It was Hurst who kept up the litany, encouraging the hostage. Catrin just beckoned, unable to speak.

It must have been as, through the tears, Hurst came

into focus and Hasanna stopped and took a step back.

Catrin whispered, "Let me."

She moved forward, saying softly, "Not far, Hasanna, not far now."

Hasanna moved forward into her arms. As Catrin held her, the odours of sweat, vomit and urine mixing in her nostrils, she found herself looking at the foliage and Amaechi Akanni's face, looking at her and Hasanna. She couldn't read the expression; it was not neutral or gloating, just interested.

Catrin switched her gaze, looking for the other hostage, Lucas, to give her a nod, a hope, as sign that she was next. She couldn't see her.

Suddenly Hurst was past her, in front of them both, his big frame shielding them as best as he could. His arm reached around, almost lifting the hostage as he spoke to her, propelling them forward. As Catrin turned to face the same way, Hasanna's T-shirt opened. Catrin caught a glimpse of the blood, the scrape and the cut caused by a signet ring or wedding ring. It ran across her cleavage, the top of her right breast and up to the collar bone above.

As they helped her back, the thought of the parallel image, the knife wound that killed Sofia, flashed across her mind and with it came Catrin's decision on her final move.

As they passed the point where Karen Moore and Liddle stood, Sayer simply peeled off, moving closer to her boss, staying a few feet away from the negotiating pair. She drew her weapon but pointed it at the ground, as if she were there simply to help protect the negotiating team.

Liddle whispered to Moore who called out, "Amaechi, come on out, with Joan. I want to see Joan. It's time. I want to talk to you."

37 CONFRONTATION

The silence continued as they saw a movement in the treeline. Catrin heard a sniper near the fence say into his radio, "He's moving closer. Target is out now."

Seventy yards away, Akanni stepped into view, holding with his left hand the upper arm of an older woman, similarly tied. They stopped a few feet clear of the copse. Akanni appeared calm, standing still. His shotgun was in his right hand, the index finger inside the trigger guard. Even at this distance it gave Catrin a momentary shiver. Police officers hate shotguns more than rifles.

Akanni yelled, "Call Sayer forward now. I want to talk to her, too. That's the deal. And Joan gets to walk, just walk."

Karen called back. "Why Amaechi? Sayer is only a member of my team. Do you know how many people report to me? I'm not a sergeant anymore. What's this about?"

The negotiator spoke up, his voice more powerful over the megaphone. "Put the gun down, Amaechi, and we will talk all you want. Place it carefully on the ground.

There are armed officers covering you, as you see. Do exactly as I say."

He hoped for but had no expectation of acquiescence. At least it was on record.

Akanni called back, "I just want to talk to Karen and this person Sayer."

His eyes were on Moore only now. "It's time, you just said. Well, I saw that sooner than you intended, didn't I? You are the one scrambling to get here now. I surprised you, not the other way around. When were you coming for me?"

Akanni's voice sounded as if he had won a prize.

In the preparations with the negotiator before Sayer's arrival, they had agreed that Karen's first response should be passive innocence.

Moore said, "Why, Charlie? I used to call you that, remember? You've done really well for yourself. Why all this, now? You have everything, a wonderful home, success and money. Why are you making a problem like this?"

He retorted, "Amaechi, it's not Charles anymore." His face appeared angry; intense. "I beat you eventually."

Moore responded, with a forced levity, "All that's happened is you are going to be interviewed about tax and duty issues around the import of art. That's no big deal in the scheme of things. Pay the fines or whatever transpires. Move on. Put the gun down and we can sort it out."

Akanni burst out laughing. "You, Karen, should work for me, you lie so beautifully. Pay the fine or do the time, isn't that the phrase? You missed that bit. If you want Joan, bring up Sayer. Now."

Moore took a step forward.

"Ma'am, stop." Liddle said quietly.

Karen focused on Akanni. It was only a yard, but ahead slightly of the others now, she felt more in control. Her voice became more combative. "You want to know why I am after you? You fell into my lap, that's why. As soon as the Welsh Police raised Rel-Comm with us, I was on to it. I have followed your progress and knew you started Rel-Comm, but I never thought of it as bent until Cardiff told me about the scam. After that, it was a priority for me."

Akanni nodded. "Sayer, remember?"

Karen spoke to Liddle. He signalled back to the group by the house. Kennedy started moving forward. Craigh's last words to her were that she should move slowly and under no circumstances cover more than half-way between the rear of the house and Moore. Even if she had to fumble with a shoe or something, she would hold to that.

Akanni called out, "Can we get serious, Karen? Cut the crap. I had the Welsh copper's hand smashed just to confirm that it was you after me. I didn't know at the time, but thought it was likely. At least talk about why you are hounding me now, after all this time."

Moore responded, "When Anne disappeared, you became a focus for me. Even when I was a sergeant. You still are. Where is she, what did you do with her?"

Inaudible to all but Moore and Sayer, Liddle gave an exasperated sigh.

The issue of the missing former girlfriend was absolutely the last resort for the negotiator, Catrin concluded, and Akanni was still holding Joan Lucas.

Akanni nodded, as if he had finally arrived where he wanted to be with Karen Moore.

Kennedy was now half-way. She stopped, staring at Moore and Liddle, who held his arm out, signalling her to come no further.

Liddle improvised. "Release Joan now, or there won't be another word. That's an order, Commander."

Akanni let go of Joan Lucas's arm and said something to her, and she started walking slowly, following the route that Hasanna had taken, up the same side of the garden, at an angle. Hurst, the tall officer, was back, moving down the lawn, beckoning to Lucas. She was crying, but also had a determined expression, as she took one firm step after another.

Liddle's arm was still out, implying that he would only lower it if Lucas made it to the safe zone unharmed. It was a lie, Catrin knew.

Akanni suffered the delusion of other gunmen, that he controlled the timing and could get one or more shots off. He would try to shoot Lucas or Moore, thinking that the rifles were focused on him, that there would be time.

They weren't, in the way he understood it. And he had no time. These snipers were focused on specific spots; the head, the heart, the elbow joint of the gun arm, each officer having a clear line to their target area. The aim was to immobilize the weapon instantly. That he would die in the process was irrelevant to them. They would act as soon as he crystallised his thinking into action and before he could do any damage.

Moore prodded further. "Is she in there, in the copse? We know you bought the woodland before the house. You have had it for years. Is it her graveyard?"

Akanni smiled. "Anne's there, yes. You have me on that one, at last. You killed her, Karen, not me. You, the hotshot sergeant. I had nothing then, not the money I have now. I had nothing! When I scammed my start-up money, you should have left it alone!"

Catrin saw that Joan Lucas was now nearing Constable

Hurst. As before, he would wrap his arm around the woman, getting himself and his ballistic vest between the shotgun and the hostage. It was going to be now if it happened at all. Her eyes focused on the shotgun barrels, still directed at the ground, apparently carelessly pointed equidistant between Moore in the middle and Lucas to one side. In fact, in a line almost directly towards herself.

As Joan Lucas reached Constable Hurst, she sobbed, letting it go. He began moving her away.

Catrin knew what was happening now. She wasn't connected into the Armed Response Unit radio-communication, but she looked at Houseman and they understood each other. Amaechi Akanni didn't have birdshot in the shotgun. Until that point, he had a target for birdshot. Lucas had been in range and available. Now he was going for Moore. It wasn't birdshot; he had slugs in the gun.

Liddle spoke up again. "There is no need to make this harder on yourself or Hasanna and Joan. You have put them through a lot. Lose the firearm and get the chance to talk to them, to explain. There is a way out of this, Amaechi. There is a positive path forward for all. Listen to me now, and only to me."

He was telling Moore to stay silent. But looking at Akanni's face, it was as if as he hadn't spoken.

In the brief silence, Moore spoke up calmly, her voice loud enough to carry, but her tone softer now. "It's over now. Let's do this peacefully, Amaechi. You've told us. We'll get her buried properly, for her family. For you, too. I know you cared for her."

It seemed to anger rather than appease Akanni.

"Cared! I loved her! Still do. You should have left Anne out of it! Not turned my girlfriend into your informer. If I can charm people into believing my lies, you bully people into believing yours. I had no choice. She was your evidence, I had to stop that before it made it worse for me. She had to go."

"No, she didn't. She didn't deserve to die for telling the truth. Again, why Sayer, Amaechi? Why her?"

"The Welsh woman, the police sergeant, confirmed it was you that was after me. But I learned that the person who got Olowe to talk was called Sayer. I didn't think he would turn on us. Karen. I really didn't. Then yesterday, what do I hear from people in KL? That a British police officer called Sayer interviewed Omar. What a coincidence! And then Hasanna talks about a police officer visiting."

"Sayer's just an officer. It could have been anyone."

Thanks for that, thought Catrin; I think.

He sneered. "No. I don't think so. I think she does your dirty work, a bully like you, Karen. I have worked that out. In the end I won, your con failed. It's over, I won."

Moore said calmly and very quietly, "I want you both to move away slowly. Liddle, move to your right and back, and you, officer, to your left and back. That's a direct order."

She glanced at Liddle and Sayer as she spoke to each of them.

Liddle grimaced at the message, ignoring it and looked at Catrin. Moore had no right to do this, was on his face.

Karen called out to Akanni. "No more discussion. Put the gun down now, Akanni. I am arresting you for the murder of Anne Krell."

It is not the way it works, thought Catrin. I am a trained security officer. You instructed me to be armed.

She took three quick steps forward at an angle, placing herself two feet directly in front of Moore and calling out loudly and clearly, "I am Sayer. Place your weapon on the ground, now!"

Her gun swung up, both arms out in front, sighting the weapon in a classic firing stance as she spoke. She saw his expression change. Surprise, then anger.

As the tip of the shotgun barrel started to rise, she didn't fire. She knew she didn't need to. His head turned red on one side as his neck snapped back and two further shots to his body twisted him as he fell. He lay on one side, one arm moving a little, then it stopped. Catrin had heard three shots.

The image of the Malaysian man, Loh Ghee, she took down years ago flashed into her thoughts, brought on by the same sudden red stains and spurts of blood, albeit, thankfully, at a longer distance away. She closed her eyes for an instant, her senses now focusing on the noises; the sound of birds, the crows, pigeons and others taking off and rising in the air.

As she looked down the garden again, a squirrel ran into the lawn towards the dog, turned, then ran sideways, up a trellis.

The following silence was broken only by the echoes and the Armed Response officers running, causing the squirrel to reverse its course and disappear in the trees. Under other circumstances, it would be comical. Houseman was giving instructions to his team; she could hear his voice as he talked into his microphone.

Catrin holstered her Glock and turned around. Moore just looked at her, silent, as the tactical officers reached the body. Inspector Liddle walked closer to Moore and Sayer.

He said, tonelessly, "It was over when he said, 'I beat you eventually'. He was waiting it out, trying to get you both. That bit by you, ma'am, stepping forward, the body in the copse thing, was out of line. That was my call. Not yours."

He was focused on Moore as he spoke, but he stopped as she looked at him, her anger rising visible. She was still a far more senior officer.

Moore shook her head. "I hoped…"

One of the officers who removed the shotgun from the body was examining it, rendering it safe and ejecting the shells. He said something into his radio to his unit leader.

Houseman called to Liddle as he walked across to them. "Slug shot, both barrels, Federals."

Akanni could have killed anyone, either by good marksmanship or by chance, Sayer understood. Slugs would have reached the house with lethal force, probably the road beyond. Catrin looked at Houseman as he joined them, but he was focused on Moore. "Federals are rifled slugs, ma'am. They would have taken both you and DCI Sayer down if he were anywhere near accurate."

Moore snapped back, "You two should have left him to me. I could have talked him through it."

She glared at Catrin. "And Gerry says I am the hard one. You had to tell him, didn't you?"

That she was Sayer, not a Thames Valley officer who had moved forward. That he had his ducks lined up in a row.

Catrin stared back, keeping her face impassive, saying nothing, containing her rising annoyance. I promised the armed response team the timing, she thought, not leaving it to Akanni's impulses as Moore talked to him. The snipers had been accurate, but her job was to shield Moore and minimize the risk of a slug coming their way.

Houseman spoke up more agressively. "I take it you didn't hear me first time."

There was no 'ma'am' now. His voice was abrasive, irritated. "The shotgun contained rifled slugs, despite all his efforts to disguise the fact, to demonstrate he only used birdshot. He shot the dog in the back end to emphasize the point; it made a greater mess than taking its head off. His sole objective was to get you and DCI Sayer here and shoot you. There was no way in hell we–."

His arm circled, pointing at Liddle, Sayer and himself.

"– were going to allow that man to discharge a weapon at a commander of the Metropolitan Police. This is our environment, not yours; it's not bloody Hollywood."

He turned and walked off. Moore, angrier still now at the Thames Valley sergeant, glared at his back, then at Sayer, before turning and walking towards the house without another word, as John Leigh ran up to her.

Roe walked past them both to be with Sayer.

Liddle shook his head. "Nor is it a movie set at Pinewood Studios. That would be more appropriate around here."

They could hear crying now from the front of the house, presumably Joan Lucas and Hasanna Akanni, hearing the shots, understanding their meaning.

Richard thought that the women were probably under the impressions that Amaechi had gone off his head. They were going to learn a lot more soon. The last thing Thames Valley Police or the Met needed was an accusation of lethal force against a mentally deranged person.

38 FRIENDS

They moved Hasanna to an ambulance, wrapped in a blanket, where they were comforting her and checking her blood pressure and heart rate. Once they had inserted a drip line, to allow intravenous medication, the team let Frances Coombs through to be with her. Somehow, that helped break the almost catatonic terror. Hasanna was now sobbing, holding her.

As Joan Lucas came around the corner, now supported by a female police officer but still walking by herself, Hasanna called out. It wasn't clear what she said, but there was relief in the sound. Joan rushed forward as paramedics came to put her in another ambulance, and John Lucas ran up to embrace his wife.

Joan had stopped crying and her face was grim. The bruise on her head from Akanni's blow was livid and already turning yellow and blue. Her arms had scrapes and scratches, and one knee was bleeding freely from a deep cut or scratch.

As John stepped back, sensing the stiffness in her, Joan said, "I need a shower and some clean clothes, ones that don't smell of urine. Then I want a cup of strong tea and to be with my husband and my friends. I need to be with Hasanna. I am still a qualified nurse, and she is my friend."

She stood still, immovable, looking sympathetically at Hasanna Akanni. The police officer with her wondered what they went through in the copse.

Then the sound of rifle fire reached them and Hasanna fell apart, her hands covering her face as the cry of anguish came.

The paramedics looked at each other. The ambulance containing Hasanna closed its door as the vehicle started its engine.

The second paramedic focused on Joan. With the woman's husband, she persuaded the second hostage into her own ambulance.

When Frances Coombs heard Hasanna scream, and the ambulance doors closed, she wondered if Hasanna's pain was from the experience of losing her husband or the fear of freedom, with no one controlling her.

She said softly, as she held Hasanna's hand, "We are going to get you through this. Me and Joan, John and Simon. We are your friends. We will get you through this, Hasanna, together. Hear me? You are going to be okay."

She moved back to the vacant seat as the paramedic made Hasanna lie flat. As something was injected into the intravenous drip, Hasanna closed her eyes.

~~

Inspector Liddle looked at Sayer. "Was there a thinly-disguised thank you buried anywhere in the criticism from the commander, do you think?"

Catrin said, "With Commander Moore, it's hard to say. I suspect that I will find out in due course. She was desperate to arrest Akanni; that's the basis for her anger. At least he didn't get one off at us."

Liddle said, "You knew, ma'am, when Akanni let Lucas move out of range, that he probably had slugs? I saw you glance over at Houseman."

"I thought it likely. By revisiting old wounds with Akanni, she prevented you telling the man he was dead before he moved, so give up."

Liddle nodded.

She focused on Roe, who was staring past her. "Richard, how are you doing?"

He had moved forward a few yards, looking at the dog and the man's body, yards away, both with blood around them and now with uniformed officers nearby, protecting the scene. The tactical team had withdrawn and re-grouped. There were procedures to be followed.

"Doing? I didn't do anything," he replied as he turned back. "Not like you."

As he spoke, the officer who substituted for Catrin, Constable Kennedy, approached holding out her jacket, neatly folded, and her ballistic vest. Catrin returned her hat saying, "Thank you. You did well.'

It was the first smile she had seen that morning. She removed the Thames Valley vest, returning it to Kennedy and put on her suit jacket.

Kennedy said, "Ma'am, it's sad that it came to this."

Catrin responded quietly as she pointed. "In those trees where he held the hostages is a body of a young woman, we believe. She told the truth about him years ago and died for doing so. That's a lot sadder, I think."

The women looked at the copse of trees. As they did so, some of the returning crows started cawing, expressing their annoyance at the disturbance, it seemed. It may be that Amaechi Akanni blasted away at them, but they seemed to be calling out that they had the last laugh.

Catrin thought of Emmie Shand and Sofia binti Awang; of the wreckage caused by the trickster, and of a remark by Jared Farra on leaving the interview room in Kuala Lumpur. He hoped it would be worth it.

In the end, it was. Akanni wouldn't be manipulating anyone else to come after Moore or her now, nor would he destroy the lives of others to feed his vanity as a con artist. All that money he earned, all his businesses, were not enough. He had to cheat others and bring a new generation of con artists up the same way.

They left the Thames Valley officer and walked slowly back to the house. Roe, walking beside her, asked, "Are you OK, ma'am?"

She nodded. "And you? I pulled you into this for experience. I didn't say it would be pleasant, or plan for you to be part of it."

"I'm good, ma'am. And I appreciate the chance to be here. But I think, unless they need you now, we should go. Do you need to be stay here with the commander?"

Roe and his constant questions, she thought. Catrin looked at Moore, now talking with the negotiator and another, more senior Thames Valley officer. Moore would be away soon, back to New Scotland Yard, she was sure.

"No, let's go, if we can. We have weapons to return to the armourer. Procedure requires me to report to the Incident Command Team here now, whoever that may be. Let's find out."

In the end, a uniformed officer took a verbal statement from Catrin. It didn't take long. She would prepare her own written report later today.

As they headed for the car, Catrin said, "When you get back, take Terry Jameson for a drink. It's your first one, and you should talk to someone who has been there."

"He'll pull my leg about it again, like when I left."

"Not when someone comes back, only on the way out. He'll be good, I'll guarantee it. Good for you, I mean."

"And you, ma'am?"

Will she call her husband? Roe knew he worked at the Met.

"I'll talk to my husband and leave early, then go around to my friends in Spitalfields. I will do something normal, focus on my pottery or collect my daughter from the nanny early."

"She'll like that."

Catrin said dryly, "Perhaps. Last time I did it, she told me off. She and Chloe, that's the nanny, had work to do, she said. She was busy. In the end, she graciously allowed me to help her make the Play-Doh cakes."

~~

In the Prince of Wales, later that day, Terry explained it to Roe.

"She's had a lot more training, for one thing. Security Officers and Armed Response Officers train together. They have different roles in the incident response."

Loretta Hills added, "And she has been at the front end before."

Richard was near the bottom of his first pint. "I felt so helpless."

Terry said, "That's because you had nothing to do. With a task, you just do it, focus on it. That's what the boss did, by the sound of it. Look, everyone would be worrying about the shotgun. Her worry would be that he would use it on the women. Once he was out in the open and they were free, it was no issue. Four snipers; he either put it down or was dropped still holding it. And that's what happened."

"She still jumped fast in front of Moore, protecting her, with her Glock pointed at Akanni."

Terry looked out through the window into the street, as the sudden rain shower arrived.

"Yes, I guess so. Training again."

That was for a different reason, he concluded, from Roe's recount of the event. But they didn't need to go there.

He smiled. "You are through it. Stone is still waiting for the psych test for suitability for AFO training, never mind get to a scene like that. They could declare him a nutbar and that would be that. We would have to keep him a cupboard in the office until he could be transferred out. Loretta, it's your shout, I think."

Garry Stone smiled, taking the jibe. He was the designated driver, to drop Loretta and Richard off at their homes. Jameson would take the Tube, he said, as usual.

Roe mused on it a moment. "But the swap with Constable Kennedy and then the boss's callout at the end, that she was there already; she tricked the trickster."

Loretta had stood, to go to the bar. She gave Terry a knowing look then smiled at Roe. "Putting it that way, I suppose she did."

Richard mused, "I'm glad I went, so next time will be easier."

"No, it won't," said Loretta. "It will be different, that's all. You will still come out feeling glad it is over. Going in, you will understand it better." She smiled at Jameson.

"Hills, Roe's dying of thirst here. Get them in."

39 AFTERMATH

It was late the following day when Gerry Lauder called Sayer into his office.

"Things should return to normal for a while, I hope. Between you and me, Karen is taking a holiday. Tom Sleiman's choice, not hers. It's been a ride, particularly for you, I know, but also for people here. I'm still worried about Tully."

"It'll take time. I've talked to her. The visit to KL helped a lot. She sees a counsellor, too."

"At least Ken and I won't have to stand in for you. Team A needs the consistency at present. But how are you doing? Straight up, now."

Catrin thought for a moment. "I'm more shaken by the aftermath of the Nine Elms killing than the events yesterday."

Lauder's face showed he understood that. "You should talk to your own counsellor, perhaps? I'll leave that up to you."

Catrin paused. "I saw Kuala Lumpur properly again with my friend Jian Li, and I got to meet my godson, face-to-face. That was good for me. I focus on that. But I will visit Dr. Herrington. He is good at picking up on the things I skip over, checking my denial meter."

Her boss was listening but focused on assessing her, she saw. "It's your call. I'm not forcing you. But I agree."

He changed the subject. "Karen's guilt following the disappearance of Anne Krell drove a lot of this case, as you know. Back then we were less effective in dealing with trauma around events. Vic Holsworth believes that counselling could have moderated her mania to follow up with Akanni. I don't agree."

"Nor do I. The commander would never let it go. Nor would you, or me. If a person disappears because you involved them to be a witness in a case, it stays with you."

Lauder spoke carefully now. She could hear the edge in his voice.

"I spoke to Karen's driver. She never said a word in the car coming back."

He picked up a piece of paper, a printout of Catrin's report.

"You went by the book, except, according to the report by the negotiator, you spoke up at the end. You included that item in your report, as well. Inspector Liddle claims Karen screwed up his negotiation strategy. He put it more delicately than that, but his meaning is clear."

She didn't comment, just waited.

"According to Liddle, there was a possibility of an arrest, as Akanni felt he had won; that our undercover investigation had failed to surprise him. The commander got in the way of him working that angle in his negotiation. He also stated that the probability of an arrest was low."

Her boss scanned another page. "Sergeant Houseman

is a very experienced Armed Response officer. His report concluded that Akanni was totally on a trajectory for 'suicide by cop' from the first exchanges with Liddle."

Catrin said, "I agree. It came up at the pre-briefing; Houseman's team member made it clear there."

She could see he knew. But all he asked was, "Anything else?"

"No, boss."

He sniffed and moved on. "Thames Valley found Anne Krell. Karen's been told. They are having Vic break the news to Anne's parents, that it still needs forensic confirmation, but it looks to be her. He may have already done that by now.

"What the Commander hasn't been told, what she won't be told until she returns from holiday, is that the dogs located another body in the copse. There may be more. Max Owens, my opposite number in Thames Valley, is pleased, but wanting more resources. He told me that the Met should be supporting it financially, dumping our bodies on his patch. I gave him an appropriate response. All he gets is a good dinner."

He gave a sigh, pushed the paper into a file folder and interlocked his fingers. "It seems to me that the outcome was for the best, all things considered. Akanni was wealthy through legitimate means. In prison, he would still have access to it indirectly and we have sufficient experience of him to show he was a vicious egotist, who would focus on retribution. I have spoken to Alec Williams in Cardiff regarding Akanni's comment about Olowe, in case he had already arranged something to happen to him. They talked to Cardiff Prison, who are thinking of transferring him, to be on the safe side."

"That's good thinking."

She was through it, she saw. Lauder was ready to close

out and move on.

"One more thing, DI Collard says that this man Gregory Clewes, your Warminster Transport friend, wants to talk. He has something he thinks he can trade."

The Warminster case.

"He may have thought on it and have something useful to offer. Can you deal with it?"

"Yes, I'll follow up."

"Catrin, you did a good job. Hopefully, things will get a little easier. I'm here, if you ever want to talk, on or off the record. Got that?"

"Yes, I appreciate it. Thank you."

She broke eye contact and headed to the door.

As she walked back to her desk, she pondered on the fact that, glancing at his printout of her report upside down, Lauder had pencil marks underlining phrases in several places, some annotations and one word, really an abbreviation, scribbled in the margin. The areas he had not touched on in his discussion were two of those; one underlined, about her raising her firearm as she spoke to Akanni. It was a classic security action; to get in front of the target and raise the weapon to return fire. At the side, in the margin, were the letters 'l.o.s.'. Line of sight.

She had seen the brief smile on Akanni's face before the anger, as she confirmed her identity and he had both his desired targets lined up neatly. She wasn't sure whether the shotgun was raised because he now had what he wanted, or he instinctively imitated her action as she sighted her weapon on him. The breech of the shotgun was closed. No armed response officer would wait as the barrels were raised.

Either way, it did not bother her. Akanni's callous, offhand comment about Emmie Shand had hit home, as had his treatment of the women yesterday. Her experience in Kuala Lumpur, in being part of Kaur's sentencing restrictions, came back forcefully, too. She owed it to binti Awang. Now Amaechi Akanni had focused on Karen Moore and her.

Enough was enough.

~~

Two weeks later, Richard Roe decided that the one thing he must not do is tell anyone in Undertow that he had seen Commander Moore cry. It was so surprising, and after the comment by her to Andy Collard, retold now in Undertow as, 'The Rain Man story', he would be lynched by Moore if it got back to her.

The funeral for Anne Krell was held at St. Saviour's, a Roman Catholic church in Lewisham. Roe was glad he was near the back. It was a large, ornate church inside, not something he was familiar with. The back gave him anonymity, at least.

Moore had been seated with Vic Holsworth near Anne Krell's parents and family at the front. June Mortimer and what he took to be some current and former CID team members were clustered further back on another row.

His decision to come to the funeral linked to his presence at the hostage incident, specifically his adjustment to the sight of first, the dead dog, then the man. Particularly, it was in seeing Akanni change from being an arrogant gunman to a body collapsed on the ground, bleeding out. What had stuck with him most, though, was his boss's comment to PC Kennedy immediately afterwards, that the victim there was really Anne Krell, believed to be buried in the woods. All through the event, he realised, she thought of Anne as a person. He had thought of her only as a body, a victim.

It seemed right to attend. He just didn't mention it to anyone else.

When he emerged afterwards in the crowd of people, he suddenly saw three women together walking away from the church; Hasanna Akanni, Joan Lucas and the woman who had approached them as they arrived at the hostage scene. Two men in suits that were better quality than his own were with them. Joan was holding Hasanna's hand. They had been in the copse, facing death, and Anne was there already. He wondered whether they felt a bond with her.

From their direction, they, like Roe, were not going to the reception in the church hall, that was clear. Others were passing them, heading there, or away.

Perhaps because he stared at them, surprised, the woman who approached Sayer and himself said something and they stopped. She walked back to him.

"Hello. I'm Frances Coombs, Hasanna's friend. You were with the other officer, I remember. Do you remember us? You said you would do what you could."

Roe gave a brief nod. "Yes. I remember you, ma'am. How is Mrs. Akanni and Mrs. Lucas?"

Coombs gave a smile and grimace. "Hasanna is not so good, still adjusting. Joan is Joan, she's fine. Hasanna decided she wanted to come to the funeral. We didn't think it was a good idea, but we are doing what we can to help her."

She hesitated. "Was it... I don't know how to describe it? We know the outcome and understand more of the background, as horrid as it is. But we were on one side of the house and Hasanna became a widow on the other."

Roe knew he was on dicey ground. "Everyone did what they could to resolve it peacefully, I assure you. I saw that. It was my first time, so it was new, but... everyone tried their best."

She whispered, "And it was quick, was it? They said it was."

Roe responded, "Almost instantaneous, I think."

She nodded, apparently satisfied. Then she looked up as two shadows fell across them. People had come up behind him, he realised. In the same instant, he saw Hasanna Akanni move swiftly towards them, followed more slowly by her other friends.

Behind him, as he turned, he saw Commander Moore and a member of the clergy, a younger man than the priest who had led the service. Moore appeared less composed than usual, and, in her face, he suddenly saw her age and that she had been crying. She was an older, tired woman now, not the tyrant from Scotland Yard.

She said quietly, "DC Roe," and looked at Coombs, as Hasanna Akanni reached them.

Hasanna said directly to Moore, "I saw you, as they helped me back. Thank you. I am so sorry..."

"You have absolutely nothing to be sorry for, Mrs. Akanni. My condolences to you. Gerry?"

The young priest said softly, "I am Gerry Krell, Anne's younger brother. Karen explained who you are. My parents and family would very much like you all to join us inside."

Hasanna started to reply that she could not possibly intrude under the circumstances, as he cut her off gently.

"We are all victims here and need God's help. Please, it would mean a lot to them, and particularly so to me."

Gerald Krell was struck by the similarities between Mrs. Akanni and his sister, the facial features, the similar slim body. They would never be mistaken for each other, but still, both were beautiful black women. It brought back memories of his sister and, if anything, his heart went out to Hasanna Akanni more.

Roe got the impression that the priest wasn't excluding anyone from being a victim, particularly not Moore. Krell had glanced at both Joan and Hasanna as he spoke and then deliberately at Karen Moore.

As Hasanna Akanni took a breath and acquiesced, thanking him, he smiled and turned, pointing the way. Her friends and Hasanna walked alongside him. Richard took a step back, preparing to turn and leave.

Moore looked at him, stony-faced.

"I have to get back, ma'am. I only took a couple of hours off."

She shook her head. "Father Krell said everyone. His was an invitation. Mine is an order. We can have a little chat, catch up. First, why did you come today?"

The face may have fooled him, but the voice reminded him of his plight. In Undertow, the phrase that Karen Moore would have 'a little chat with you' was one of the great threats of life, along with, 'Lauder will have a word in your ear' or, 'you are on the verge of being transferred to uniform duties in High Barnet'.

Perhaps he could escape by talking to a priest?

As he walked up the steps, letting Moore enter first, he replied, "It was some things DCI Sayer said in Iver, ma'am; they resonated with me."

It was a Roman Catholic church, after all. He had been told that confession was good for the soul.

40 LECTURE

At ten a.m. in Lecture Theatre 4 at the University of South London campus, the door opened and, instead of Professor Ward entering with his breezy opening comments, the Dean of the Faculty of Business Studies led two other people, both considerably younger than him, to the front of the room. The black male was in a suit and priest's clerical collar, wearing a pectoral cross. The white female, slightly older, was in business attire.

As the Dean switched on the microphone, he said, "Professor Ward is not with us today. I will be speaking to alternative course arrangements shortly, but first these visitors have some important information for you. Father Krell?"

The man stepped forward, obviously comfortable at a podium and microphone. "Good morning, everyone. My name is Gerry Krell and as you can tell, I am a priest, a Roman Catholic priest. To a class of students expecting a lecture in a course on cultural anthropology, it should come as no surprise that I am here to talk about beliefs. But not my own, I should add."

He looked at the woman now standing by the Dean. "With me is Detective Sergeant June Mortimer with the Metropolitan Police, based in Lewisham, one of the police officers many of you have read about and perhaps some of you have written about in the last months."

The lecture theatre was large, but the change in the atmosphere, the rise in tension, was noticeable. Several faces suddenly turned hostile, others looked suspicious or sullen. June stared them out, looking impassive, undaunted.

Krell waited a moment, letting the small body shifts, breathing changes, and eye movements associated with the growing discomfort settle as he faced them out.

"My sister Anne was a student here, fifteen years ago, during the formative years after the transition to university status. She never completed her degree, as some of you will have read. She went missing.

"Her body, as the media reported widely, was found a month ago in an area of woodland owned by another former student, Amaechi Akanni. I have no need to say more about that, as again, there has been a lot said in the media surrounding the death of Mr. Akanni.

"And, of course, there has been speculation, many allegations and conspiracy theories arising from some quarters, not the least from people at this university, students and staff. The subject has gained a life of its own, an energy, a set of beliefs. We know how strong they can be, don't we? Well, I do, at least; belief is part of my job and the whole of my motivation. Hopefully, I am motivated by love, not anger. I try, anyway.

"Two weeks ago, we were able finally to put Anne to rest, to have her funeral and in some way, give our family closure. Present at St. Saviour's were a lot of people you would expect and some you wouldn't, but among them

were DS Mortimer and a group of her colleagues, some
of whom have never wavered over the years in seeking
the answer to why Anne disappeared, and the identities of
the perpetrators involved in the crime. Much of what they
know, they can't talk about, it is *sub judice*. The coroner's
verdicts on my sister and on Amaechi Akanni are awaited.
These are long processes. June?"

Mortimer stepped forward and joined Krell at the
microphone.

"Good morning. Around now, the Metropolitan
Police will release that Professor Darius Ward was arrested last night in connection with the death of Anne Krell.
He has been charged with conspiracy to murder and is in
custody pending a bail hearing. As Father Krell said, I am
not at liberty to say more at this time; not, I should add,
because it is a matter before the coroner, it is now *sub
judice* before a court of criminal law."

She moved back, standing by the Dean again. Gerry
Krell centred himself on the podium again.

"I am sure all of you are shocked by that, as was I.
Some of you are wondering how you can support Professor Ward now. He is your professor; you know him,
respect him, find him insightful, whatever. And he is
innocent until proven guilty, as he should be in this
country. Please, do not hesitate to do so, practically or
spiritually. We are not here to inhibit such support in any
way."

He paused, reflecting on how to move forward.

"But what will some of you write? What will others
read, arising from anger and prejudice? If the recent
months are any guide, it will be painful, emotional and, if
I may say so, very hurtful to many people.

"I ask you, in finding your own way forward at this sad
and shocking time, to consider two things.

"First, be a good student; by that, I don't mean that you should be prissy or politically correct. Be honest and kind in your support, be critical and objective in your thinking."

One person raised an arm and started to speak, but Gerry said, "Hold your comment or question for a moment, please? I want to show you one image first, and make my second point, and then I will answer any questions I can. Is that OK with you?"

The student nodded. Gerry pressed a button on the podium and an image, a photo, appeared on the screen behind him.

He continued. "The Dean tells me that the average age of this class is 20.5 years. Amaechi Akanni was twenty-three, Darius Ward was twenty-one and my sister Anne was twenty when she disappeared. There they are: a family photograph of mine, of Anne and her friends, young people, like you.

"You are hearing about the arrest of a professor now and have heard or speculated on the untimely death of a successful businessman, a valued alumnus of this institution. But look at them, remember how old they were. Do we, do you, really know what happened? Particularly when the facts, the evidence, are still protected from publication by law.

"What I see, and you as students of your field should see, is that beliefs grow with or without facts and, to me, the recent coverage and distortion of the motivations and actions of the Metropolitan Police is part of that. Look at these three people. Whatever happened, it was not about race, they are black, like me, like many of you."

He paused again. "Now my second point. I ask you, before you write something about Darius Ward's arrest, if you are so inclined to do that, to read the internet coverage from sources at this university about the police harassment and attempt to arrest Amaechi Akanni, a former student, a benefactor, a former board member. It's plentiful. Then check for any similar coverage of Anne Krell, also a former student, killed before she could even graduate. It's sparse, I will tell you that now.

"Then ask yourself, who truly spoke up for Anne?"

He let the question sink in a moment then pointed. "You had a comment or question, I believe?"

The student who had raised his arm a little earlier shook his head, thinking through something. Krell panned across the audience, waiting. After several seconds, he looked at the Dean and June Mortimer and said, "Thank you for the opportunity to address the class."

As the Dean moved to the microphone to talk about course arrangements, that today's lecture would be rescheduled and given by another member of faculty, Kim Lee Sung from Singapore looked at the photographs still on display. They looked like other students on campus, although their clothes dated them. But they were simply students.

Kim was an amateur portrait photographer and had followed the events of the last months from a distance. She was struck by the image of Anne Krell, the eyes, the smile, the dark, ebony black complexion. It reminded her of another person. Not precisely the same, not a twin by any means and not even the same age. She thought for a moment, then recalled the image of Amaechi Akanni's wife she had seen in the media coverage. She was an older woman, but there was a definite resemblance. It set her thinking.

~~

When the prison officer informed Peter Olowe that his solicitor was waiting, he thought it must be about the change in prison. Two weeks ago, he had been moved, for security purposes, from HMP Cardiff to HMP Parc, near Bridgend. The precise reasons were never explained, but he thought the news item about Amaechi Akanni's death must be linked to that. He had worked it out.

When he was shown into the meeting room and saw Rowena Paston, it was obviously more serious, from her face.

"Peter, you are to be arraigned on a murder charge. A police officer is waiting outside, to make the formal arrest. I said I would give you a little time to prepare yourself."

The colour drained from his face. "I thought... with the letter during my interview, the agreement, I would only be in prison here for a short time. It's not fair!"

She reminded him that the agreement with the Crown Prosecution Service was for leniency on his sentence, removal of the more serious charge and, in prison in Wales, he could not simply be sent home or anywhere else. There were procedures.

"When? How soon?"

The dread of being sent back to Nigeria or to Cameroon loomed over him.

"The Norwegians have to go through the process I just mentioned. The charge is the first step."

Norway.

Rowena Paston read his face, understanding. He probably did it, she concluded. Relief isn't the emotion you show after hearing you are going to be charged with murder, even if it is not the murder you thought it was. She pressed on.

"They have your travel details from Birmingham to

Olso and back identified. The same type of gun that the Metropolitan Police officer demonstrated was used."

His face revealed his disbelief. That was insufficient to warrant a charge. An interview, perhaps, but no more than that.

She pressed on. "They have also the report of the interview at Cardiff Hospital. Now they allege that your fingerprint was found in the same place on the weapon used in their case. For some reason, it was missed initially, but the South Wales Police report made them re-check."

"You don't have to plead or say anything. They just need to charge you. I will help deal with the process afterwards, representing your interests here, and my firm will locate a lawyer for you in Norway, at least for your arrival there."

"I can't fight extradition?"

She shook her head. "Britain and Norway, for a pre-meditated murder charge? No. We can try, but it will be rejected out of hand, I think."

"What are the penalties in Norway?"

"That's for the court to decide. Generally, the country is very progressive on sentencing. Your legal counsel there will advise."

He nodded.

She asked, "Are you ready to see the man, let him do this, get it over with? Remember, stay quiet, just accept the charge being read, that's all."

As she left to talk to the police officer, Olowe thought about his plan, how it would need to change. His initial idea was first to fight the case, but if they had that sort of evidence, it would need a technical or procedural loophole to be found not guilty, or have the case dropped.

It may be better to confess to the hit there if the sentencing elements were appropriate.

His next problem was to decide on the way to handle the job in Cameroon, if that also surfaced; the one that brought him to the attention of Amaechi Akanni.

He faked his story to the Welsh police officers convincingly, about only hearing the name Akanni once, in the context of the scam operation, but the reality wasn't far off that. He had only met Amaechi Akanni alone one time, at a meeting in Lagos, with Olowe's own boss at the time.

He had been nearly eighteen. The job in Cameroon had been his first kill. He had babbled on to Akanni about the Ruger being a great weapon for the work. He wanted in.

Akanni had listened. How Peter, in a stolen school uniform, hair slicked and looking anxious, had asked about the chance of getting supplies to become the new dealer at the high-end private school. It got him close enough to the target.

Amaechi Akanni had asked only one thing. "What was the best part; the kill or fooling him into seeing you?"

Peter said instantly, "The trick to reach him. Shooting him doesn't do anything for me. It's a job."

Akanni took him on. They never spoke directly again.

Now he was going to Norway, at least, rather than to Cameroon.

The key thing, he decided, was to work the system to the hilt, find support in Norway and sympathetic ears among the prison rehabilitation groups. If it reached the point of a guilty plea, he would appear a reformed man in a strange new country.

Akanni, he found out after joining Serval Enterprises, always said that the joy was in the con. Peter understood that.

41 HANOI

Armita Montaigne had chosen the package tour carefully. 'Discover Vietnam' promised good travel arrangements, talks and guided tours with 'windows of time' for its guests to relax and recharge or explore on their own.

It was important that the trip should be seen as a holiday, with a return date, part of a tour group yet one where she had the freedom to move around unaccompanied and unobserved. Montaigne was an experienced traveller with no need of any group arrangements, but it gave excellent cover for the real purpose of the trip.

After the recent events in Iver and London, she was on tenterhooks. Having survived the raid on Rel-Comm and the arrest of Roland McKewen, she had hoped for easier times. But the last month had been still more traumatic, with the news about the violence around the death of Mr. Akanni, and now the arrest of Darius Ward.

She was the last of their core group, wondering when any renewed investigation into Amaechi Akanni's businesses would end up at her door. Darius wouldn't betray her, she was sure.

The final call from Mr. Akanni still chilled her, despite all her experiences as a fraudster. While he was not a friend, they had the same goals in life, the same drive to con people. He had called unexpectedly on a burner phone and told her to get a paper and pen, as he had some inportant information to transfer.

On the free afternoon in Hanoi, she took a taxi to the Orient Maritime Bank downtown after making one phone call to the telephone number provided by Amaechi, asking for the Expatriate Accounts Supervisor.

Mr. Pham was in his late fifties or early sixties. She had been kept waiting twenty minutes in the reception area before being shown into a private office and introduced to the man.

After settling her, he went straight to the main point. "The account number you provided to me. What is your relationship to the account holder?"

"I am a business colleague."

"You have been given the account access, you say. Do you have any documentation validating that?"

Armita stared at him. "No. Nor is any needed, he said. I have the account password."

She waited him out.

"So, Mrs. Montaigne, if you have the account number and the password in these times of online banking, why do you need to see me?"

"There is a limit set for online withdrawal transactions and also a cumulative cut-off. I am not looking to draw from the account, but to transfer most of the funds to an account in my name that I will establish here, today."

"For that you will need the account holder with you here, in person, to validate that claim or..."

He left it open.

She smiled. "Or another validation method. Do you have a female staff person I could see?"

He looked sombre, his voice carrying his regret. "I will call in my assistant. Unfortunately, no alternative is permitted, I must witness the validation. The instructions of the client were quite explicit. We must avoid all confusion or error."

Armita nodded.

The woman who was called in wasn't introduced, just shown a file card by Mr. Pham, presumably carrying the account instructions. She read it, her face revealing nothing as she nodded her understanding.

Armita stood and opened her blouse, removing the right arm from the sleeve. As the silk slid down at the back, the tattoo of Anansi became visible on her shoulder blade. Both bank staff moved behind her.

The woman said, "You will need to hold the bra cup as I release the strap, please. The skin in the area must be flat and unstretched."

The tattoo of Anansi was not large, about eight centimetres in length. It had been well executed and was still clearly delineated, although the colours, black and red, were faded slightly, indicative that the work was not recent. Anyone familiar with the folk law image of the trickster spider would notice this image was elongated compared with most images of Anansi. The spider outline was black, the compound eyes were red, and two additional red spots were positioned symmetrically on the carapace.

The assistant moved forward with a small metric ruler, measuring first the distance between the red spots depicting the compound eyes of the mythical spider. She then measured the distance between the two red spots, one on either side of the carapace.

"Two point eight and four point five, as best as I can establish. I am required to repeat the measurement two more times. Please relax your shoulder, stretch a little then relax for each repeat measurement."

Despite a sudden sense of alarm, Montaigne followed the instructions without comment. Again, the assistant made the measurements. By the third touch of the ruler to her skin, Montaigne was smiling to herself; she knew the figures were correct.

Mr. Pham made note of the figures and then averaged the findings. "The ratio between the eye separation and the carapace spot separation is correct; one point six."

Armita nodded. One point six one, the golden ratio. But the measurement would never be that accurate, the tattooist had told them.

Amaechi had chosen it. "The golden ratio is a sign of beauty, of growth, of relationship. These Anansi tattoos will be unique."

Mr. Pham thanked the assistant and, once Armita Montaigne was properly dressed again, dismissed her with a smile. After the door closed behind her, he said, "Let us talk about the account you want to set up. Will you be staying with our bank or is this a short-term transitional account until you make other arrangements?"

"A standing account here. Under similar arrangements as Mr. Akanni. It is my intention to relocate here in the near future."

He smiled, pleased with the response, other than a slight frown as he added. "I heard through the news of Mr. Akanni's death. It is most unfortunate. However, the account cannot be closed; it must remain open until formal advice is received by the bank from the estate."

She nodded. "Shall we say a a reserve of five thousand

US dollars, to meet any ongoing account costs?"

He nodded. "That would be acceptable."

It still left over a quarter of a million dollars available now to Armita.

"And I would like a suitable letter of introduction to Mr. Ngygen at Hunan properties. Mr Akanni told me you made the preliminary arrangements for the property lease for him. Under the circumstances..."

Mr. Pham smiled. "Of course. I will have it prepared for delivery to your hotel this afternoon and I will also call him personally to advise him of the change in arrangements."

As she left the bank to return to the hotel and join her tour group, Armita reflected on the presience and vision of Amaechi Akanni. Years ago, she had a call from Darius, at USL. Could they grab a coffee later, in Lewisham?

When they met, he came straight out with it; would she object to a tattoo of Anansi? She could choose the size and location. Amaechi had arranged for a specific tattooist to do the work for three people, Amaechi, Darius and himself.

When she asked the reason, he said that he wasn't quite clear himself, other than it gave a unique identifier for the three of them, a special permanent link. Even Amaechi wasn't sure what he would use it for, but for him it identified the three people with the drive and vision to keep the Rel-Comm operation growing, people committed to the development of others with the skills and discipline needed.

"What about Roland? Will he be tattooed?"

Darius paused. "I asked the same question. No. He is loyal, but Amaechi said if Roland weren't working the con game, he would be running an operation stealing high-end cars or dealing drugs. It's not the same. You are from India, Amaechi and I from Africa. We have each risen from poverty by our wits and ability to trick wealthy people. We have lives that would otherwise be beyond our wildest dreams and can show others how to do the same. Anansi will be the specific link between us."

She had thought little about it, afterwards. It was just a tattoo.

When Amaechi called the evening befor his death he went straight to the point. "Armita, it's falling apart. The police will be at my doorstep soon, I think. I'll tell you what I told Darius. There is a fund and a house set up in Thanh Hoa, in Vietnam. Either or both of you can access it, so get a piece of paper; write the details down."

Once that took place, and she read back the string of numbers and letters, he advised her to choose her timing, but pull up stakes and start again. Keep the best who will go with her to Vietnam, but centre the business there.

She had wanted desperately to ask him when he would contact her again, how they would work together. Something in his voice stopped her doing that. All she said was that she was honoured that he entusted her with the role and she would talk to Darius.

As she carefully picked the words to explore their new relationship, Akanni said, "The final verification by the bank will be Anansi. I have every confidence in your ability to do this."

He had rung off without another word.

The following day, she heard he was dead.

Darius had made the decision to stay in London. He was a univeristy professor, a man of standing. His links to

Rel-Comm were more tenuous than hers. His cameo as 'Reverend Doctor Fisher' has been his closest direct exposure risk in recent years, but the only person who could identify him, the Maesteg *mugu*, was dead.

With Amaechi, Darius' primary role was one of talent spotter, to locate the people with the strength of character, skills and ruthlessness to become predators, tricksters; young people who would study well at university but make their money from unsuspecting victims.

She only clued into his major error when he was arrested, charged with the death of Anne Krell. She had no idea about the murder of Krell before that. It was before she joined Akanni's operation. She was suprised at Darius; he should have realised that more sensitive and sophisticated DNA testing could incriminate him if he had helped Amaechi kill her, as the media reported.

When she heard of his arrest, Armita fought the urge to flee, choosing to plan her own exit properly. The tourist trip to Vietnam was the result.

Now that the assets were hers, she would return to London and carefully monitor any further police investigation into Rel-Comm, or the activities of Amaechi Akanni. The company in Lewisham was now clean of scams, it was simply a legitimate business. She was in steady employment there. She could live a normal life.

But she knew in her heart after Ameichi's call that she would move to Vietnam. First, she would develop a reason to return to Kolkata, in a month or so. Armita would work with the Rel-Comm's board to ensure a smooth transition of leadership and take the accolades, farewell dinner and best wishes. She would exit in style, not do a moonlight flit.

In Kolkata, she would have a battle royal, no doubt,

with the local office, but would make it clear who was now in charge. It was her world, her background. The Lagos office was still in shock. Amaechi had been very hands-on there, to the extend that the supervisor of the little team was a great right hand support player, but no leader. He would be happy to see her show leadership.

Armita would then reach out to some of their people past and present, ones who were mobile. Study visas to a university in Vietnam could be arranged. First, Miri Udoh would be brought over from Frankfurt.

She would honour her commitment to Amaechi, to live a more dangerous but exciting way of life, finding people like them, ready to take what they needed to get on in the world.

They would begin again.

The one new rule she would introduce would be a complete ban on in-person contact. Never again.

It had been the Masteg fiasco which started the whole problem. That, and the fixation that Amaechi Akanni and a police officer called Karen Moore had with each other as a result of their pasts.

42 RED WITCH

DI John Leigh called Catrin.

"Commander Moore asks you to be in her office at 2.50 p.m. on Wednesday, ma'am."

"What about, John? Did she say?"

She had heard nothing from Moore directly after the events in Iver. A month after her return following her enforced holiday, the commander appeared her normal self. But, as Catrin told the negotiator, sometime or other she would find out the meaning of Moore's remark, and the consequences.

His voice conveyed that he knew, but his answer was standard. "No, ma'am, she didn't ask for any preparation from you. She said don't cancel or be late, or she will give you hell."

That sounded like Moore.

On Wednesday, Catrin went over the river to New Scotland Yard at lunchtime, working on other items in the early afternoon. At 2.50 p.m. she walked into Moore's outer office. Barbara, her assistant, met her.

"Commander Moore says you are to go to the Commissioner's office for three p.m., ma'am."

"Is the commander there?"

"No, ma'am, she and DI Leigh are away today."

Returning to the Executive Floor, with its quite different layout in the new building on the Embankment, brought back to Catrin her time working with Assistant Commissioner Hunt.

As she entered the outer office, Commissioner Worthington's administrative assistant stood and led her directly to the inner office door and opened it.

"Have a seat, Sayer. You know Colleen Barrington, I presume?"

Commissioner Worthington sat behind her desk, but she looked up and spoke as they entered. Dressed in a pale blue blouse and navy-blue pants, the matching suit jacket had been hung on another chair back. She appeared busy with her mobile, thumbs moving swiftly, her eyes now on the screen.

The assistant pointed to a chair at the meeting table, diagonally across from Barrington, with an empty seat on the other side directly opposite her, presumably for the commissioner.

Catrin had seen the personnel chief sitting at the table, a laptop open. She glanced at Sayer and returned to her reading.

"We haven't spoken, ma'am, but of course, I have seen Miss Barrington around and heard her speak to us."

For some reason, it brought a fleeting smile to the commissioner's face.

The assistant asked, "Would you like a coffee or tea, DCI Sayer?"

Not knowing what she faced, she said, "Thank you but

no, not right now."

As the door closed behind the admin assistant, and Sayer sat down, she took in the Director of Human Resources. She wore a cream silk shirt and charcoal grey skirt, a woman in her late forties with makeup not doing the best job of hiding a lined, worried-looking face.

The only time I get close to her, she's not in red, was Sayer's fleeting thought.

Barrington had been hired as the Deputy Director of Human Resources during a major reorganisation five years earlier. Her nickname with the rank and file then was 'Axewoman'. It derived, apparently, from a Kensington constable's loud shoutout in the station after hearing news of their local reorganisation; 'The axeman cometh, and she's from Fermanagh'.

With the appointment of Commissioner Worthington, Barrington's boss announced his retirement and Barrington got the top job. Having warmed to her, and knowing her penchant for red in her wardrobe, the forty thousand or so kind-hearted members of the Metropolitan Police Service now referred to her universally as 'The Red Witch'.

Catrin was trying to work out if this was a 'make your visitor completely ill at ease' opening, or they were just busy as hell and on a roll, that she was just one in a line of people filing in and out of the Commissioner's office that afternoon. Recalling Sandra Hunt's working days, it could be either.

Barrington glanced up and asked, "Surprised?"

Even with the one word, the Northern Ireland accent was apparent.

Catrin was surprised; you could say that.

"Yes. I thought I was meeting Commander Moore." No 'ma'am'; Barrington was a civilian, not a rank officer.

"Good. Karen did as she was told."

Barrington did not finish with 'for once', but the words were there, the tone clearly inferred that meaning. The Commissioner was still lost in her phone.

Worthington's finger stabbed at the return soft key and then the send button as she said, "That'll do."

She placed it on her desk and moved over to the table, sitting opposite Catrin.

The Commissioner took a moment to take stock of Sayer, then said, "You are a fast-track officer; have been identified as such since you joined the now-defunct Art Crime Unit. Not, I notice, from your initial recruitment; you spent three years in Lambeth and Brixton before that, which is unusual and unexplained, or buried too deep in your file. How has the 'fast track' label worked for you? What is your evaluation of it?"

It caught Catrin by surprise. She assumed it would be a case-related element she would be questioned about. On the way up, she had worried that it was a complaint related to the Iver incident although, if it were, she could not believe Moore would pass it up the line without talking to her face-to-face.

But this meeting wasn't exactly starting with 'let's give her a nice welcome and an easy question or two to settle her in'.

"In what way, ma'am?"

"Have you felt left behind, pushed too soon, gone in the right direction? That sort of thing."

Catrin had started nodding halfway through the explanation.

"When I was a DC in the incident in Scotland, and that is in my file, I was thinking of leaving the Met. I felt, in making an arrest and getting injured, I had caused problems for us with Police Scotland. It was Assistant Commissioner Hunt who came to see me while I was on medical leave and told me to start preparing for my sergeant's exams. I was amazed. DCI Worsely then told me I was 'fast track'."

Barrington, she noticed, was scrolling through a document, her eyes moving constantly from the page to her and back.

She paused, thinking it through.

"Then I was given the chance to be her security officer, and a promotion from there to inspector. I have felt pulled into opportunities rather than held back.

"I think that fast track is only partly about me and my capability and performance. It is also about trusting people that I don't even know and what works for the Met and how I fit into that. Or not. It involves me and my career but is bigger than that, for everyone labelled as such."

She stopped, wondering if her instant soliloquy was too much of a ramble or off the mark. Their faces were revealing nothing.

The commissioner responded evenly with, "I think that's well put. And appropriate for why you are here. We are going to share some information with you and ask you to think on it. In complete confidence. You, me, Commander Moore and Ms. Barrington are the only ones involved. Colleen?"

Sitting up straight and focusing on her, Barrington said, "Superintendent Lauder will be retiring in four months. He has had an exemplary career and, in developing Operation Undertow and turning it into what it is today, it is his crowning achievement, if I can use that term. He won't announce it to others, though, until a month or so before that date."

Catrin's mind shot to the obvious. She was being prepared to be his successor.

The Northern Irish melodic flow continued. "We will promote DCI Osborne to Superintendent, to lead Undertow, hopefully for a considerable period, for the stability. How do you feel about that?"

She leaned forward, eyes on Sayer's face.

What a stupid question, was Catrin's first thought. She swallowed, trying to remain impassive and not quite succeeding.

"Ken is older, more experienced. He and I work well together if that's what you are asking?"

The Commissioner butted in, her clipped accent contrasting with the Red Witch's charming lilt while delivering the bad news. "Not necessarily, although that could be, from my perspective, a satisfactory rather than a desirable outcome."

She paused.

"One of the more intangible elements that define a senior police officer is critical decision-making under pressure, making the right and often hard decision. It is not easy to assess in training sessions, and there are not that many occasions for most officers when it is tested to the extreme. In your case however, you have had more than your fair share of those. Including, I might add, the incident in Nine Elms recently and its aftermath.

"We want you to consider a long-term plan, an opportunity, not a promise. I think your comment earlier tells me you see that each of us is part of a bigger picture."

She looked back at her colleague.

Barrington continued. "About a year from now or perhaps less, when Osborne is settled and his replacement up to speed, no doubt with your help, we want to announce that we are placing you in the next MPhil course in Criminology at Cambridge University. As you know, it is world class, attended by people from the law professions who are on the rise, whose careers will handle the strategic aspects of crime management, the future direction of criminal law, the future direction of policing. The 'what if' stratospheric stuff."

She was looking conspiritorial. Listening, focused on her, Catrin noticed a coffee stain on the cream blouse front that had been unsuccessfully attacked with a cleaning pen. So, they had been at this for a while, she concluded.

"The course is an academic year. Afterwards, on this plan, you will not return to the Met immediately. You will receive a superintendent position or equivalent elsewhere, probably Wales or the South-West, Devon and Cornwall. You are known in those police services."

Commissioner Worthington jumped in again, "We like that one, particularly North or South Wales, with you having some experience with both. And being bilingual. Remember my mantra on building bridges with other services? This fits well. It could be anywhere in England of course, but not Scotland. Some up there have long memories and, frankly, I don't think you would want that either, given your experiences there."

Barrington ground on. "On this plan, you return to the Met in about three or four years at the Chief Super-intendent level. From there, well… it is obvious. It will depend on how far you can go. At that rank, you will still be at the bottom end of the age bracket, but also at the cusp of senior operational command and its interface with executive leadership."

She sat back in her seat with her eyes still boring into Sayer. "How does that sound?"

Catrin replied, "I haven't thought about it like that. It's… great that you are thinking so far ahead and that I could do those things. It's a lot to absorb."

"Which is why we are laying it out now. And remember, this is not a promise, it's a plan. Other things can happen. Flunk the MPhil. course and it goes nowhere – and the Commissioner can tell you Cambridge isn't an easy ride. But it is an opportunity with parallels to the experience you had working with Sandra Hunt, seeing the picture from the top. Few police officers get to go on that course."

The softer voice of Worthington came in.

"What is most important is trust and honesty. We undertake to tell you in a timely manner if anything changes that would render that plan invalid or seriously changed from our perspective. You undertake to tell us if anything changes for you. If the secondment to Wales or wherever, let me call it that although it will never be referred to that way outside our little group, results in you wanting to stay there, tell us. This plan is your career plan, but we both own it."

The room went quiet. Catrin did not know what to say without repeating herself.

Worthington continued, "There is one more thing unique to you. Your art, your business with your friend. That must be considered. No one is saying you shouldn't continue to do that. What we ask, if you accept the plan, if we make the investment in time and money to develop you this way, is that the Met comes first. And it will absorb a lot of time. Senior management jobs do that. Think about that aspect, too. You need to be honest with yourself, with us and with your artistic partner. And your family. With your husband working for us, that makes it easier, but his career interests need to be considered, too."

She looked at her colleague. "Have we covered everything, Colleen?"

Barrington looked at the Commssioner and nodded, her job clearly done.

"Now, you have plenty of time to work through this. Colleen will be your link. You will meet at least quarterly with her, and she will be available if you have any questions. You can speak to Commander Moore also."

She paused. "One more thing. Your comment earlier, about Osborne having more experience. He is a little older, yes; his experiences are different. When I asked each commander for recommendations, making it clear that we would be putting very few into the mix, the criteria did not include zeal, or experience, or current performance. They were simply asked to put forward names of people, with reasons, who, with training and time, could replace them and do their job as well, if not better than them. Commander Moore put forward only one name, yours. She thinks very highly of you and sees you can go far."

The Red Witch gave a little waggle of her left wrist within sight of the Commissioner, her wristwatch flashing. Catrin, focused on Worthington, caught it in her peripheral vision. The Commissioner gave no sign of seeing it.

"I remember your briefing after the Nine Elms surveillance operation went wrong, how you handled it, and your remark to Commander Reed that the focus was not on operational justification but on Constable binti Awang. I thought then that this is an officer who can trudge through a sea of mud and still come out the other side properly focused. You must have been devastated that there was a fatality, but you handled it well and faced up to a more senior officer trying to hijack the agenda.

"Please give our idea serious consideration. And now, Colleen, I have forgotten who is next?"

Worthington stood, signalling that the meeting was over as she offered Sayer her hand. Catrin stood also and shook it. Barrington half-raised herself out of the seat to shake Catrin's hand also. All Catrin could do was say, "Thank you. Both of you."

As Catrin left the office, Barrington sank back into her seat and returned to her laptop.

Catrin closed the door behind her. Sitting in the outer area was an officer in uniform she knew by sight from a training course several years earlier, but his name escaped her now. They gave each other a brief smile. Catrin looked at the clock; it was 3.28 p.m.

As she reached the outer door, she heard, "The Commissioner will see you now, Superintendent."

The new broom was working through the candidates for her organisational development plans at half-hour intervals, Catrin concluded.

As she walked back to the office where she had left her coat, her phone rang. It was Karen Moore. She will want to know how it went, Catrin concluded.

"Catrin, I never said it, but I want to thank you for everything you did on the Akanni case, particularly the last few steps in the garden you took that day. I was too close to it, I'll admit."

"It was my training, ma'am. I thank you for the news I've just received, I am bowled a little sideways by it."

Moore laughed. "Glad it went well, then. Thank me when you are stuck behind a desk dealing with headcount numbers, budget changes and being bothered by Home Office bureaucrats.

"And no, it wasn't just training, getting between Akanni and me. Not at all. And you bloody well know it."

The phone went dead.

Commander Karen Moore was back on form.

EPILOGUE

The follow-up surgery on Emmie Shand's hand led unfortunately to a secondary infection, producing a high fever and more tissue damage. She stayed in hospital the second time for nearly two weeks, not for several days.

Dealing with the consequences of the setback and waiting for everything to heal meant that she remained off work for nearly four months.

When she returned to duty, she wore her plainclothes equipment harness under her coat a little differently. She now used her left hand for the telescopic baton and torch, not her right. At the end of her physiotherapy, the outcome assessment noted her right-hand grip was dextrous enough, but its strength would be permanently reduced. She could write easily, do a lot of things right-handed, but for heavy work or using a baton, her left hand was needed. She trained herself accordingly.

Her fitness recertification proved to be no problem. The examiner insisted he hadn't given her any leeway, but she never knew if he told the truth or not. Some of her colleagues now treated her like fine porcelain. She would have to work through that.

The analogy with porcelain also made her think of DCI Sayer and her friends. Emmie's injury had overshadowed the Maesteg case. Coming out of it gave her a memory she would keep; to be part of a different world of policing for a short time, and to have senior officers from two police services showing their concern and support.

She checked online the website of the Cwmbran Kiln, deciding to buy a vase, a keepsake, and paid using her Visa Bank Card.

The parcel that arrived was larger than she expected. It contained two items; her vase in a Cwmbran Kiln box and another, a vase in a box with the markings of a gallery called Liz's Place. For a moment, she thought the order had been packed in error until she saw the card, written by Jean and signed by her and someone called Melanie - and by Catrin Sayer, wishing her well on her return to work. They said she should visit London again.

On the back of the card, Catrin had written in Welsh, "Tell Alec Williams that I still have a car waiting."

It would not be needed, thought Emmie. She was happy to be at work in Cardiff, for her world to return to normal.

When she checked the second box, it too contained a vase. She could tell instantly that the pottery was from the Sayer-Hughes art Jean had mentioned. Checking the website of Liz's Place, she saw similar items, each unique, selling for £400 or more. The image of her vase simply said, 'sold'.

A week later, checking her bank card statement, she found that her original payment had been refunded.

~~

The wind was up and a bit chilly, but they were gardeners. They knew the little gathering was to be inside at Hasanna Akanni's home, but they wanted to see the garden, too. They came suitably dressed for both locations.

Hasanna had prepared the refreshments, with several friends. Everyone would have pitched in, given the chance. She had decided to stay in the house in Iver, not sell and move away. They thought that was a miracle, considering what she had been through in that garden.

That the copse was for sale was a different matter. They understood that. But Hasanna had been adamant; this is my home and my garden. She wasn't leaving it. Her husband had, and the less said about that, the better.

Several of the Horticultural Society members had maintained the garden for the first few weeks after the police allowed access to the Akanni home. Joan, with some relish, supervised arrangements with a contractor for the complete returfing of the bottom thirty feet of lawn near the copse, and the erection of the new tall privacy fence separating the woodland completely.

Hasanna couldn't face doing it and Joan said she wanted to; so that was that.

The only time one of the workers mislaid a strip of turf, he heard about it and didn't repeat the mistake. John and Simon did the aftercare; the watering, occasional seam-filling and rolling. By the party, it looked fine, at a distance.

In the afternoon mix of sun and cloud, as the light changed across the garden, Hasanna thanked them all for their support through the last weeks, particularly John, Joan, Simon and Frances. They had done so much. She had one request of a few others, if there were any volunteers, some simple tasks, really.

Which is how Mrs. Jacinthe (call me 'Jackie') Howell ended up at Lavender Hill police station.

DS Ian Underhill called Loretta Hills with the simple opener, 'Where are you and how long to get back?"

Loretta was shopping over the lunch break.

"About ten minutes, why? What's up?"

"Get back and when you come in, you are Constable Sykes, recently transferred from Slough. There's a woman here to see you."

"God, no. Not–."

"No, not Akanni. Another woman called Howell. She's with the boss."

Loretta, shopping bag over her arm, was walking faster now up Lavender Hill.

"Inside Undertow or downstairs?"

"In the boss's office. I doubt this one has any links to organized crime gangs. She's a retired schoolteacher turned eighty, if she is a day."

When Loretta dumped her things, she straightened her jacket and went to Sayer's office. She first saw the flowerpot peeking above a cardboard outer with its tall, ornate wrapping. It was sitting on the desk, to one side of the back of a smaller, older woman in a tweed suit. Catrin stood as she entered.

"DC Sykes, this is Mrs. Howell, from Iver, a friend of Mrs. Akanni."

As the older woman stood and Loretta bent a little to her as they shook hands, Sayer, all smiles, said, "Why don't we do this in the main area, Mrs. Howell? I'll carry this pot out for you."

Loretta looked askance at her boss as they trooped out

and Sayer called others around 'for just a minute or so'.

Jackie Howell said, as they moved to the centre, "So you were promoted to a detective, in London. Good for you. Hasanna will be pleased to hear it."

Catrin said to the small gathering, "Mrs. Howell is here with a presentation for DC Sykes. Mrs. Howell?"

As a former teacher, Jackie Howell regarded her new class.

"Good afternoon, everyone. Yesterday, we had a party of sorts at the home of my friend Hasanna Akanni. You may know from the news, or through your colleagues at Thames Valley Police, about the 'awful event', as we refer to it?"

Several nodded vigorously, not wanting a regurgitation of the story. Richard, who was on a stakeout for Ken Osborne currently, had more than covered the bases.

"Hasanna asked a few of us to deliver plants grown by her to the police officers who helped her, and I drew the one for PC Sykes, as she was then, before she became a detective with you. I thought it was for the Slough police station, you see, but a kind officer there telephoned someone, and I ended up talking to DCI Sayer. So here I am, by train and taxi. It's quite a while since I ventured into London."

She eyed Loretta. "Hasanna virtually emptied her greenhouse; and I gather you, a fellow gardener, got to see that at its best. This is for you, from Mrs. Akanni, in appreciation."

As Howell passed over the box and Loretta thanked her, she reached into her bag and brought out a card in an envelope and held it out. Loretta opened it first and, on reading it, gave a small smile.

She said, "It says, 'to PC Sykes, who was the human face of Thames Valley Police the day before many of your colleagues, whose faces I don't recall, came to my aide. I cannot thank everyone and will never be able to thank enough all those I should."

As she opened the tall box and delved inside, she brought out the earthenware pot and tall plant, the long white petals of the spiderlily catching the light through the window.

"It's beautiful. Thank you for bringing it. Please, thank Mrs. Akanni for her kindness, if you would." It was all she could say.

After Jackie Howells accepted a ride in a brightly coloured police car to Paddington Station for her return trip to Iver, full of her day's adventure, Loretta was finding it hard to concentrate. In the end, she picked up the plant and walked to Sayer's office, just as Super-intendent Lauder came around the corner, with plans to see Catrin also.

She stepped back.

He said, "You go first. So, this is one of the Akanni plants, I hear. Thames Valley is buzzing about them."

"Yes, boss, I came to give it to DCI Sayer. She deserves it, not me. I felt such a fraud, accepting it."

Lauder could see Sayer shaking her head and he smiled.

"She's not going to take it. Do you know why?"

Loretta looked surprised. "No."

"Hasanna Akanni went through hell and when she came out of the other side, in gratitude, she sent flowers to the people who helped her. She didn't know everyone, but in less than half an hour, you managed to make such a positive impression on her. Am I right?"

He looked at Sayer.

"That's right. You put it better than me. It would also

remind me constantly that you got the last laugh, Loretta, on the joke I started about you going undercover as a police officer. Keep it out in the office and occasionally remind the others; a swift jab or two, when it is needed."

NOTES

The Pinewood Gardener arose from two observations. First, people become incensed by many issues, but internet fraud doesn't seem to rank high on anyone's list – unless you become a victim, then it becomes personal. For most people, they accept it as part of the internet. That a segment of society lives by arms-length theft from others is taken as a sad fact, rather than an indication of a societal malaise. In some cases, as reported by a number of journalists, the scammers who live an extravagant lifestyle are admired as an aberrant interpretation of 'Robin Hood' style folklore.

The second observation that drew me to the more difficult plotline of internet fraud was the early stages of the COVID19 crisis. In lockdowns, and with reduced services, we were so dependent on the internet, yet every morning my email in-basket would contain the next batch of scam mail, with ever more preposterous proposals. How can this vital global communicatoin system be allowed to be constantly abused in this way?

The answer is that somewhere between one and six billion US dollar equivalent in global theft occurs annually by internet fraud, according to various sources. As large a figure as that it, is still hard to quantify. As one report put it, 'people at home in pyjamas and slippers can rob a bank'.

Or steal from a well-meaning man in the village of Maesteg in Wales.

My wife Gill and my friends Jack Soule and Fred Grigsby read drafts of the work at various stages, which helped me significantly. I thank each of them for doing so. Any remaining errors are entirely my own.

ABOUT THE AUTHOR

Allan Jones lives in Ontario, Canada. He was born and grew up in Merseyside, England. By profession an industrial chemist, he worked for many years as a consultant on international chemical regulation. He has lived in or travelled to most of the regions featured in the Catrin Sayer novels.